CW01202599

ANGELS AND ALIENS

Do you have the capacity to imagine the future with a prophet? This tale has the whiff of that future.

CERN, Geneva, not merely a particle physics laboratory and the birthplace of the WORLDWIDE WEB but a hotbed for things both earthly and divine.

Cathy Burkert and Matt Mallard are part of a global team to save earth from certain annihilation as a wormhole stretching from the Andromeda galaxy to the Milky Way is causing a collision 3.75 billion years earlier than expected. The team use their brilliance to gain access to the stellar and planetary world of the heavens encountering an alien mode of being: the stuff of visionaries and magical thinkers.

Iran invades Iraq and Russia is backed into a corner to bring about the downfall of its President. Will the select group that rule the world, The Opus Signori, command the tides or are they ambassadors of death? Will one demonic manipulation of a machine despoil pure thought for eternity? Will the decoding of the prophetic Seven Seals in the Bible celebrate a reality of scientific vision for today's world?

The chain unfinished started with characters in *The Conduit*, finds an ending in steps immortal -Adam and Eve, DNA sequenced through the millennia and the arrival of the new era of quantum thought: Beautiful Physics and the Absolute Mind.

ANGELS AND ALIENS

CHRYSELLE BROWN

TO

My Sons: Kristian and Luke and my Husband Tim - my champion always,

My Father Tom Antonio, My Mother Lucy and my Mother-in-law Patricia Avery Wendy Brown

"Knowledge is limited.
Imagination encircles the world"
Albert Einstein

With special acknowledgement to:

Mr Matthew Coombes, MPhys

Thanks for your generosity and patience.

ANGELS AND ALIENS

PROLOGUE

January 2012

He was seated at the bank of screens, slouching, his mind busy analysing the data, his eyes hunting for quasars, those extremely bright and energetic distant objects in the universe, otherwise known as quasi-stellar radio sources - radio emitting material in the hearts of enormous black holes.

The AMS (Alpha Magnetic Spectrometer), the particle physics detector was sending this continuous flow of data. The AMS located on the only habitable artificial satellite, called the International Space Station, in low earth orbit. He brought up an image of the ISS on his screen.

INTERNATIONAL SPACE STATION

The rest of his team seated at a bank of computers at the Payload Control Operations Centre at CERN, were making sure the data was properly processed, before distribution to the regional centres for specific detector related analysis and calibrations.

He suddenly jerked upright; there again was the blueshift of gamma rays – otherwise known as photons or light. It was moving towards him. He stared at the screen; his eyes could barely comprehend the significance. The increase in the frequency of wavelengths was visible and terrifying. It signalled an approaching object. He shouted out loud in his excitement and consternation. Something big was approaching earth.

Space-time was being bent with negative energy. My God, this was his first wormhole. Was it a natural phenomenon or was it man-engineered?

His mind was feverish. Think, man, think. Normal wormholes or Einstein-Rosen Bridges as they were scientifically christened, in all experiments to-date collapsed, if anything crossed from one end to another. This *mother* of a wormhole on his screen must contain negative energy or exotic matter to be stable. As exotic matter bends space-time, it had created this traversable tunnel, this gigantic wormhole, stretching from one end of the cosmos to a yet undetermined distant part. Worse, there was something in the 'throat' of the wormhole.

He had to work it out painstakingly. He had to get it right. He summoned the others from their desks. Each subsystem had a dedicated monitor desk, his was the special position devoted to data flow. They gathered around the oval desk in the middle of the room. Others started entering the room. The word was out. There were no secrets in science. All the physicists at CERN talked excitedly of analysis and calculation.

They consulted data from telescopes around the world and had confirmation of fluctuations of star brightness caused by the wormhole. Starlight would be flickering and wavering because of gravitational lensing, when a massive object (such as a galaxy) warps the fabric of space and bends light around it. The effect, similar to the distortion of objects behind a thick lens, was exaggerated with increasingly massive objects. And this was big, bloody big. Just to be absolutely certain, CERN fired up all seven of the particle detectors, constructed at the LHC (Large Hadron Collider). Many hours and many minds later a conclusion was reached. The AMS had confirmed the phenomenon.

One end of the wormhole was in beautiful Andromeda with its central bar of stars pointed directly towards the earth and the other end in the heart of the Milky Way, a region of extraordinary and violent activity. The wormhole was just outside our solar system, half a light year away. The cause of the wormhole was pinpointed to a dark matter particle; they christened it the Black Widow.

Expanding in size the wormhole due to gravitational effects was carrying a devastating payload, swallowing the hot subdwarf star Damocles. Lodged in its throat, Damocles was headed for the solar system and earth. An estimate put it at 0.25 light years away, travelling at half the speed of light.

The overriding factor in every calculation left the physicists unable to comprehend the magnitude of the threat. For not only was Damocles on a trajectory to annihilate earth but the expansion of the wormhole tunnel was creating a breathseizing scenario.

An Intergalactic Stimulation resulting in a collision of cataclysmic proportions 3.75 billion years earlier than expected!

Earth might feel the aftermath of being swallowed whole by the Andromeda galaxy, a galaxy which stretches across more than six times the width of the Full Moon.

The vast distances of the galaxies would mitigate the effects on earth was the thought each man of science confidently nurtured.

NASA had simulated images of the collision. An observation exercise was conducted.

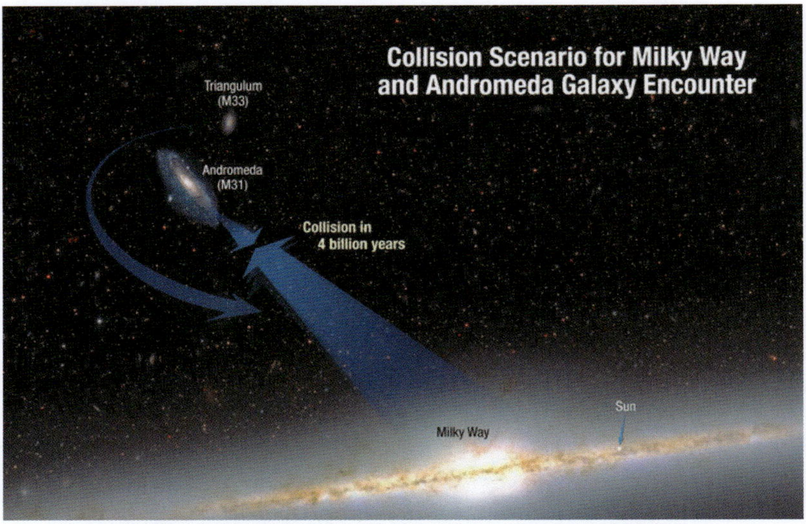

Credit: NASA, ESA and A. Field and R. van der Marel (STScl)

Credit: NASA; ESA; Z. Levay and R. van der Marel, STScl; T. Hellas; A: Mellinger.

Aloud they clocked the advent.

Collision date: June 20th 2012.

Humans had six months before annihilation.

The Seven Seals

The scroll was ancient, it was papyrus and its inks were of the 2nd century AD. Sheaves of the ancient parchment tightly rolled, all sealed with clay. Seven Seals.

Fingerprints of the ancients visible on the fabric, the scribes copying the Biblical words of Revelation. The text of long ago, steeped in secrets and only the chosen one to break the heavenly code.

Once revealed, the truth would herald cataclysmic change for the Universe. So St. John of Patmos wrote in the Book of Revelation. To break his symbolic seals risked chaos - The Day of Judgement. Would Physics, the religion of today deliver a new Apocalypse?

St. Petersburg, Russia. The Hermitage Museum.

The man held his hand and begged his son to take good care of the package. His face betrayed his life. He looked old and worn.

He said, 'This is the papyrus I have safeguarded all my life. It was entrusted to me by your grandfather. It must never be given to anyone but the woman I speak of. Swear it on our family name'

'How will I find her?' asked Dimitri

'You will know her from the colours of the earth, the stars and the heavens. Soon the time will come.' Dimitri Sosnovsky made the vow. His nephew, Sergei Boystov, his sister's son and the old man's grandson, would obey too.

Dimitri Sosnovsky searched long and hard both in his native Russia and the world beyond. No clue emerged. Five years passed and the old man, his father, grew frail but with a strength of will and purpose that was indomitable. He would wait to die until after the woman and the papyrus were inseparable.

Then, an obscure article came to Dimitri's desk. As editor of The Russian Weekly, he would sign it into print. A man and a woman from London, England had taken photographs of the earth's surface not with ordinary means. Mentally airborne, they had orbited the earth. A Brain-Computer Interface hooked up to their visual cortex produced glorious 3D images. The pictures were like no other Dimitri had ever seen, a panorama beyond the heavens.

There was a profile of the man and of the woman. The woman was a Classics scholar and had deciphered ancient papyri.

Dimitri knew he had found the woman his ancient father had spoken of. That evening he handed his nephew, Sergei Boystov, a lacquer box with strict instructions. The box contained the precious papyri and one other item, a document of such import to bring about the downfall of a President.

Two days later Dimitri was found dead. He had been poisoned.

October 1963, USA

John F. Kennedy, President of the United States was making a speech.

He was going to expose the Gnomes of Zurich. The 'Gnomes of Zurich' were the ultra-secretive and powerful Opus Signori, translated from the Italian as 'Work of Lords', a group of very rich and powerful businessmen. They were rumoured to plot the fates of the world. Exercising immense control of the World Bank and the IMF (International Monetary Fund), they were constantly accused of conspiracy and meddling in world affairs, through governments and corporations to establish a New World Order.

Kennedy was talking tough.

A month later, Kennedy was assassinated.

January – June 2012

CERN, Geneva

They arrived from all over the globe. Thousands of learned men, all specialists in the study of particle physics. Every conceivable theory was tested, every one failed. First, they waited for the radiation feedback to destroy the wormhole naturally, just like sound feedback if not checked could destroy equipment like amplifiers. They waited in vain. Then they tried to reverse the negative energy density in the centre of the wormhole with the gravitational pull of micro black holes, thousands of them. CERN powered up the LHC, sent commands to the spacecraft Voyager 1 and tried to squeeze energy into very small spaces and the physics allowed small black holes to be created but the weak spots in the wormhole could not be destabilized.

Discounting nuclear explosive charges, which would do more damage with debris circling the entire globe, they then talked of diverting the sub-dwarf star, Damocles in the throat of the wormhole from its heading, once it was closer to earth – by using spacecraft propelled by solar sails, giant mirrors that fly through space via the force of sunlight reflecting off them. Lasers, balloons and harpoons were also suggested.

The trouble was that Damocles was estimated to be big. Too big for earthly contraptions?

Tension was high as they waited and watched. The mouth of the wormhole near the solar system was too far away to be reached and the other end of the tunnel was millions of light years away in Andromeda. Time to these learned men, seemed like a river, hectically fast-flowing and looking set to burst its banks. A decision was taken.

They knew there was only one recourse. They had to find the Black Widow particle, the particle that had caused the wormhole, isolate and eject it. They could not contain it with magnetic fields. It was neither stable nor charged.

It had taken 20 years and the LHC were still on the hunt for the Higgs particle. They had a fortnight to identify the Black Widow. And time was running out.

June 2012 Tehran:

Mahmoud Ahmadi, Iran's President looked defiantly at the man standing across from him. The supreme leader Ayatollah Ali Khomenei ignored the look. He always tended to ignore this imbecile anyway.

It was widely known that the two had fallen out. Publicised and pondered over by the World press eager to see the hard-line Ahmadi go and along with him Iran's nuclear ambitions.

The world did not know that an Iranian nuclear arsenal was already primed and a stockpile growing. For Mahmoud Ahmadi's departure they would have to wait a while.

'Are you crazy, Mahmoud?' said the supreme leader. Do you mean to go ahead with this plan? Annexation of Iraq?'

Ahmadi said, 'Our Intelligence sources have formulated a plan. The Americans have long gone from Iraq. The country is seething again with the old unrest – the Shias pitted against the Sunnis – they cannot abide each other and the Haj pilgrimage is their only meeting ground. Civil strife looks inevitable.

The Guardian Council, our band of clerics, agree the time to move is now. I have a man in a very high place; he has the means for us to seize our explosive neighbour. The world will not do anything in retaliation, not the second time around.'

June 2012 Geneva:

The heat was stifling in the room, Cathy had to get out. She opened the backdoor and stepped outside onto the balcony, shrugging her dressing-gown off her shoulders. Her nightie, black and silky draped across her body in the slight chill. It was 3 a.m. and she had to rush but the darkness for a moment was welcoming and inky-black with only the moonlight. Cathy gazed upwards, the moon was a perfect orb, a silver so intense that she exclaimed softly in awe. Clouds drifted and suddenly an aura appeared, 18 carat burnished gold within the vapour, a ring of tones like a nimbus that took Cathy's breath away. Was there a demi-god around that translucent silver of a moon or was Andromeda in her starry sapphire constellation beckoning her in pure thought? A good omen for what she was about to embark upon?

Cathy thought of the anti-God particle that haunted every waking moment, every dream. Working at CERN was proving tough, tougher than she had ever imagined. She had been chosen, selected to determine a solution vital to the future of mankind- why was she the privileged one, her friends asked with kind envy – science and God, how do you manage to separate the two ?, was the other question. She had to come to terms with both. God was breathtaking, a benevolent power source. Her friends knew that she had recently become intrigued by that concept. After years of disbelief, the perfect symmetry of the science had brought about her renewal of faith. The science of course was The Large Hadron Collider (**LHC**) – the world's largest and highest-energy particle accelerator.

It was built by Cathy's current workplace, located on the Franco-Swiss border deep underground, in the suburbs of Geneva. Named the European Organization for Nuclear Research (CERN) and constructed over a ten year period from 1998 to 2008, its aim was to allow physicists to test the predictions of different theories of particle physics.

Cathy tied the silk robe and went indoors. 4 am. Cathy dressed quickly, chewing on a piece of Swiss Emmental cheese, took the lift downstairs and rushed around the corner to get the bus in to the huge industrial complex that was CERN. Transport throughout the night had been arranged in these urgent days. Cathy could only describe CERN in the words on their official website – a utilitarian 'the buildings crowd untidily around the large machines devoted to the production of high-energy particles.'

The office allocated was a room white and clinical with Swedish looking furniture. It had a glass wall on the one side and the other displayed huge photographs, depictions of the Atlas detector and superimposed shots of the wine-growing countryside surrounding them. Cathy knew from the notes she had compiled, that the ATLAS detector is about 45 meters long, more than 25 meters high, and weighs about 7,000 tons. It is about half as big as the Notre Dame Cathedral in Paris and weighs the same as the Eiffel Tower or a hundred empty 747 jets.

This was the detector that would help to uncover that deadly particle, the Black Widow. Cathy's extraordinary ability for astral projection had led to her urgent presence here. And Matthew Mallard's. He had weeks of prep with the scientists.

Matt turned towards her as she entered the office. Tall, dark and handsome, with chiselled features and piercing grey eyes. He said, 'We have to dash. Scheduled for LHC results on the psychokinetic dark matter searches, I attempted 3 days ago. The detectors normally have proton-proton collisions to unearth the Higgs boson but now they are urgently looking for missing particles, mainly the Black Widow. I, employing my perspicacity, have been attempting to influence the discovery of this particle pinpointing large amounts of unaccounted for energy which should be present from the decay of the collisions.

An announcement will be made shortly. First, and this gets more imperative by the second, we have to take part in what you and I have successfully embarked upon many times.' He took her by the arm.

'Cathy I know you were briefed thoroughly re: the protons collisions, so just to summarise - the protons are accelerated in opposite directions in the Large Hadron Collider, (LHC) an underground accelerator ring that crash together in the centre of the ATLAS detector, - It's an amazing piece of technology Cathy, this tubular structure, (its innards are like a gigantic hair curler). The particles will produce tiny fireballs of primordial energy. LHC recreates the conditions at the birth of the Universe – 30 million times a second.

Relics of the early Universe not seen since the Universe cooled after the Big Bang 14 billion years ago, will spring fleetingly to life again. The LHC is in effect a Big Bang Machine -trying to find the Higgs boson until this catastrophe.'

Mallard ushered her towards the door, 'Did you know, the search for knowledge of the Universe that is being conducted here at CERN mirrors the discovery of the electron, the chemical property of an atom?

Why Cathy, it's amazing – I find myself utterly fascinated, the electron's existence manipulates or harnesses phenomena such as electricity and magnetism, that is why we have TV, radiotherapy treatments for cancer patients, lasers, etc and of course the LHC. We will be attempting stuff, the success of which is impossible to determine but promises new paths of discovery.

'Let's go, I'll explain in the lift.'

With urgent steps they made their way to the lift. Cathy understood how desperate the situation was but her mind was straying. She reflected on how she had first met up with Matt Mallard, 5 years ago. She had gone to see him as she was sorely in need of answers.

She had at 26 years of age, visited Cyprus acting as a researcher on ancient papyri discovered in the country. Her educational background in Classics had landed her the position but once there, her mind had been attacked by a rogue Turkish faction seeking to push the Greeks to vote 'yes' in a referendum on the 2004 EU treaty between North and South Cyprus.

A thought transference machine developed by Matt Mallard had been stolen and used for that purpose.

Cathy had escaped but the British official line had been to allow the label of a psychotic on her person. Cathy had known she was nothing of the kind, she believed she had inhabited an alternative reality of cutting-edge mind technology; but the medical world needed to suit the diagnosis to their profession. Cathy endured hours of therapy but could not shake off the invitation to her destiny.

She had decided to find the man she been communicating with telepathically. His paranormal gifts mirrored hers.

Matt pressed the buttons on the lift. He looked at her. 'I know what you are thinking. We have been fortunate, you and I, working together for the last couple of years. We have to talk at length, when this is over.'

'Do the press know we are here?'

'I've managed to keep them at bay but if we succeed today. ..We are doing the unthinkable, Cathy, we are attempting through Psycho Kinesis or PK as it is commonly known, to influence the path of the Black Widow particle and Damocles, the dwarf star. We hope to overcome today decades of scepticism.

The scientists here at CERN, despite major opposition from within their own ranks, contacted the ICRL, the International Consciousness Research Laboratories. The ICRL is an offshoot of PEAR, the Princeton Engineering Research facility that ran for 30 years under the aegis of the Princeton University's Engineering School.

PEAR, described their activities as conducting extensive research and experimentation of the interaction of human consciousness with sensitive physical devices, systems, and processes, and developing complementary theoretical models to enable better understanding of the role of consciousness in the establishment of physical reality. In other words, PK applied to science, mainly physics. The ICRL are doing the same, on a global basis.

The ICRL contacted me after we became a household item when we did the last astral circumvention of the earth. The photographs we took mentally of earth's orbit were proof that we had actually achieved an out-of-body state. Today, we will prove to the scientific community and to the world at large that PK, the movement of our minds, can alter the fate of the world. Cathy, don't look so scared, we have nothing to lose. CERN has tried every other source and resource. We are all they have left. We cannot fail.

Here we are..'

The lift stopped, they exited the building and walked the short distance to the wooden structure that was The Globe. At 27 metres in height and 40 metres in diameter, it's about the size of the Sistine Chapel in Rome.

The globe of the European Organization for Nuclear Research, CERN, illuminated outside Geneva, Switzerland, on March 30, 2010. (AP Photo/Anja Niedringhaus

They walked up to the 1st floor, entering a very large conference room with a huge TV screen showing images of the LHC and wormholes, and a plethora of high-tech electronic computers arranged on the sides with men and women seated in front of them. Physicists and scientists from all over the world. A dais at one end of the room had men standing in front of a microphone. More electronic equipment was visible behind them.

The ceiling was a spectacular domed vision more than 12 metres in height. A recent addition, a vast elliptical screen studded with a cornucopia of projected stars and planets decorated the ceiling, stunningly beautiful in its etching.

There were other people there. Many different languages sounded. Cathy started to get very nervous. There were 5 beds in the middle of the room, hooked up to lots of electronics. Cathy nodded to the other three, professional astrophysical surfers. Astral Cosmos-nauts from Russia, India and the USA. Together they would attempt to find the Black Widow particle and in so doing, Cathy hoped, find a teleogical explanation for the universe.

Teleology being a philosophy that imputes a final cause to nature, where life begins, ends in death and then, Cathy believed, the final spiritual ascent into the heavens. Would Andromeda, with its spidery tendrils, be full of that afterlife? What of the entire cosmos, would some form of afterlife exist in stars big and miniscule, saturated with particles, energy soaked and full of light? A mass of electrons with protons in the star-studded nucleus.

Assistants dressed in futuristic metallic grey overalls came towards them.

Cathy looked to the public space in a tier high above them, she was reminded of theatre boxes clinging to the sides – recently constructed, to afford a vantage point over the proceedings, they held many important people there. Government officials from both France and Switzerland, Britain's ambassador, America's too and officials from the 20 European member states and my God, all were relying on her and Matt and the 3 others to achieve a miracle. The gentleman on the dais in front of them started speaking into a microphone whilst Cathy and the others made their way to the energisation chambers. His voice was heard on speakers throughout the structure.

'Ladies and gentlemen, I am Professor Christoph Benjamin and all of you present are the only ones aware of the imminent arrival of the dwarf star Damocles and the predicted merger of the constellations. The information has the highest priority restriction; the news must be contained for fear of panic among the general populace. While the cosmos-nauts are preparing, I will attempt to explain some details of this undertaking.

You have been informed that earth faces extinction. If our attempts over the next hours do not succeed, earth will be annihilated. Ever since we learnt of the wormhole and the deadly cargo it carried, we have been trying to collapse the wormhole and eject the Black Widow and Damocles. We have worked around the clock – our people are exhausted – each and every calculation, every variable has been attempted. We have not succeeded. The wormhole is stable and the expected delivery to our solar system is now estimated at 24 hours or less. We have run out of days.

Scientists at CERN cannot close their minds anymore to extraordinary solutions to this anomaly that confronts us. We have to try the quantum mechanics of consciousness on this phenomenon. The theory that human consciousness can exert direct influence on nature was born in antiquity and is still prevalent today. Just look at religion where prayer is assumed to have an effect on physical events. Metaphysics, alchemy attest to inescapable links between the mind and the physical world.

To explain what we are about to attempt and to provide a solid scientific base for the decision to use a movement of consciousness (which includes perception, cognition, intuition, instinct and emotion), also known as Psycho kinesis - Psycho kinesis or PK, for those unaware of this type of energy, comes from the Greek word psyche meaning mind, soul, heart or breath - And it literally means mind movement.

Jahn and Dunne of the ICRL conducted extensive experiments and proved that the phenomena of physics at microscopic levels i.e. quantum mechanics- such as mass, momentum, energy; electric charge and magnetic field; the quantum and the wave function; and even distance and time –well all this variation has to be organised in the mind as the mind receives as well as emits this chaos of information, therefore quantum mechanics and human consciousness interact with each other and with the environment.

Their book, (*Quirks of the Quantum Mind)* by the way for those interested in reading further, provides evidence-based detailed correlations.

For our purposes today, I quote from the book - ‘if consciousness had a wave pattern and it was relaxed or penetrated in any way, consciousness could escape to a ‘free-wave’ status thereby achieving access to a more remote environment.

The mind could then escape beyond environmental constraints, beyond physical space and time and be able to redefine the ‘here and now’ into the ‘there and then’.’

For the non-scientists present, I ask you to imagine a light bulb filament giving out a photon, seemingly in a random direction. Erwin Schroedinger came up with a nine-letter-long equation that correctly predicts the chances of finding that photon at any given point.

He envisaged a kind of wave, like a ripple from a pebble dropped into a pond, spreading out from the filament. Once you look at the photon, this 'wavefunction' collapses into the single point at which the photon really is. Here’s a picture on the screen.

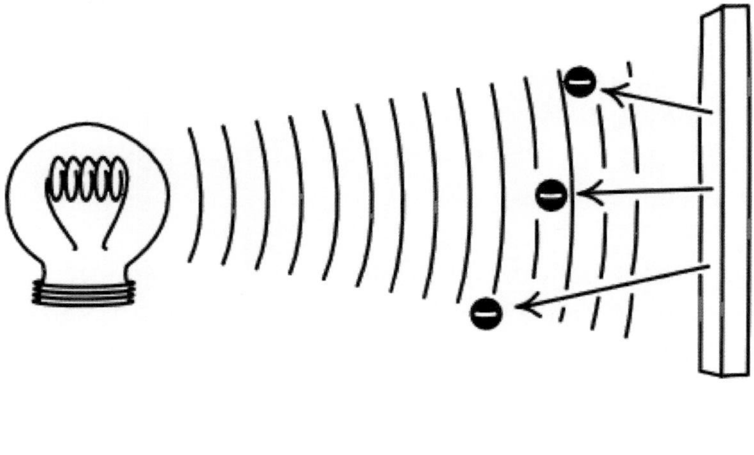

So here we have consciousness, PK or mind-movement, with all the associated precognition, engineering a ripple effect towards an object and finding it. This is how we hope to isolate the Black Widow and eject it, thereby collapsing the wormhole.

Ladies and Gentlemen, I hope I have demonstrated with such phenomena as telepathy, psycho kinesis, out of body or remote perception inextricably linked with quantum physics, a decision was reached to undertake Astral projection/travel or what's commonly known as an 'out-of-body experience' or as we, men of science prefer to call it OBE. In this instance I will continue to call it astral projection as it is amongst the stars, the mind will adventure forth. The mind assumes the existence of an "astral body" separate from the physical body and capable of travelling outside it. Rigorous training to achieve the highest level of mental concentration accompanies the out-of-body state.

There are 5 stages the cosmos-nauts (a word coined by our Mr. Mallard) go through to achieve supreme consciousness: 1) the withdrawal stage - from the physical environment, 2) the cataleptic – an impairment of movement occurs, 3) the separation-free from earthly perceptual viewpoint, 4) the free movement stage – movement within a certain radius and achievement of visual and mental clarity and finally 5)the re-entry stage – of a fast snap back to reality.

We cannot reach the end of the wormhole any other way. Our particle detectors are not up to the task here and cannot be transported as the wormhole is too many millions of light years from earth. The mouth of the wormhole near our solar system would take years to reach, so cannot be accessed either and it is feared any interference as it heads closer to earth might hasten Damocles' journey and certain extinction for humankind.

On the screen now is an example of a wormhole. The entrance of our wormhole is in the Andromeda galaxy, and the exit is the Milky Way.

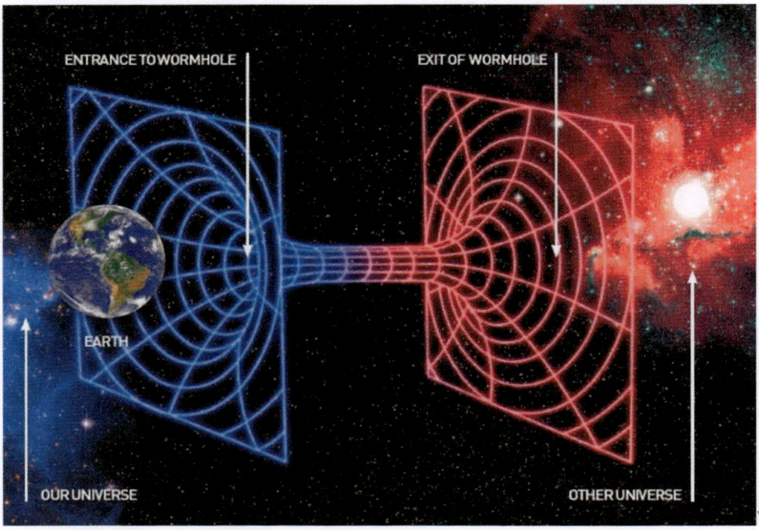

Wormhole visualised as the contours of a 3D map

Our very experienced astral cosmos-nauts will attempt through mental flight to find the wormhole, isolate and eject the Black Widow using lasers to trap it, replicating the procedure electronically, which will cause the collapse of the wormhole tunnel, and we hope the particle gets pushed in the direction of Andromeda's black hole, where all will be sucked in. Black holes are regions of space-time where gravity prevents anything, even light from escaping. The screen shows black holes in the Andromeda galaxy.

Credit: NASA/Swift; background: Bill Schoening, Vanessa Harvey/REU program/NOAO/AURA/NSF

Obviously, for research purposes we would like to contain a sample of the Black Widow in a vacuum for detailed analysis here at CERN but that is an outcome that seems remote at the moment.

The large TV screen behind the dais continued projecting images of the LHC and other related matter the Professor was detailing.

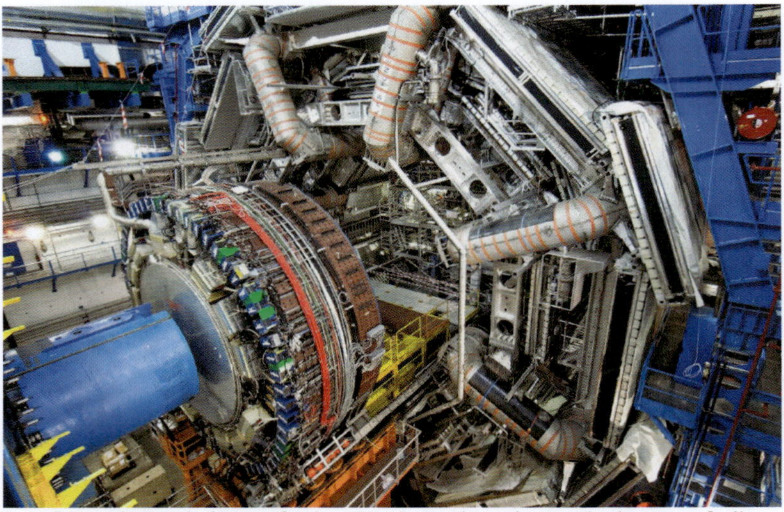

One of the end-cap calorimeters for the ATLAS experiment is moved using a set of rails. This calorimeter will measure the energy of particles that are produced close to the axis of the beam when two protons collide. It is kept cool inside a cryostat to allow the detector to work at maximum efficiency. February 16, 2007. (Claudia Marcelloni/© 2012 CERN

View of the Compact Muon Solenoid (CMS) Tracker Outer Barrel in the cleaning room on January 19, 2007. The CMS is a general-purpose detector, part of the Large Hadron Collider (LHC), and is capable of studying many aspects of proton collisions at 14 trillion electronvolts. (Maximilien Brice/© 2012 CERN)

During the past week, we have been attempting to influence discovery of the Black Widow through PK energy coupled with the LHC output, without success. Today we attempt both, PK and astral projection. A combination of the two interacting with the power of the LHC will ensure a result today, I firmly believe this. These are desperate times.

We have special energised superchambers where the projectionists are currently absorbing propelling intensity. CERN as you all know has never tried this before. We have no choice, it is only a matter of hours before Andromeda and the Milky Way collide, which will either form a new giant elliptical galaxy or the antithesis of the Higgs Boson – the Black Widow will help blast it into oblivion.

For the non-scientists present, I will explain very briefly the nature of the workings of our LHC and the Atlas experiment.'

Cathy her body pulsing with energy in the superchamber, felt she was breathing in a heady perfume, where synapses and electricity combined and molecules were firing up receptors in her nose, transmitting signals through a deluge of excited neurons illuminating the dark recesses of her brain, and all the while the Professor's voice explaining what Cathy already knew.

Particle physics, exciting stuff not boring as she had thought before this job came about, a branch of physics that studies the existence and interactions of particles, ingredients of what is usually referred to as matter or radiation.

CERN was the ultimate discoverer of high-energy physics and until the Black Widow, the hunt for the Higgs boson particle was conducted through the Large Hadron Collider (LHC) – The LHC, always extremely active, colliding protons. Protons are one part of three particles of atoms (empty space)the other two being electrons and neutrons. The LHC's hunt for the Black Widow requires the careful study of thousands of trillions of particle collisions at incredibly high energies.

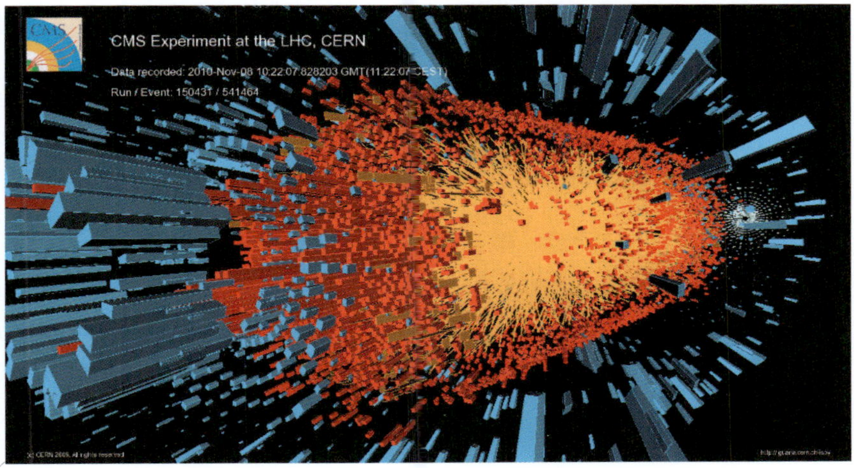

A lead-ion collision as recorded by the CMS detector at the LHC. © CERN for the benefit of the CMS collaboration

The large TV screen behind the dais, was showing stunning images of the collisions.

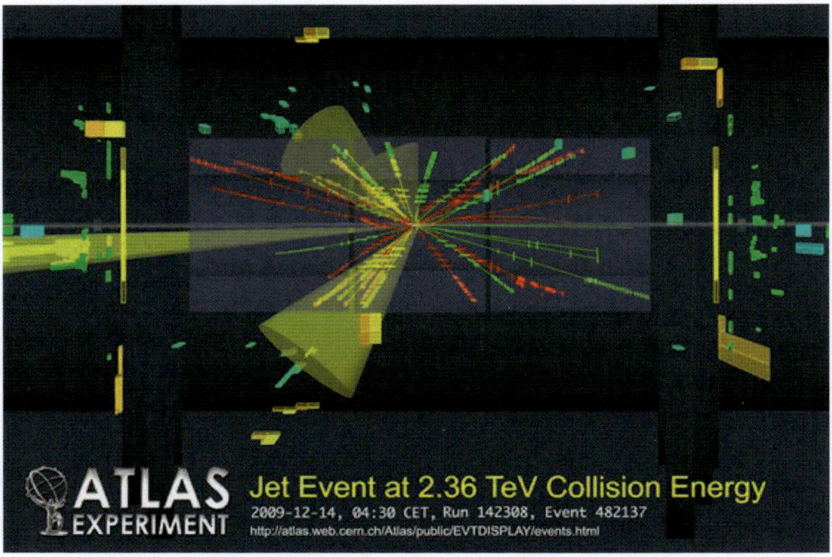

The Speaker, Professor Christoph Benjamin continued, 'What we are attempting is similar to our quest for The **Higgs boson,** the latter, as you all know, has been widely publicised. Every day, we are in the news and on the TV. Some of you will have seen the physicists Doctors Brian Cox and Michio Kaku, in TV documentaries, who have explained that the Higgs boson is a massive elementary particle (a particle is a minute portion of matter or energy) that is predicted to exist by the Standard Model(SM) of particle physics.

The SM is a theory developed by physicists to explain how the various types of elementary particles that make up the visible Universe interact. Results from other particle physics experiments match the SM extremely well only if one missing piece, the Higgs boson, is assumed to exist.

Based on the particles discovered so far, The SM could not otherwise explain why some particles have mass whilst others don't. Cathy smiled, recalling the picture detailing the SM she had seen on the net.

A pony picture, but one that appealed as an aid to recollection.

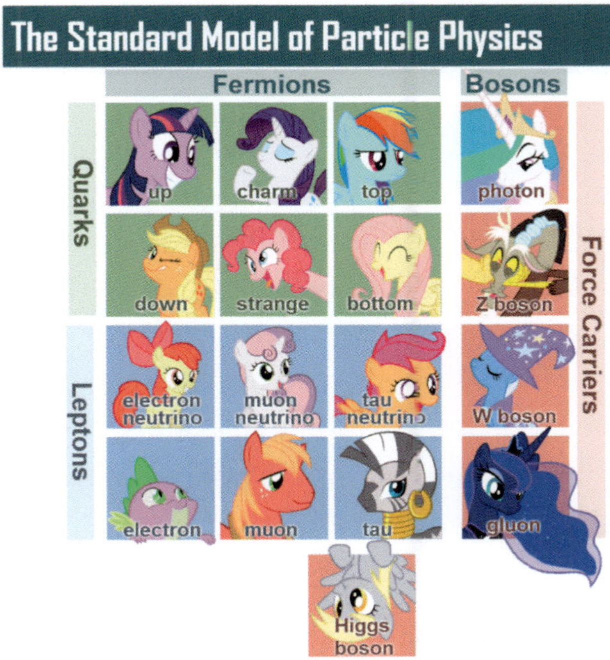

The Higgs boson poses the question what is the origin of mass?' Cathy knew that mass was the amount of stuff in something. In this case, the question was what was the origin of the amount of stuff in the Universe?

Cathy a week ago, in the midst of packing for the trip, having said a casual goodbye to her family (she was under strict instructions not to disclose the gravity of the situation to anyone), had pored over sheets of printed paper on The Higgs mechanism - a theory by the Scottish theorist, Peter Higgs who said that space is not empty which leads to the search for a particle that other particles bump into – the Higgs particles –and the quest for the elusive Higgs boson.

Eating Chinese takeaway in her flat in London, Cathy had thought of the fortune-hunt for what the press had dubbed 'the God particle'. The particle which in a Higgs quantum field stores mass and with the Big Bang all those billions of years ago, resulted scientists believed, in the creation of earth. However, the crock at the end of the rainbow could be a tragedy for mankind.

For in the last few weeks, as the Prof. said, the LHC had to cease looking for the Higgs boson and had to hunt for the Black Widow, the dark matter particle in the wormhole, which had been interfered with and corrupted through man-engineered missile radiation.

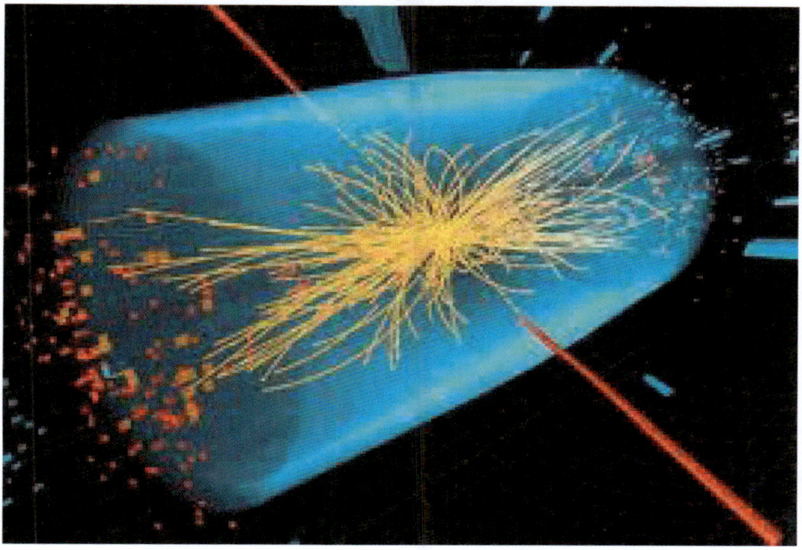

This image made available by CERN shows a typical candidate event including two high-energy photons whose energy (depicted by red towers) is measured in the Compact Muon Solenoid electromagnetic calorimeter. The yellow lines are the measured tracks of other particle produced in the collision. The pale blue volume shows the CMS crystal calorimeter barrel. (AP Photo/CERN)

A nuclear missile misfired had imbued the Black Widow with negative energy density, causing the wormhole and gravity had done the rest. The hot subdwarf star, Damocles massive enough to devastate earth was heading towards the solar system and the wormhole was expanding with the threat of a collision between Andromeda and the Milky Way.

World leaders had to prepare in haste. They had found they had such little time.

It was essential that Cathy, Matt and the rest of the team succeeded in finding that elusive particle, the Black Widow that could devastate earth within a matter of hours. Eject the pesky particle or introduce positive energy density into the wormhole somehow, making it collapse. That was the latest last-ditch measure but like such plans there was an intrinsic flaw. They would have to get hold of mass, any bit that they could find. Unfortunately, there wasn't enough in the solar system.

Eight months earlier

Karoo Region South Africa:

A tumbledown tin-roof shack. The man was young, barely graduated from University. He had wanted to live a rustic life in this vast semi-desert covering more than 100,000 square miles of South Africa's Cape region but living was sparse. He had lived from hand to mouth. He had a couple of ostriches, a vegetable patch that did not yield much and a ride from the locals into town once a week. Then his money ran out.

But fortune had smiled upon him today; he had a call from an old mate. Yes he was willing and able.

He would get employment at the Ionospheric Research Instrument (IRI) a high-powered radio frequency transmitter facility operating in the high frequency (HF) band, which Teheran had set up in the Karoo region.

Teheran had worked jointly with the South African government to explore the potential to energize a small portion of the ionosphere for radio communications and surveillance, much like the HAARP Station manned by the USA in Alaska. But Teheran had a different itinerary as to its workings. An intent of evil.

The facility had its own choice personnel but this time they needed an outsider. Someone like him, trained in scientific research on nuclear physics. The job was to temporarily send out this massive electromagnetic pulse. He had to disappear after the job was done. Hal Heinberg had few regrets. He knew his life would begin again somewhere else. There was one other further instruction. Do some research on IRI and mind control.

CERN, Geneva

Matt Mallard was instructing her and the other astral projectionists as to the order of events. First, they had been superenergised, after which they would take their places on the beds in the centre of the room hooked up to digital-age systems, which had been crafted with the minute precision and skill of a watchmaker. An audio-feed had been provided which would enable them to hear each other and also to hear music or meditative chanting that would enable a level of mental clarity to achieve astral transport.

Cathy was only half-listening. Her mind was worrying at the toxic particle Black Widow, believed to exist in the core of Damocles, the hot subdwarf star in the wormhole. It had been created by man's greed and avarice and the need to subjugate his fellow beings. And Andromeda, utterly unsurpassed in beauty had been despoiled with one end of the wormhole firmly ensconced in its centre.

GALEX: The Andromeda Galaxy Credit: GALEX, JPL-Caltech, NASA

Cathy felt Andromeda in her very soul, a galaxy clad in David Bowie's Ziggy Stardust outfit, a dazzling cobalt.

M31: The Andromeda Galaxy Credit & Copyright: Robert Gendler

She had been spirited across its surface in pure observation, not long ago. Thanks to the Space Telescope Science Institute, which analysed data from the Hubble Space Telescope. They had allowed her and Matt to have ringside seats at their base in Baltimore, USA.

The scientists had informed her that Andromeda's core contained, in one of the latest Hubble Space Telescope images, a dual nucleus one with blue stars around a supermassive black hole. Intelligence existed here with unabridged streams of pure thought, was her immediate intuition.

These heavenly blue stars in the NASA images from the Hubble Space telescope, that Cathy had avidly gazed at, were surrounded by a larger ‘double nucleus’ of Andromeda. The double nucleus is actually an elliptical ring of old reddish stars in orbit around that heavy black hole but more distant than the blue. Matt Mallard would have reason to remember these stars in the next few hours.

Cathy, her mind automatically absorbing the drill from hours of constant practice, which Mallard had instilled in her and the other three, remembered her recent research. The prestigious journal, Science, ran an article that claims of 300 to 500 million years after the Big Bang, the earliest stars had appeared and burned for a few million years, then died out. This was untrue. New data suggests that some were not extinguished but have continued to burn to this day. Cathy felt a frisson of electrical awareness in the pit of her stomach.

A deadly star, Damocles was just such a star newly discovered and intensely frightening. Cathy, Mallard and the other three astral surfers had to halt it before it reached the Milky Way and Earth.

Today! At best tomorrow.

Chapter 2

Eight months earlier:

Teheran

Sohrab Reza strode in to the ornate gilt and rosewood decorated bedroom. The girl lying there was young, barely seventeen. Russian. She was naked and nubile, of great beauty. He stood for a moment looking at her legs splayed on the cream silk covers. Ivory with a hint of a tan that she had picked up on the French Riviera. He had paid for it of course.

'Hello Sohrab' she said, smiling shyly

'You are early. I expected you in two hours time. If there is to be a next time, I expect you to obey my instructions. Anyone in the palace could have seen you. Did you use the back elevator as I told you?'

Natasha climbed gracefully out of the bed. He was undressing. He had taken off the blue ancient Persian head cloth that he favoured. She approached him and took his hand. 'Do not be angry Sohrab. I was so anxious to see you. I just want to please you. You are my hero. You have given me so much.'

'Hum, the jewels I gave you. You are not wearing them. Put them on. I want to fuck you with them on. Nothing else'

The diamonds glittered against her throat. He kissed her and said, 'Open your mouth.' He penetrated her mouth. She was choking. It seemed interminable. At last it was over.

He rolled over and said roughly, 'You can go. I have work to do. Take this.' He clutched a handful of notes. 'Buy yourself something nice. You are a good girl.'

An hour later, he was at his desk, the machine in front of him. Enhanced electromagnetism at its best. A mind reading, mind tampering device enabling thought transference with radio wave technology. He had come across it unexpectedly. The Turkish corporation he had bought six months ago had yielded unexpected results. Within their archives were the blueprints of this device, digitally stored along with a name, Nasr Al-din.

Al-din had bent over backwards to help the new buyer of his corporation. He had explained the function of the machine and verified that it actually worked. 'Just think of a real-time remote functional MRI scanner. This machine works on the same, if not far superior, principle. It deciphers a thought process, for regardless of a person's native language or history, certain parts of the brain light up at certain nouns and also emotions. This baby sequences all of it and thought recognition is achieved.'

Al-din dropped a hint that he had his henchmen perform a mind manipulation exercise in Cyprus some years ago on a young woman. Unfortunately, he had been stopped by the British and his own government. They had confiscated the machine. He would be delighted if a British subject was a likely target once again.

Within weeks Reza's technicians had the machine up and running.

Reza's telephone rang. The scrambler was active. The voice at the other end was business-like and curt. A man from the Iranian Guardian Council.

'Have you got the information the President requires? Ahmadi does not like to be kept waiting'

'I have already given you most of the information on the nineteen other minds in the group. Details of their personal and business transactions. They are programmed already.'

'What of the Israeli bastard among the 20? Ben-Ami Efraim and his country's Ofek 9- the spy satellite that is spying on our nuclear programme. They must never discover that we have gone atomic. We must protect our arsenal. The President has further plans which under no circumstances, can be discovered by Ofek9.

Keep this in the strictest confidence: Iraq is going to get a bombshell soon.

First, we will end Ofek9's lifespan. We are going to blow it up. That way no one will find out our nuclear and neighbourly options.'

'How do you plan to do that, Mashhadi?'

'Sabotage- we have installed a powerful radar in the vast isolation of the African desert and we plan to transmit an extremely powerful electromagnetic pulse to interfere with the probe and make it crash into the earth's atmosphere. I will send you all the details. Make sure you have a man in place.'

CERN, Geneva:

'This was rather like a full body CT scan, thought Cathy as she lay being supercharged. Cathy thought of the task ahead. Psychokinetic energy among the constellations, Gemini, Orion so much more. Stars, crystal-like in their stasis, spiritual stalagmites from where all beings ensue. Professor Brian Cox explained in his TV series how all 92 elements on earth, including those that are part of our bodies, originate from the death of stars.

Products of theories that were abounding in the world today as humans probed the heavens looking for the afterburn of life on earth. Cathy liked to think of Earth rendering its bodies to exist eternally in infinity.

Were Cathy, Matt and the rest of the team, destined to be forever stranded in that infinity as they made their ascent through space and time or would earth's vicinity beckon them home with its own pull of energy, the kinetic and the potential?

Cathy had painstakingly worked out that Kinetic energy is motion while the Potential energy is an object that has the promise of motion. The best analogy she could think of was what had been spotted on the news back in February, when Iran had demonstrated its show of potential primed and ready to go lethal anti-air and ballistic missile systems.

The trajectory of the missile follows a laser beam; the potential energy is the trigger being drawn back before the missile is released. Think of a rider on a bicycle or an Iranian anti-air missile, she had said to herself.

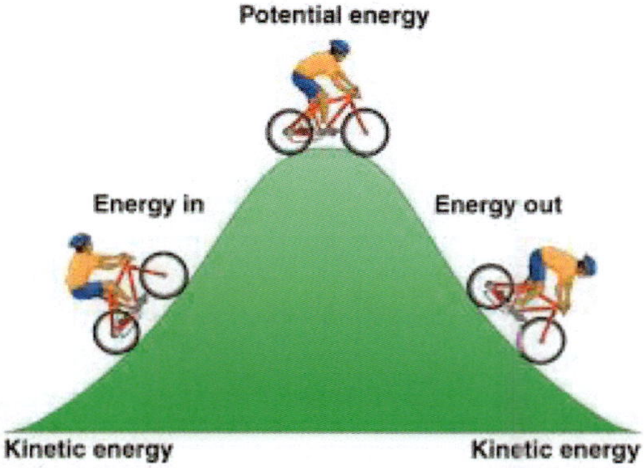

When the bike climbs, its kinetic energy changes into potential energy. If it is a missile, deflecting air-strikes from Israel, it climbs to the very top and then it reaches its maximum potential energy. The missile explodes. It has achieved its potential.

Now like the missile, the bike speeds down the hill back towards earth and potential energy turns into kinetic in its movement. Potential energy is the stored energy of position, like a drawn bow. The other, the kinetic is of movement. Rather like the latest news of Israel's actions – of concentrated movement planned - with the promise of air strikes on Iran's nuclear facilities.

More relevant now, the Black Widow was the potential energy. That left them, the kinetic connection. Or rather the psychokinetic connection. Cathy and the others. They had to go to the top of the swing, like a pendulum, psychokinetically high up in space, to find amongst the stars earth's nemesis. The wormhole, with Damocles and the Black Widow particle.

Was there also the collective secret hope that the insight of the five humans would provide a definite outcome in space? Finding Spiritually-charged potential energy- unexplained sources of energy, mere silhouettes that she and Mallard had recorded on their last astral projections.

Angels or Aliens?

Were they the dark energy in the Universe that permeates all of space and is responsible for the acceleration of the expansion of the Universe? Was the Black Widow also part of that dark energy or dark matter? Cathy knew dark energy makes up 70% of the universe and dark matter 25% with only 5% that of normal matter; and everything ever observed with all earthly instruments was the normal kind.

The rest was unknown.

Einstein's theory of gravity said space is not empty, it is energy filled, so with the expanding universe containing more space and therefore more energy –

were there different forms pulsating with that energy? She must discuss the idea with Matt.

Perhaps, as she and Matt had proved, all it needed was a state of consciousness raised to such a level that it interconnected with other phenomena in space. They had told the others to exhort their minds- reach as high and as far as you can. All extra-sensory powers would have to be brought to bear. Her forte and the others like her gathered here today. Charlie McCarthy, Chandra Gupta and Sergei Boystov. They had been introduced when they had arrived here in Geneva.

Here was Sergei Boystov approaching her now as they both walked out of the energisation chambers.

'I have to give you something. It's very important we meet. We need to talk'

Cathy said, 'Sure, after this session I'll be heading to the cafe. Why not join me there?'

Sergei nodded. The man on the dais, Professor Christoph Benjamin, his rhetoric changing from explanation to an instant of sheer panic as an assistant approached and whispered an aside to him.

He started sweating. Wiping his brow he said shakily, 'We now have twelve hours. The latest tests which the eminent Mr. Mallard has attempted have not succeeded. Atlas has not found Black Widow. The wormhole is impenetrable.

Roll back the screen. The projectionists please take your places. The lady and the 4 gentlemen will begin in the next few minutes. They are just emerging from the Stimulation Superchambers. They are volunteers and they are pre-eminent in their fields and affiliated in some way to the Monroe Institute which is a highly-respected organisation based in Virginia, USA, specialising in a higher consciousness, reaching levels that are renowned.

Let us begin. We have no time to waste.

Cathy after being supercharged in the energised chamber was high, adrenalin rushing through every pore, her skin tingled, she felt as though she was in a fever, yellow-gold it engulfed her. She donned the energised oversuit, the assistants plugged all leads into the console by the bed, and settled her in adjusting the visor. Her mind was in tune with Matt's. Together they would do this. The others had no idea they were telepathic partners. The only two in the world as Matt was fond of telling her. She tuned in her audio guidance headphones. Matt's voice, hypnotic and soft was lulling her into a familiar place. A level of consciousness in the highest ethereal zone.

The last time they did this together had brought about an experience where God, angels or aliens had transported them to the heavens and beyond. The earth's blue, its turquoise and jade were displayed in huge swathes of glorious colour. She had felt herself borne on the backs of smoky spirits. Andromeda, only in its outer bounds, they had skimmed together, cloaked in stars and sapphire – An indescribable astral experience.

They were euphoric but their findings brought consequences – dire consequences. They had thought the world would see them as pioneers in space projection, physical bodies' earth-static, while they achieved mental astral flight and an incredible search for proof that life existed in the seething mass of empty space. But they got it wrong. Shortly after, they were to be hunted down as common criminals.

Matt Mallard was finding it difficult to concentrate. He needed to reach that special place, a stratosphere of consciousness. He was the leader of the 5 and all the world was a heartbeat away from a massive collision- the Milky Way and Andromeda. In twelve hours time.

He willed himself to focus but his mind kept turning over a little quatrain he had read in his student days, recurring incessantly of late. A quatrain of Michel de Nostradamus, the 16th century physician, astronomer and seer:

'Shall be born a strong master of Mohammed. He will enter Europe wearing a blue turban. He will be the terror of mankind. Never more horror'

The Antichrist. One of the Opus Signori.

He had met them a month ago. Mallard had been summoned to a meeting. The hotel conference room was anonymous, buried in the heart of London. Twenty men gathered around the oval table. An ante-room housed the assistants, choice personnel armed with computers and tight security. He shook the hands of the twenty, names sounding softly almost whispered. Men dressed in the finest cloth, their minds a closed book to him. All he knew was the impression of potent power they emanated.

Faces, none he recognised - white, brown and black, a mixture of nations. They were men infinitely removed from the public arena. Behind closed doors, they were sentinels of world order. Whispered rumours abounded of the need for insatiable control. Had they ordered a deathly sanction on President Kennedy all those years ago? One man stood out from the rest, was he the leader? A man dressed in blue, a Persian name. Sohrab Reza. Mallard sensed a dark presence. A thought, formed from the middle distance, the way it always did impinged. Mallard recoiled. The familiarity was ugly. A catastrophic technology of Matthew Mallard's own making was in use. His hair stood on end, was he the target or was it someone else in the room? Or was it all twenty of the sleekly-clad power-soaked men present?

Chapter 3

CERN, Geneva

Cathy, slipping into a trance at the CERN private gallery, started dreaming of Andromeda, it's primary star, the Alpha whose Arabic meaning refers to the 'horse's navel'. Andromeda, in Greek mythology was the daughter of Cassiopeia and Cepheus.

Unfortunately her mother, Cassiopeia, was so vain that she thought herself to be more beautiful than the daughters of Nereus, a god of the sea. This angered the sea god Poseidon.

To punish the mother, Andromeda was chained to a rock off the coast as a sacrifice for a sea monster, Cetus. She escaped this deadly fate when she was saved by Perseus, a demigod. Perseus had beheaded Medusa, and used the head to turn Cetus, the sea monster to stone, thus saving Andromeda.

After rescuing her, Perseus demanded Andromeda as his wife, which the parents gladly accepted. As an eternal reminder of her vain folly, her mother Cassiopeia remains forever chained to her royal throne, and doomed forever to turn over and over in the starry skies whilst Andromeda reigns supreme as a large northern galaxy.

A Greek myth. As Greek as Cypriot Hektor. He started intruding in her mind. Hektor Xanthis her former lover. She had stopped seeing him just months ago. Hektor, whom she had met in her former job as an interpreter in London. His ambitions to be President had been the reason for her being a mental conduit in Cyprus 5 years ago. Cathy had been attacked through her mind so that Hektor would be coerced into promoting a consensus for a positive vote on the EU treaty. Cathy had resisted and Hektor had succeeded in his ambition of doing the opposite, but had to step out of the presidential race with the demise of his only son. Had his son been deliberately murdered? The aching question still haunted his every waking thought.

Three years ago, his wife too had died and he had sought Cathy out. His ambitions to be President had re-surfaced. He was powerful and wanted her. He had serious intentions. She had agreed to see him again because she believed she loved him. But she had been unhappy. Cathy tensed thinking of the reasons why. Hektor reminded her of a time of mental turmoil. Methods of persuasion had been attempted on her mind to thwart Hektor in his ambitions in Cyprus. Cathy could not forget that terrible time.

Matt's voice intruded. His tones were soporific, soothing, and hypnotic. He could read her mind. He could feel the stress taking hold of her.

'Calm Cathy, they are starting to unfurl the canopy around that vast screen above us.   - Look, we have stars. We have weightlessness. Glasses okay? That visor certainly looks fetching on you -You know, I believe, CERN's and NASA's techies collaborated to produce these navigational aids after the latest research where apparently, eyes need to be wide open to access all the other senses to the full.

We can access system diagrams and imagery live from the ISS and space probes to pinpoint our location. The built-in goggles give us almost X-Ray vision with infrared light to extend our sight through all the dust and gas clouds that exist in the heavens. The imaging spectrograph is based on the Hubble telescope and will allow us to hunt for the beginnings of the wormhole in Andromeda.

I have the sole task of applying the optical laser tweezers also present in the glasses to the Black Widow once we identify it – fascinating stuff Cathy- the boff's used highly focused laser beams in the tweezers based on programmes like Windows and the Kinect to give me full body control over tiny particles. Particles like the Black Widow can be picked up using body, hand and arm movements.

Previously, trackpads and touch controls like the iPad were used but this technology is the very latest and I've had some intensive training in the past few days. I needed it as I have to initiate movement purely with my mind whilst retaining my contact with sensory input from my body. For, I as you know will be nowhere physically near the Black Widow - just my mind in the astral projection but there is an imprint of my stored brainwaves in the array of sensors in my headset and the data collected allows me to control objects by just thinking about my actions.

All this wizardry has lastly, depth sensing cameras installed in the goggles which send back the images to the screen up above us. The computers will of course analyse all the info. and simulate my actions, replicating them until all the Black Widow particles (if there's more than one in the wormhole) are ejected and the wormhole collapses.'

Mallard kept the disquieting thought to himself that the scientists had shared. They feared there was no way any amount of computers could achieve such a gargantuan task. The wormhole stretched too far and too wide.

He said aloud, 'Approaching Orion and Taurus. Look how close we are. Left and there's a constellation you might remember from before. Why the sudden fear? You are shaking. Imagine I am holding your hand. Don't worry, this is our first session and it will be of short duration. Our concentration will slowly expand at each attempt.

Can you feel the power?' His voice was creating a febrile excitement. Her stomach was clenching, not with fear but with yearning. She watched as Gemini came close, her breath almost stilled.

A cavern – superman's like in the film- was it ice, serrated and elongated surfaces? - She was floating – she tried to touch it, she couldn't, her body in the astral projection was not working; a voice, Matt's, spoke of matter, she knew matter and energy were equivalent and all the energy was being used up psychokinetically. Her body was in a void, whilst her mind performed callisthenics.

The ice, no it was quartz, virginal white with edges of blue, sharp and clear. Shimmering, glowing, glistening she felt drawn to merge in its depths. She remembered Gemini was a constellation, one of 88 modern constellations – its name was Latin and meant twins.

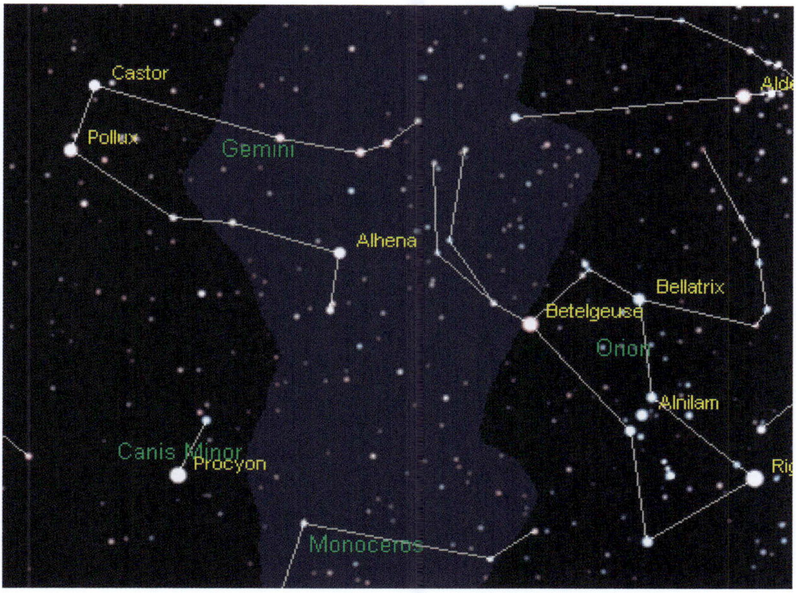

She approached Pollux. Matt was near the other one Castor. She suddenly remembered what had happened on their last astral flight. Matt's machine had recorded the event – had he re-jigged the memory? His machine was of mind technology so advanced that Matt had taken extreme precautions, setting up all sorts of alarms and firewalls to ensure its secrecy.

Cathy shuddered as she now recalled in full, the souls of the ancient Chinese Tang dynasty had fiercely tried to detain her. Twins echoing in her mind, born of the Li family, an injustice done – a murder, their spirits seeking surcease. Were they angels?

Cathy's mind had been torn from pure abstract thought to the plaintive voices telling their story. An account of what had befallen Li Yuanji and Crown Prince Li Jiancheng. The Li brothers belonged to the military aristocracy in the reign of the Sui emperors. Li Shimin, a sibling, who was proficient with a bow, sword and lance, was famed for his aggressive cavalry charges. He deposed his father in 626 AD and in a terrible fratricide, murdered his brothers - the Li twins, who were invading Cathy's mind. They talked in shrieks mentally inputting their sorry tale.

Cathy had felt overcome on that occasion, she had felt so close to death and now the Li twins were resurrecting their influence again, as images of lotus blossoms and soft Chinese accents filled Cathy's mind – could she stay forever, they wanted to know.

They knew her thoughts were contained in a vessel- a vessel that radiated good in the world. She could influence life on earth, she must stay. Cathy was settling into Pollux's immortality, the twin who had pleaded to share that immortality with his brother, Castor and the gods had listened and made them stars in Gemini.

The other cosmos-nauts noticed her whereabouts on their locator screens.

‘There are famous sculptures of the twins, resident in the Hermitage Museum, St. Petersburg. I will see if I can get CERN to send you the image in your visor screen’ was mentioned in her earpiece by Sergei Boystov, the Russian cosmos-naut.

Castor and Pollux. Hermitage, St.Petersburg

Cathy observed the image in a daze. No form beckoned. Just sheer influential thought.

It would be so easy for her mind to let go of the physical body. Death of the body, but eternal consciousness amongst the stars. Adrift, sensually and emotionally unable to be rational, Cathy, disoriented, heard the whisper of names of these stars of Gemini, Castor and Pollux, in Chinese. They were the White Tiger of the West and Vermilion Bird of the south.

In this world of sky with no borders, she was cocooned in a microcosm of self. She would die in this sheath, this covering. Star-struck she would curtsy to the grandeur of this vast expanse – colour-bright, hues impossible and impudent, like all the light, and the birds and the fish in the world put together, as far as her eye could see.

Cathy's mind, sensing the death-throes of her body, started the struggle for survival.

Matt's voice issuing instructions, punched through the yards of sentient wall and jolted her, she started. Concepts of mind and intelligence which she had explored, to better understand Matt's tutelage, came back to her now. She must concentrate!

Recently, on a tube journey in Central London, a sudden quickening of the senses and Cathy wondered if all the people present in the carriage, could affect each other's thoughts. If ideas, likes, dislikes, popped into each other's heads; a shared Telepathy that would determine a trend in thinking, in fashion, in a taste for knowledge. The concept of Zeitgeist and the collective consciousness which moved in a certain direction and dictated the actions of its members.

Cathy had googled for more knowledge on the subject and came across the philosopher Arthur Schopenhauer who proclaimed that if it is certain that our ideas appear to us in succession, then they must move themselves because they are not moved by things that are not ideas. Ideas are also capable of moving things that are different from themselves.

The fascination lay in a thinking substance as a separate entity removed from her body rather like what she was doing in projection, an idea, a thought that moves itself and other substances. Psychokinesis and the reason for today.

For that matter, if her physical self died, could she influence the outcome of their quest and communicate it to the others purely as spiritual telepathy? Cathy was doubtful and as long as such doubt existed, she must stay alive. She felt herself trying to drag her consciousness back into order; she must overcome this mental lethargy. She had a role to fulfil, a reason for her continued existence on earth. Desperately, she fought the influence of the Li twins but her mind teased with possibilities instilled by a Classical background.

The Li's seemed to occupy a separate realm of consciousness where spirits dwell. Were they evil or were they angels? Were they mind and intelligence surviving, pure and unadulterated, from the demise of the human body? They seemed to be able to communicate with the higher consciousness that Cathy and the others had achieved.

Now here on Pollux, another mad spirit or sprite or an angel, Friedrich Nietzsche the German philosopher of the late 19th century entered her thinking. Hadn't he said that *nous* or intelligence created the universe?

Cathy was interrupted rudely in her beads of soft thought. The Chinese twins, the Li's, were strident in her mind. A Bloody Loud Spiritual Telepathy, thought Cathy. Cathy was jolted back. Thinking of Nietzsche had brought her back from the brink of staying in Pollux forever. She looked across to Matt. Castor seemed only wisps away in the visors specially developed for the cosmos-nauts.

Matt Mallard looked towards the shimmering around him. Canis Minor and Orion close by. He felt close to God. His thoughts turned to his childhood and Sunday School. Genesis 15:5-6. '*He* *took him outside and said, look up at the sky and count the stars- if indeed you can count them...*Gemini, now what was that the Bible had said of the twins, dressed in the garb of a man and a woman, words of ancient meaning, 'After the man was created to bear witness of the truth of God, the woman was added to verify the truth.'

Procreation had been on his mind of late. Was Cathy, his Pollux? The female of the twins of Gemini, represented in the ancient Denderah Zodiac (the Egyptian bas-relief dated at 50BC), the only complete map of the ancient sky now on display at the Musee de Louvre, Paris. Faint fingers of Latin brushed his memory of the figures in the Zodiac - *Clusus*, or *Claustrum Hor* - the place of Him who cometh.

Image: Wikimedia Commons

God warning him of imminent danger. One of the Opus Signori or all of them.

His mind snapped back. He took himself back to that place of ultimate consciousness. He heard Cathy's voice, she was exclaiming in wonderment for there was a shape appearing, a supernova.

NASA's composite image of the Tycho supernova appeared in his memory

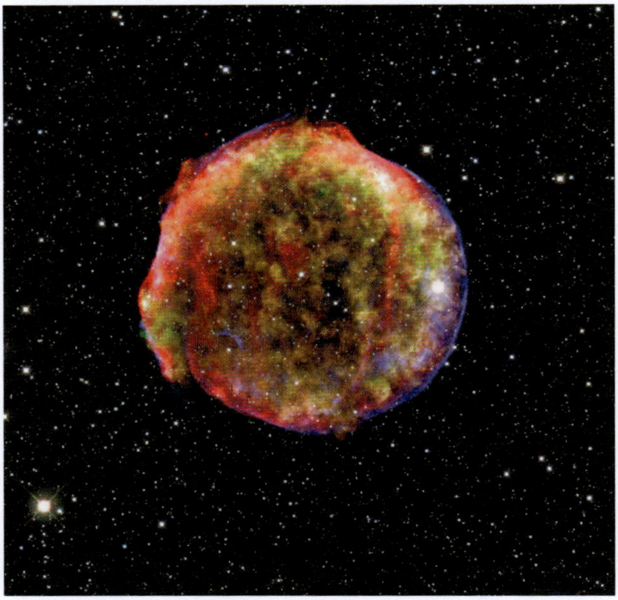

He knew Cathy liked to think supernovae were caused by stars preferring to end their lives rather than just fading away.

They explode in massive cosmic displays of beauty and grandeur. For Cathy and Matt, in their astral projections they were safe from the debris but their minds ingested the knowledge that heavy elements like iron only exist in supernovae, and as our bodies have traces of such elements, all of us carry the remnants of these distant explosions within our own bodies. 'Further proof of the connection between all things in heaven and on earth,' Mallard said to the others.

Mallard was a man of extraordinary gifts. Acute extrasensory perception, telepathy, psycho kinesis and high doses of electrical energy had brought about the need to heal. He had become world-renowned for his healing powers alone.

The gift of prophecy and insight had brought him closer to an understanding of the growth that existed under the earth, a lifeblood of ore and minerals and fertile roots, above it lands and seas where man and creatures walked and bathed, and in the universe where all things interact with each other and with planetary life. Interaction through mental pathways above all. Telepathy, his lifetime occupation.

He had built a special machine creating thought transference electronically, helping those in need. However, the machine had been appropriated by the British Government a few years ago as Cathy had been inadvertently caught up in a Turkish plot on the island of Cyprus and the machine had been used for nefarious purposes. They had never discussed that time. He must talk to her about it.

Here on Castor, with his vision adjusting to the fantastic palette displayed from the colours of the supernova, his electrically charged consciousness emitting beams of pure light, he sensed that telepathic hotwiring which brought a trembling in his gut. A prescient of an amoeba forming- a form of new life emerging in the universe, on a planet not too far distant from our solar system.

Matt in a flash of inspiration, chose Shakespeare's nickname to baptize the planet. 'The Bard's Muse.'

He must tell Cathy. He must also inform the Opus Signori. He signalled to Cathy they would start descending.

Chapter 4

JUNE 2012

CERN, Geneva:

A short break and the sounds of a dozen different languages with broken English predominant in the cafe at CERN. Cathy thought of her pet 'tube' theory. Telepathy, ideas hopping from one mind to the next but of course that too could be perverted. Mind tampering, used as she knew, on unsuspecting individuals.

Cathy smiled when Sergei Boystov took the seat opposite. He seemed terribly in earnest as he said, 'I know all about you'

'Yes, they gave each of us the other projectionists background info. before we got here'

'No, I mean I really know all about you' He looked fixedly at her. As Cathy started to look uncomfortable he said, 'Do not be afraid. I mean well. I have a story to tell you and something to give you.' He handed her a painted lacquer box. It was beautiful and looked old.

Cathy listened as he told her a strange tale.

She said with something approaching awe, 'I'm so sorry to repeat all this to you but I want to get it straight in my mind. My understanding is that an old man, a Leonard Sosnovsky, your grandfather, who is still alive and as a collector, was exhibiting at the Hermitage Museum in St. Petersburg. Your uncle met him there.

He had saved this box for ages and gave it to your uncle who died and entrusted you to give it to me. It is a box containing the scroll of the seven seals, ancient papyri containing what was first inscribed by St John in the Bible. You tell me that throughout the centuries men have pondered over St. John's meaning. And, Sergei, the package also contains incriminating evidence about the Russian president, Putinov. Your Uncle was murdered because of this evidence. You say these are meant for me alone.

You, Sergei, fought to be here. It was very hard for you but you succeeded and all because you wanted to give this to me. The papyri have never been opened and are an ancient artefact. The package is to be unsealed if all else fails today.

Sergei, I am really honoured to be chosen but I'm not sure I am the right person you seek. Yes I have knowledge of Ancient Greek and I have done translations before but I am not special in any way. I'm quite ordinary. My knowledge of the Bible is limited'

'My uncle and I have been looking for you for 5 years. We checked you out when we saw you were in the newsfeed six months ago. My uncle before he died tragically was in no doubt that you were the one. I am too. You flew across the earth's surface using your mind, astrophysical flight and you have photographs to prove it. That is very special Katya.'

'Matt did it with me. The photographs were reproduced because of his special machine. Here he comes now'. Sergei hurriedly stood up. He said, 'I must go. Look after this with your life. As I said it contains the Apocalyptic seals. Today we will have need of it'.

Matt had been closeted with one of the team of astrophysical surfers. Cathy, sitting in the cafe and sipping a coke, reflected on what Sergei had told her. Her phone rang. Ten minutes later she switched off the phone and thought, 'A rather disturbing call.'

Hektor Xanthis. She had told him where she was. He said he would fly over for a visit. He insisted he had to see her. He would arrive in 2 hours.

She had loved him. She still did but her relationship with him had ended a few months ago. Funnily enough, it was Cathy whose character changed texture. From confused youth she measured up to her given insight and acknowledged a liberating force deep within, a right to command the wind, to dictate the bounce of the ball.

Hektor was as he ever was but he had no latent feelings encompassing the elements. Matt had explained that it was the old animal brain of Homo sapiens, considered defunct that caused all the psychic activity in her and others of her ilk.

Hektor was all business and ambition. Cathy on the other hand had been all liquid gold – a sixth sense, a sensitivity that was affected deeply by waves of human thought. Other people's thoughts. Current events/global thinking/personal ties of family and friends - their thoughts would impinge on her consciousness without any access to media or conversation. Episodes of psychosis were the clinical diagnosis. The psychiatric world had discounted the paranormal and stated that she came under the umbrella of schizophrenia when she had related that she had heard voices. Cathy, full of self-doubt, had taken the medication and continued to be monitored by her physician.

Now at CERN, her entire being soared. She felt like a pilot lying prone, being his own aircraft, arms outstretched and propelled with priceless privilege while the floor beneath him ripples into pinpricks of light, infatuated with the world under as it becomes his flight path.

Matt walked towards her. Cathy thought recently she really fancied him. Tall, dark and sooo macho. He had impinged on her mind when she was a young girl. She had read his books and had been introduced to paranormal activity. Subsequently, their minds had known each other. Then she had met him in the flesh. She was sexually aware of him from that moment, but all she remembered was a mental communication years ago, a dream, of sepia tinted sketches of body outlines- his and hers. The deed had never been done. And Hektor, her Greek lover had always been in the vicinity of her affections.

Now that she had created a distance emotionally from Hektor, and seeing Matt continuously, since she had started to work with him professionally, she was drawn to his magnetism. They had spent many an hour in astral projection. He had taught her everything she was able to do today and she felt absorbed by him, of the same star-studded aura as the constellation Andromeda.

Blue Velvet with the blackness of eternity.

Matt, though, never seemed interested. Cathy had never referred to his involvement in Cyprus when she was used as a mental conduit with attempts to control her mind and influence Hektor.

She gazed at him, green eyes concealing her deep interest in him, as he took the chair opposite her.

Matt smiled at her as he sat down. He was always in her mind. He ordered a coffee and said, ‘I have to talk to you about something very important that occurred up there in the ether. I think I have touched on something of a monumental nature. I don’t know how to impart information of such magnitude. I’ll put it plainly. I think I have sixth-sensed Amoebae in space, embryos of the silhouettes, faintly reproduced in the images of our last astral flight. We could not figure them out, nor could the boffins we shared them with- but you and I, in all humility, could not then believe in the possibility of extra terrestrial life being displayed for our private viewing. I made sure those photos of the silhouettes were never put in the public domain.

Now, Cathy, I am overcome. I believe.’

‘My God, Matt, you are never wrong with your intuition. Shouldn’t we tell somebody?’

‘I feel the urge to get on my knees and pray Cathy. Not only did I sense the presence of such life but I actually understood Spiritual Telepathy among other things. He told her of the divination – a message that God was close by in the ancient Latin etymology.’

'Matt, I've got to tell you what happened to me out there as well.' Cathy repeated the story of the Li twins and Nietzsche. 'I also had this sudden notion about dark energy. Do you think dark energy is a realm of consciousness where these spirits dwell? Cathy sounded eager as the words spilled out of her. 'What if, as the human population expands and to fit them in, so does the universe?'

Mallard held up his hand, 'Cathy, whoa there, I've been speaking to the others. They have had similar experiences. I suggested when we meet in less than an hour's time, as our consciousness is raised; we get high on each other's stories. Will buoy us up. Each of us may have stumbled on or been divinely led to an existence after death or perhaps the alien life I sensed are doing the educating.'

Mallard flexed his shoulders and put his hand on her arm. 'Another matter has arisen, we have so little time --but I must tell you --about the group of men I had occasion to meet once recently. I had forgotten all about them but just before I entered the energised chambers I felt a faint resonance, a voice touching faintly on my brainwaves. Briefly, he told her how he was summoned to the meeting with the Opus Signori and what had transpired.

'I think they got hold of my details when we had all that fuss with the press and MI5 on our last astral trip, photographing the earth - the publicity proved negative in some ways. The positives were we got funding, and were able to use all major facilities like NASA's great observatories, earth and space based telescopes, to assist astral travel and of course CERN contacted us to do our best today as a result of that publicity, but the suspicions aroused outweighed the joys.

We both felt like criminals with the grilling we received from Government security officials. We are still being hounded and should the press get hold of what we are doing.. well, we hope CERN is keeping everything under wraps at the moment'

'Matt you will have to tell someone if you have sensed alien life out there.'

'Cathy, I fully intend to. This group I mentioned, the Opus Signori, have promised that because they are above and beyond governments, we would be taken care of. We would never be pursued because of our professional calling. We could go about our business of deciphering phenomena earthly and in space without the gutter press ridiculing and probing every venture. The Opus Signori would keep us safe and in return we would share all our findings with them.

I trust most of them. I believe it's best I tell them of my discovery. I will make the call in a minute. Cathy out there, you told me you sensed the pull to stay. I felt a similar thread – a drawing on my mental reserves. There is a danger to our mental well-being and with that in mind before our next venture out there, I have to refer to the time when life was rather unpleasant for you.

Cathy, we have never talked about your time in Cyprus. I tried to help you but had to step back and deny all knowledge of you being on my machine's wavelength, when you went to the British Embassy for help. They of course branded you with a psychotic tag and I had to stay silent. I would have been shut down. My entire life would have evaporated. I could not touch it. I always knew you would commit to me someday. I hoped but I did not coerce you mentally. I held off until you came to me but now ...' he was interrupted by the futuristic metallic grey clad assistant, beckoning them back to the Globe.

Cathy spoke quickly on the walk back, telling Mallard of Sergei Boystov and story behind the lacquer box. She needed to put it in a safe place. Matt suggested they store it in the office they had been assigned. Cathy proceeded to the office. Before he entered the honeycomb that the Globe resembled, Mallard made the call.

Mallard's ESP was interconnecting with minds of great cognoscenti – especially well informed people, the Opus Signori, they knew what was happening at

CERN, and they were waiting for confirmation from him.

Chapter 5

JUNE 2012

ENGLAND:

The 5 men were seated in the home of the former British Prime Minister, Winston Churchill. Chartwell was closed off to the general public today. Yellow drapes shut out the summer sunshine. They talked quietly of the possibility of earth's annihilation. They had been informed that experiments were currently taking place. Results would be called in real time – microseconds of the event happening- the other fifteen members of their strata were being loop-fed, via their personal satellite ensuring utter communication security, including video conference calls. The five at Chartwell needed to make their peace with God. Cardinal Jules de Fleury sitting in their midst had already heard their confessions, even though they were atheists. They were, in the end, taking no chances.

The Cardinal said, 'I informed you that I have a man, a very spiritual, gifted man at the CERN experiment. He is a man who has the gift of all nations. The ability to see all in the past and the future. He is the one who I have been in constant touch with. He just telephoned. What he had to say must be contained in this room. Gentlemen, I suggest we pray. I believe we have life after death.'

CERN, Geneva:

Mallard adjusted his goggles and led the others via the audio feed which had been jigged to include all five participants. The other three, Russian, Indian and American were eager to settle in to listening mode as they prepared to raise their levels of atmospheric awareness.

Charlie McCarthy, the American, was the most assured. He had done it all. He was at the top of his game. Lauded by the press in the USA for his achievements in astral transport and psychic phenomena, he was wildly popular through TV, bestselling books and films. He was a man of 30 years of age, and he had a story to tell.

The Big Dipper is an asterism of 7 stars, it's also known as The Plough, and Charlie was heading there in his astral persona. A Native American myth told by Charlie's grandmother appealed to his mind.

The Big Dipper Cluster
Credit & Copyright: Noel Carboni

The bowl stars of the Big Dipper form a bear. The stars of the Dipper's handle are hunters. The tiny star near the elbow of the handle is a small dog named 'Hold Tight'. In autumn when the Dipper is low to the horizon, the blood from the bear's arrow wound drips on the trees and turns them red and brown. Trees jogged the memory and he told the others his story.

His grandmother was Cherokee and she had sat on a cold winter's evening, when Charlie was young, in a faded old armchair and told him the legend of the cedar tree. Charlie had listened enrapt and he told the others how it had led him to the present day. He said, 'A long time ago when the Cherokee people were new on the earth, they thought life would be much better if there was never any night. They prayed to the Creator (Ouga) and he answered their prayers. It was day all the time. Soon the forest was thick with heavy growth, paths were difficult to tread, and corn and other food plants were choked.

The heat was intense; people found it difficult to sleep and became short-tempered. They asked the Creator for their request to be reversed. They wanted it to be night all the time. Soon, the crops stopped growing and it became very cold. The people spent much of their time gathering wood for the fires. They could not see to hunt meat and with no crops growing it was not long before the people were cold, weak and very hungry. They went back to the Creator and pleaded for it to be as it was in the beginning, divided between light and darkness.

He obliged. Thereafter, the people were grateful but during the long days of night, many of the people had died and the Creator was sorry they had perished so he placed their spirits in a newly created tree. This tree was named the Cedar tree. When you smell the aroma of the cedar tree or gaze upon it standing in the forest, remember that if you are a Cherokee, you are looking upon your ancestor.'

Charlie said, 'See, river recovered cedar is used in the drums of the Indian religious ceremonies. I heard grandma's story, attended the gigs and heard the drumming, it was electric, wired to my brain - I could raise the mental bar- every time it got clearer- I tasted the ether!

Later, with scientific analysis, they told me that I became receptive to other brainwave mechanisms'

Now, as Charlie finished speaking, his grandmother's spirit beckoned him as he surfed the Ursa Major. She was telling him many things now, of trees networked between roots and fungi deep under the soil, transferred from one generation to the next, rather like a tree possessing a brain, a metaphysical presence, passing messages back and forth, giving nature the resilience to withstand strife.

Recently, he had read an article on trees having sex- how intermediaries like a bee or wind can pollinate female trees at a great distance. Tears rolled down Charlie's cheeks as life took on new meaning. When this was over and if the world survived Charlie was going to go for mad, glorious sex with his girlfriend, all day, every day until she felt his seed growing within her. Like his grandmother's stories of the trees, he had to ensure continuity.

For Charlie was dying. He had just 6 months to live. He had had no idea the cancer was growing within him. With all his powers of prediction he had been unable to sense it. Charlie heard the other projectionists emit sounds of sympathy.

The Big Dipper loomed in front of him. Chandra, his team mate was uttering his own form of reassurance for Charlie. He was saying,

'Look at the stars Charlie, the Eskimo says the stars are not just put in the sky to light or guide the wandering traveller. They are living things, sent by some twist of fate to roam the heavens forever, never swerving from their paths. Just think Charlie, there's hope. Do wish upon that star!

Eight months earlier:

Karoo, South Africa:

Hal Heinberg had managed to get the night shift. He had been hired just yesterday. The facility needed a transmission technician, urgently one like Hal, with a degree in nuclear physics from Cornell University, USA. They thought they were lucky to have him.

Hal settled in front of his screen and charted the position of Ofek9, the Israeli spy satellite. The co-ordinates had been sent just yesterday. He worked quickly.

Ofek9 was lying in that rarefied region of space called the ionosphere, about 70km above the earth. Hal pressed the buttons on the computer. The high-powered, high frequency phased array radio transmitter with its set of 180 antennae started their electromagnetic interactions. He needed to get the fucker out of the sky and crashing downwards. He only had one shot at it. Ofek 9 was only going to be in position within the next 5 minutes. Hal had to do the job and be out of here tonight. Two hours later, Hal left the building.

He had not succeeded.

Teheran would have to seek another option.

JUNE 2012,

GENEVA:

Hektor Xanthis left the airport building with his bodyguard. Of course he had cleared officialdom through diplomatic channels. He had no time to waste. Meetings were set up for him and he had to see Cathy. The Cyprus embassy car purred along the streets eating up the miles. Cathy had said she would call when she was free.

In the meantime, he had two meetings to attend. The first was with a Swiss Government official. The Swiss gentleman, Dominic Anderhub, was also the honorary Chairman of the space lab Columbus. Columbus in which the Swiss Government have a stake in had been shipped to the Kennedy Space Centre, USA back in 2007. From there it had been transported to the International Space Station. Hektor recalled what he knew of the ISS. It was a habitable artificial satellite in low earth orbit which could be seen with the naked eye from earth. Its research in space environment on various fields like biology, astronomy, physics and a myriad of others was lauded all over the Globe.

The second meeting was with a specialist photo laboratory here in Geneva. Proof was required.

Anderhub shook hands and got straight down to business. 'We have the photographs of course. They came through on the ISS screens. Mr. Xanthis I'm at liberty to tell you that these pictures were not taken by any known technology ever developed.

Four months ago, routine research was being conducted on astronomy, among other things, when the pictures started coming through. These photographs are unbelievable. We think we have proof of alien life. We believe we have connected the dots- it is a matrix of unbelievable proportions. Having read an article my secretary picked up in the British press, I had to get in touch with your man. We now know these important photos were taken by the human mind.'

An hour later, Hektor made the call. Cardinal Jules de Fleury listened intently. 'I know of this already. Mallard is keeping us informed. I knew of Cathy Burkert but I didn't know of your involvement with the girl'. He carried on speaking.

‘The girl in question is very important to me. I plan to see her shortly. Yes my loyalty is clear. I will let you know every detail,’ said Hektor. He was an Opus Signori after all.

Cathy stared breathlessly ahead. Betelgeuse, the red star of the constellation Orion the dying star, was just off to the right of her. She was connecting with the other four through the audio feed. Chandra was saying, ‘The Mughal Emperor Babur at the beginning of his memoirs states that there is a twin mosque called the Jawza Majid- It has been suggested that Jawza is the name for Orion and the twins are Castor and Pollux. When the moon leaves the evening sky by late February, you can draw an imaginary line from the Orion star Rigel through to Orion’s Betelgeuse to star-hop to the twins’ location.’

Cathy knew that Betelgeuse was due to run out of fuel someday, and have a stupendous explosion into a supernova. The Earth would have ringside seating.

From Mughal emperors, Chandra started to talk about the oldest scriptures of Hinduism, the Vedas. First, he would tell them his story.

A truly gifted highly intelligent man, Chandra had been born with a silver spoon in his mouth. Fabulously wealthy, he was protected and cosseted all his life by indulgent parents but in his early teens

Chandra developed a liking for girls. Not just one at a time, he liked them in twos and threes. He craved sex and his increasing lust needed to be fulfilled several times a day. His endless bank account bought him women, choice girls who commanded choice fees. That proved insufficient as his needs changed. He wanted virgins. He started stalking women, young girls barely out of school.

Chandra turned 21.

His parents, totally ignorant of Chandra's obsession decided Chandra was reaching an age he needed a wife, and they would select a suitable bride. Chandra married but that did not stop the pursuit of his craving. He would hold parties in his penthouse and invite girls, plying them with drink and drugs and expensive presents. They would put out for generous Chandra. His obsession was fulfilled.

Until the day he killed the young girl. 'You see,' he said to the others, 'she told everyone' – his wife, his parents, his friends. They rejected him. His wife divorced him and his parents cast him out. The word 'paedophile' was mentioned within his earshot by his friends. So enraged, he took her for a drive in his car. To berate her and reduce her to an abject being. There was an accident. She died, Chandra was flung clear. Chandra survived without a scratch but was found guilty of death by dangerous driving.

Chandra was lucky. His parents sacrificing their own distaste came to his rescue, they hired the best legal mind and Chandra got off with community service but the girl's death buried itself deep in his psyche. He was unable to eat or sleep. He was convinced her spirit haunted every moment and extreme guilt writhed within in daily torment.

To change the path of his tormented thinking he started to concentrate on yoga and meditation techniques. That led to recognised institutes like the Monroe that educated his thought projections. Over years of dedicated study, he turned his life around. He agonised over the holy books of all religions looking for absolution and finally the Vedas had an answer. The girl would live again.

Cathy started relaxing, his soft voice with the Indian chant, acting hypnotically on her. She was drifting and the Vedas were infiltrating her soul.

The soul of Re-incarnation as stated in the Bhagavad-Gita. Chandra related how his Vedic soul passed from one body to the next. Life is truly a circle of birth, death and re-birth. We never die; we merely change our physical form.

'Nietzsche would be turning over in his grave. Reincarnation was abhorrent to him' said Cathy.

The other four cosmos-nauts wanted to know more. Cathy obliged them.

'Nietzsche of course believed that intelligence created the world as a game. The freedom of thought and creative will is in direct opposition to the way the Universe works.

The Universe is based on the fact that everything is cyclical and all that happens has to happen and cannot be otherwise. *Nous* is referred to as a mind (Geist) that has free, arbitrary choice. The created world, *physis,* is a determined and mechanical piece of machinery. Cathy listed Nietzsche in order of her idea of importance:

Any order or efficiency of things is random, an outcome of purposelessness.

Earthly reincarnation was a punishment without end as there was no escape.

Humans needed to free their minds and not rely on a God.

Therefore there is no god who moves things with a purpose in mind.'

Mallard said, 'Have you heard the old joke about Nietzsche inscribed on a loo wall? God is dead: Nietzsche. Nietzsche is dead: God.'

Sergei, Charlie, Chandra, Cathy and Matt, each trying to relax their minds, talked softly of the relevance of Nietzsche in the light of their encounters up here in the ether. Ideas flowed back and forth. Questions crowded the air -Did Nietzsche's idea of Intelligence or *nous* translate as pure thought without form, as Cathy had thought of on the tube in London. What, if he was right and Intelligence did create the world- his famous saying: 'I think therefore I am' - an eternal consciousness in the vastness of the universe- the dark energy Cathy had thought of earlier. Was God then pure thought only?

Do we owe this consciousness the creation and demise of every organism? Intricate laws of physics devised and etched for us to discover through the millennia. Was the human race being drip-fed knowledge as the world grew older by this after-life, popping thoughts into human minds? Perhaps giving us our Eureka moments - A Spiritual Telepathy.

The American, Charlie McCarthy, felt he had stumbled upon the holiest of secrets. The chance of an after-life, of spiritual continuum, did what repeated bouts of chemo had never done. It spelled hope.

As the cosmos-nauts underwent the cataleptic and separation stages of their physical bodies, their mental drive for dynamism churned out ideas – new or the same message haunting humans, distilled through the generations?

They wondered aloud if the dark energy in the Universe was feeding them cordon bleu courses of sumptuous brain food, as mental and visual clarity became acute.

Nervously, aware of the eternal question: Why do good men do evil things- was the dark energy increasing their mental pulse for a deathly, dark reason? Would the re-entry stage - snapping back to their physical selves be hindered? Did death await them any moment? Or madness?

The fear of the unknown presence in their minds was all-pervasive.

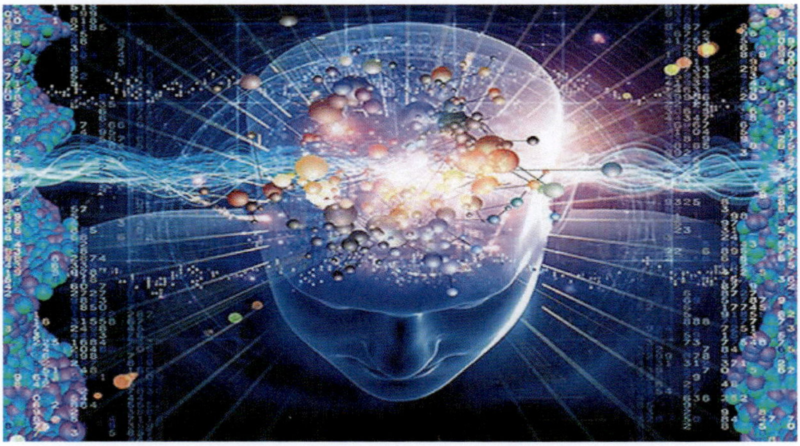

Image: Fate of Consciousness on CSglobe.com

Their pulses racing, the screens in their visors momentarily displaying an image that Mallard had purposefully uploaded, they tried to listen to Matt attempting to channel their thinking again to pure curiosity: Do we return to that consciousness in the after-life? If such consciousness, both Good and Evil influenced the living, therefore could humans be absolved of crime?

Or like the Buddhist belief of attaining enlightenment or *nirvana*, human progression to this after-life would be a passport to pure thought and eternal good.

Cathy offered soft reassurance continually. If in their current elevated consciousness, they were penetrating this universe of intelligence, then their thoughts jostling in the cosmic star-washed expanse would filter through to others – people would begin to re-examine the mysteries of the universe, rethinking the laws of physics, in this era of the quantum mind.

And thus panic subsided and reason resided once more in the minds of the cosmos-nauts as purpose was established.

They empathised with Cathy's analogy of sand on a beach absorbing solar heat and then releasing it into the atmosphere, and a smile came to their lips when Cathy said, 'Surely the great Nietzsche's theory of randomness would then be disproved. Purpose therefore, would be the science of telepathy- a god instilled messaging service!'

'Why according to the Vedas do we keep coming back to life?' said Matt in her earpiece.

Chandra answered, 'The teachings state that we are reborn to exhume our karma. We build our karma during our life and we must come back to face the results of all our actions.

He carried on, 'Further teachings reveal that beyond the universe is transcendental knowledge. Meditation that we are indulging in right now; all knowledge exceeding every expectation.'

The melodic tones ceased and Cathy was there on that astral plane. So was Matt. Together they were of one mind.

Andromeda was up close and personal. Not far in the visor's system intel – Cathy adjusted the hi-tech goggles, she knew the cameras on the outside of the visor were feeding high resolution images into the helmet.

Matt was speaking, 'Concentrate now, we need to get near the black hole of Andromeda. That's where the wormhole begins. If we were on a spaceship we would have to orbit at intermediate speed so as not to get sucked in. The pattern of approach would be complicated and is called a Rosetta orbit. I am going to try to achieve that pattern near the wormhole.

Damocles the ancient star is nestling cheek by jowl in there with the Black Widow particles.

Think darkness in your mind, there is only black velvet. In the inkiness, you should see the edges of the event horizon, a boundary in spacetime around the black hole. Steer clear. This is the point of no return for the outside observer.

Beyond lies the gravitational pull where nothing can escape, not even light. Andromeda, we are skirting the fringes now. Cathy, transcend billions of years, now don't think of the black hole, think colour and light, starbursts and supernovae, patterns of sheer light, pinks and reds, greens and blues. Deep breath and think again, think life. The amoebae is nearby too, alien life now growing quickly, I sense it with every fibre.

'We are so close to the black hole, I'm terrified.' whispered Cathy

'Take your time. No need to rush. Let your mind float on the swell.'

An hour later, the concentration of the five cosmos-nauts, started to wane. Getting close to the black hole of Andromeda was proving more difficult than anticipated. Matt called a break and they started the fast snap-back to reality.

CHAPTER 6

CERN, Geneva

Hektor Xanthis put his arms around Cathy as she walked in to the room. He had managed to get a coveted room in the Hostel at CERN. The room was by no means luxurious for a man of Hektor's means but it provided easy access to Cathy who had grown in his estimation.

From the naive young woman he had met more than 5 years ago, she had blossomed into the most sought after woman on this earth.

He kissed her, passionately. She was unresponsive. He took her by the hand and led her to the bed.

Cathy sat on the side of the bed and said, 'Hektor I agreed to meet you because you said it was urgent. What is the matter?'

'Cathy what are you doing here? What is going on? All the buildings are restricted- no access to outside personnel. Even with all my influence I can't get anywhere near the facility. Are you involved in something earthshaking?'

'Funny you should say that. It is rather earthshaking. Well Hektor I know you are absolutely trustworthy so I will tell you something of what we have been attempting today.' Cathy told him the broad outlines of their space venture.

She finished with, 'We haven't succeeded on the second attempt but we are getting closer.'

'My God, ten hours. I knew of course that there would be a major catastrophe but I wasn't aware the timing scheduled for oblivion was just ten hours. There will be pandemonium if the world knows.'

His brow furrowed, 'If on the other hand, we survive as a giant galaxy with Andromeda and the Milky Way in fusion, we need to be prepared. Humans need to be aware of what is out there. It makes the reason I asked to meet you urgently today even more important. I wanted to see you of course, you know you are really important to me, but also to talk to you about the photographs of the earth- you know the ones you took with your mind- , is that correct?'

Cathy looked at him in surprise, 'How did you know?'

'I have my sources. Are they real? How was it done? All we know is that you and a man named Matt Mallard' He touched her cheek affectionately, 'You are romantic, eh?, what would you call it, brushstrokes of cloud? ..aahh, I see you like that - You went around the earth, hour after hour. Such a mental feat, it has never been attempted before'

Cathy was shaking her head.

He said, 'Please don't lie to me *koukla* (doll). The Swiss authorities have the photographs from the science laboratory in space, Columbus. Columbus has a machine with the technology of a combination of brain imaging and computer simulation and has succeeded in decoding and reconstructing the visual images. Mallard made sure you both were interconnected with every device that would submit proof of the mental orbit. The results were amazing.

You and Mallard and the incredible photographs of the universe. I believe the photos were leaked to the press and they started to come after you. I have had the photos examined by experts. We believe there are images of alien life and now with this collision taking place, those photographs have become of vital importance. The world must prepare for alien beings. I believe you are in danger. You will be inundated if the world knows what you saw.

He took her hand. 'I love you. Let me protect you'

'Oh Hektor, you are kind'. They kissed. His hands touched her breasts. Cathy started to feel the familiarity of his embrace. He was hard. She was getting to be amenable.

There was a knock on the door. Hektor's bodyguard called out to him. Hektor spoke to him in Greek.

Cathy remembering some of her Greek knew he was instructing the bodyguard to come back later.

She couldn't do this. Not now. Not with Matt on her mind.

Cathy decided to leave. She had to be back at the Globe. The next attempt was due shortly.

She said to Hektor quietly, 'I have to go but I hope to see you before you leave.'

'Cathy you are in danger. There are people out there who think you are evil and are bringing about the end of the world. Take care. I will help.'

Cathy wished him good bye.

London -Vauxhall Bridge and MI6

The cherubic-looking blonde man looked at the contents of the file and remembered Cyprus as he looked at the photographs of the two individuals. He had monitored the female, Cathy Burkert when she was a Turkish target. The male had proved to be a loyal subject.

Mallard, sterling bloke then, but now he wasn't so sure. Mallard had surrendered his machine in Cyprus 5 years ago. The British Government had put the machine to good use ever since. And kept a close eye on Mallard.

What the devil was he up to now? Calling Cardinal Jules de Fleury. The content of the conversation was still in the mix, being defragged but Jesus the stupid bastard was being swallowed up whole by that beast– the ultra powerful, sleekly fed, Cardinal.

The MI6 man also knew he needed to put a trace on the location of the good Cardinal. It was somewhere in England. His request for the trace was denied. Unusual. There was something fishy going on.

Instead, he had been given access to the machine that Mallard had developed, clearance not normally granted, the photographs of the universe were displayed, frame after frame of unbelievable dimensions, clarity of colour and the smoky images..Fuck, were they silhouettes? What beings were they?

The suggestion had been put forward by the one other man who was in the know, his superior high up in the chain of command, that the images were the transcendental images of Mallard and Burkert. He had to verify this. Immediately. Moreover, with the imminent collision between the galaxies, a new planet could be forged. British interests had to be protected. He had booked the next flight to Geneva.

Paris,

The Louvre

The old man unpacked his belongings in the hotel in Paris. Leonard Sosnovsky felt weary after his travels but he must not flag. He walked outside the hotel and hailed a cab.

The Dendera Zodiac had led him here to the Louvre. Gazing at the ancient bas-relief which represented a map of the stars – a planisphere, he knew from his research, that the Zodiac's origins were from the ceiling of a chapel dedicated to Osiris in the Hathor temple at Dendera, Egypt and had been moved to France in 1821.

The Denderah zodiac had paid homage to one woman, the goddess Hathor, and the old man knew his grandson even now was engaging with, (he was convinced)- her reincarnation in Geneva, Switzerland.

Sosnovsky noted the thirty-six spirits or 'decans' around the circumference of the Zodiac, which symbolised the 360 days of the Egyptian year. More importantly, they also symbolise 36 stars or small constellations and rise every ten days in the ancient Egyptian clock. The number 36 made the old man's veins protrude in his forehead as he tried to recall its significance. A group of men, a tale of yore. The thread of memory, spun of gossamer wafted gently away.

Sosnovsky shook his head and reminded himself why he was here. He had to see the Zodiac on this day. His grandson had told him that the ancient prophecy of the rising of the decan of *Andromeda* was about to be fulfilled. On the Zodiac, Andromeda is pictured in chains, and these chains will only be broken by Perseus, pictured in the square Denderah zodiac as a crowned king with a bull's tail, riding on the famous steed Pegasus.

The old man's mind was seething with so many questions. Did Perseus, as the ancients say, have the gift of prophecy, a momentous figure, yet to emerge on planet earth? Or was he already here? Was he, in fact the other half of the duo his grandson was interacting with in Geneva?

Matt Mallard. The thread, a thought transference, with the old man was established across lands and borders. Mallard, who had a short time previously, remembered the Dendera Zodiac on the constellation Gemini and the words 'He who comes' had been engraved on his mind.

The old man had seen the photographs that his son Dimitri had published in the press before he was murdered. Earth reproduced through mental avionics. Mallard was Cathy Burkert's partner in astral transport. 2012's Perseus or was he yet to be born?

Leonard Sosnovsky's grandfather had entrusted him, Leonard, with the seven seals and his grandson Sergei Boystov had the task of handing it on to the one woman Sosnovsky knew was part of a present–day planisphere. Sosnovsky gazed at the decan of Andromeda and knew with absolute certainty that the ancient calligraphy was to be rescripted. Cathy Burkert would hold the quill.

Leonard Sosnovsky had one more task to undertake. He stroked the amulet on his wrist. He must live to reach Syria.

England

He was ruggedly handsome. His wife loved him. Other women did too, frequently. What his wife didn't know didn't hurt her.

He met them in the apartment he rented in Fulham, London. Two men with leather cases. They showed him their wares. Semtex and thermonuclear weapons packed tightly with deadly intent.

He would call them when the time came. They would have to be prepared to move swiftly. The targets would be meeting amidst strict security, virtually impossible to break through. Did they know a way? They nodded. Surveillance had begun a long time ago. They had a foolproof plan.

He spoke to them ironing out all the tiny details. Their faces showed their deep respect. They knew he was a man highly valued by his Government. His agenda was blind compliance. And the British trusted him absolutely. He was above suspicion.

JUNE 2012

CERN, Geneva:

Sergei Boystov, the Russian, one of the five astral cosmos-nauts, had achieved his own out of body experience. His teammates were waiting for his story as they undertook the third quest for Black Widow and the mouth of the wormhole. All had mentally tucked in their cerebral wings and were rolling like stunt pilots on the updrafts.

Sergei was approaching Phoenix, the minor constellation in the Southern sky. Visible to him, through his application goggles, and to the naked eye in Australia, he remembered the legend of the Phoenix. He adjusted his audio-feed to a Phoenix musical score - violin friendly, the instrument a passion. Now he could explain clearly in English. He began, 'In Slavic folklore, the Firebird/Phoenix (Russian *zhar-ptitsa*), is a magical glowing bird from a faraway land. It could prove a blessing as well as portend doom to its captor.'

The words were uttered in a monotonous tone and the others, their senses attuned to raising their mental bar, did not hear the despondency lurking in the clefs. 'The Phoenix is described as a large bird with majestic plumage that glows brightly - a red, orange, and yellow light, like a barbecue with coals burning brightly. Fairy tales portray the Phoenix as the quarry in a hunt, and the hero must jump through many hoops- you say? Yes – to capture the bird. A lost tail feather of the Phoenix begins the search and the hero sets out to find and capture the live bird, sometimes of his own accord, but usually on the bidding of a father or king.

The Phoenix can signal doom for the hunter. It has a 500 to 1000 year life-cycle, near the end of which it builds itself a nest of twigs that then ignites; both nest and bird burn fiercely and are reduced to ashes, from which a new, young phoenix or phoenix egg arises. The hunter dies but like the new phoenix is reborn and destined to live as long as his old self. It is said that the bird's cry is that of a beautiful song whilst it arises from the ashes and its ability to be reborn from its own ashes implies that it is immortal.'

Sergei stopped talking and chased the faint emissions of light from Phoenix, the minor constellation. Yet again, spiritual immortality was uppermost in the rare atmosphere that was his and his teammates' mental plateau. Sergei longed for that spiritual freedom. Like the phoenix, to rise from the ashes of his old life. He had done what had been entrusted to him. He had handed the scroll with the seven seals to Cathy. She would take the others through. All the world in fact.

Sergei didn't want to go back to his physical self. Like the music in his earpiece, his melancholy was a language beyond words. He could not tell the others that Russia was a constrictive place to be in. He was virtually alone. His only living relative was his grandfather and they had exchanged their farewells in the event death tripped up the heart. His Uncle had been killed and Sergei felt utterly helpless. He could never avenge his Uncle's death at the hands of the Soviet authorities.

Another case of Polonium poisoning, which induced acute radiation syndrome, just like Alexander Litvinenko, who had been poisoned in London in 2006. His uncle had been living in Russia, the editor of the Moscow Weekly, the paper a fierce critic of the power-hungry Putinov. He had found out details of the Litvinenko poisoning, details that would incriminate Putinov.

His uncle had been hushed up with the same poison, Sergei suspected. In Litvinenko's case, the British

Courts had pursued the case and tried to extradite the man responsible to no avail. The Russian authorities had refused to give up the accused, one Andrei Lugovoy. Instead they made him a member of the Duma, so he would have immunity from prosecution.

Did that son of a bitch, Lugovoy contract cancer, with his handling of the Polonium 210? Sergei hoped so. Sergei felt himself letting go. His spirit was descending into a black hole. He was drifting close to the black hole in Andromeda.

Black hole of Andromeda

Black holes caused by a lack of a hydrogen fuel supply, the remaining gases thrown off which results in a supernova, leaving a core. The core keeps collapsing becoming so minute that if one can imagine a grain of salt might measure 0.0001 metres, to describe the size of the minute core, called a singularity, you would have to stick 35 zeroes in front of that number one.

Sergei remembered that impossibly small speck had the mass of several suns inside it. Space and time, drawn to a focal point (the singularity) cease to exist at the said singularity and Sergei was in a place where his heart rate was slowing down, beat by beat. He could feel the lifeblood draining from his body. His mind could not get back to his physical self. He was being sucked into the black hole that was Andromeda.

The spinning black hole at a 1000 times a second pulled everything into its cavity, including light, stars, other black holes and he most of all- it was pulling him into the vortex. With the violin concerto reaching the cadenza in his ears he felt like a very heavy ball sitting on a sheet of rubber. The indent caused made him feel like water falling down a plughole – the supermassive black hole in Andromeda- millions or even billions of times the mass of our sun. Sergei felt pulled like a strand of spaghetti, his head felt the difference in gravity from his physical feet. He had to let go. He whispered a breath of something faint, lost in the audio feed as the others tried mentally to override the gigantic spin of the singularity. The next instant Sergei Boystov was gone. Mallard brought the others quickly down to terra firma as Sergei was not communicating in Mallard's audio-feed. His lifeless body was found within seconds. The four that were remaining were deeply shocked and felt real fear at what they were attempting.

Six months earlier:

Teheran

Sohrab Reza's mind made cold calculations. Two days ago, the machine he had constructed from Al-din's blueprints, had picked up the photos transmitted by the mental images of 2 British individuals.

Sohrab Reza had not understood the significance of the photos. He had no access to the minds that had taken the photos but he gave a sigh of deep satisfaction - He definitely monitored the minds of key personnel in the world, which allowed him unlimited access to their personal data.

Sohrab thirsted for such knowledge. With immense riches and power, only the impossible attracted him. Mind control. The machine in his possession with printouts issuing forth of minds that controlled the world. His fellow Opus Signori, patterns of their brainwaves stored and accessed.

Iran had issued a final instruction. The weapon had to be fired. Only one individual was to be used. The utmost secrecy to be maintained. Hal Heinberg was on his way from South Africa. Hal and Sohrab would be heading to the heavily fortified site of Fordo near the holy city of Qom. The site was producing Uranium enriched by 20%; nuclear weapons were being churned out.

Everything went like clockwork. Almost.

The missile was fired, directly aimed at Ofek9, the Israeli spy satellite. Hal Heinberg had no practical experience of firing a missile. Due to his inexpert handling, the missile exploded into outer space, missing its target completely. Not harmlessly as the world found out.

The radiation released vast amounts of energy causing a Dwarf star, one as big as the sun and close to the black hole of Andromeda and its immense gravity to fling out a stream of a pair of particles. One of the pair was swallowed by the incredible suction of Andromeda's black hole but the other survived; this surmise was met at first with general disbelief among the scientific community, whose experiments to date had concluded an ephemeral existence for such a particle. The Black Widow Particle which in its turn, created the wormhole.

Now six months later, Sohrab Reza remembered and checked the images again on the screen. In front of him were pictures of the earth taken from outer space by the English duo- a male and a female. Because of the incredible clarity of the photographs, even he had to feel amazement. Doesn't the earth look like it is hung out in space by NOTHING? And indeed, isn't gravity, the force we now know holds up the earth, something that is NOT seen? It reaffirmed Reza's fanatical faith in God – Allah the unseen, Allah the all-powerful.

Sohrab Reza had many a discussion about religion with his fellow Opus Signor, Cardinal Jules de Fleury. He remembered what the Cardinal had told him what the Bible said about gravity and God. The Bible says in Job 26: "He stretches out the north over EMPTY SPACE. He hangs the earth on NOTHING."! ...The Koran had a similar script, '*And He holds the sky so that it would not collapse upon the Earth, except by His leave. Indeed, God is Kind towards mankind, Merciful.* (22:65).

How did the ancient scribes know that the earth was thus positioned? They had nothing – absolutely no technology, no space travel or exploration – nothing at all!

Nothing was *not* on Reza's agenda. He had the technology. He had the machine.

He had tried to blow up the OFEK9 satellite. He was icily aware of the consequences of his failure to do so.

But his mind-machine had been churning day and night since his failed attempt.

Now months later, as he sat in front of the device, he reflected his monitoring of the Opus Signori had led him to CERN in Geneva.

There, Reza thought it prudent to tap into key CERN physicists. That had resulted in a detailed, mostly indecipherable science-speak. He passed the information on to the scientists here in Teheran.

They got back to him. Penetration of the wormhole was being attempted through psychokinetic energy. A surplus of positive energy from the human mind and the power of the LHC. The opening in Andromeda, millions of light years away, could not be accessed any other way.

Damocles was lodged in the throat of the wormhole and the wormhole was expanding vastly pushing the dwarf star towards the solar system and earth.

This information was highly classified. Only certain government leaders and certain Opus Signori were informed. Reza checked his printouts of the Opus Signori minds. The information tallied with the intel he had received.

Earth would be blown to smithereens.

Or the galaxy would be absorbed into a super galaxy. A Merger between Andromeda and the Milky Way. Mergers occur when two galaxies collide and find they do not have enough momentum to keep going after the collision. Instead, they fall back into each other and eventually merge together, forming one galaxy where there used to be two.

Now Sohrab, skulking from his recent reprimand by no less than Ahmadi himself for his bungled attempt at destroying Ofek9, looked again at the photographs on the machine. The 2 individuals, who had taken the photographs on Al-din's machine, were displayed in full colour. CERN was utilising their paranormal abilities.

Although, the latest reports from that facility, via his sources, was the last-ditch desperate attempt to hire not just the 2 astral projectionists but a total of 5 from Britain, Russia, India and USA. It was hoped the astral voyage would uncover The Black Widow particle and the scientists would be able to eject it. Sohrab Reza was heading for Geneva.

He had to find the two who had taken the earthly images - Cathy Burkert and Matthew Mallard.

Chapter 7

JUNE 2012

CERN Geneva:

Matt Mallard reflected that despite his verbal assurances to the British Consulate in Cyprus to the contrary, he had with a great deal of help, gone about building a super-deluxe facsimile of his original invention. It had paid off. Everything was recorded on the new machine.

The machine, much like the one in Sohrab Reza's possession, but of far greater spec was laid out on the table. Complex applications of Electromagnetism resulting in tecno-enabled telepathy or psycho-electronics- A remote fMRI machine which recognised stored brainwave frequencies and recorded thought patterns. Mallard looked at his machine spewing forth the printouts. Fortunately he had packed the innocuous looking black apparatus, much like a laptop.

Mallard had used up every favour in the scientific community. He needed to store energy – vast amounts of it. His physicist connections, close friends hit on the idea of storing energy as data. They had delivered a state of the art prototype based on Photons, the most basic units of light, carrying two kinds of momentum, a kind of energy-of-motion.

One, spin angular momentum, is better known as polarisation. Photons "wiggle" along a particular direction, and different polarisations can be separated out by, for example, polarising sunglasses or 3D glasses

But they also carry orbital angular momentum - in analogy to the Earth-Sun system, the spin angular momentum is expressed in our planet spinning around its axis, while the orbital angular momentum manifests as our revolution around the Sun.

Matt's laptop aimed to exploit this orbital angular momentum, essentially encoding more data as a "twist" in the light waves. The "twist" of the waves is a way to carry vast amounts of data – Mallard's natural gift - a huge reservoir of electrical energy.

His extra-sensory perception had been hackle-raisingly acute, over the last month. He had to find out the cause. He triangulated his calculations. Yes he was absolutely certain. There was another machine in use besides his and the one at British SIS. Matt worked it out. It had to be the Turkish connection and the machine that Al-din had appropriated five years ago. He must inform the British Government and of course the Opus Signori.

The MI6 man intercepted the call from Mallard. It had been rerouted via Cyprus and Mallard's contact at the British consulate, a Nigel Brainthwaite. The MI6 man remembered he couldn't stand that fucker, Brainthwaite.

Brainthwaite was of the hope that Mallard's ESP was accurate. Mallard had been useful over the years.

The MI6 operative on the telephone assured Mallard that the matter would be pursued. The Turkish connection would be investigated vigorously and immediately. He would have an answer within minutes. The machine would be traced and destroyed. It was crucial that British minds were not being accessed via the machine.

Britain had taken apart the technology surrendered 5 years ago. No, it wasn't in operation. Absolutely not, we don't do any of that nonsense here. The MI6 man switched his mobile off. He had just landed in Geneva and was on his way to his hotel. He patted the laptop next to him on the front seat of the rented car. Certainly no nonsense from the British.

Mallard phoned the good Cardinal next. He had half an hour before the next astral take-off. He decided to take a shower. He stripped off.

Cathy knocked on the door. Matt opened the door a couple of inches.

'Just a mo,' he said, grabbing a towel.

Cathy felt a sudden intense physical reaction. She was thinking sex. She was feeling wet. His chest was bare, bronzed and hard, no doubt due to his gym workouts – a hotline to her senses and Jesus, she felt overwhelmed with raw sensation. She literally wanted to tear off the towel and plead for him to enter her, now.

She said breathlessly, 'A bit winded, the stairs...'

'I wanted to tell you the latest and also to plan what we do in our next...Christ Cathy, I know what you are thinking. I feel the same when I am near you but this is the wrong time.'

He looked at the big green eyes with all her sexual allure glowing and beckoning and pulled her into his arms. They were on fire, kissing passionately.. they were on the bed. Her clothes were being taken off.

Matt was saying in his head, 'Slow it down but – Jesus, what if there was no later?'

He paused, his breath moist on her breasts and said, 'Cathy I want to enjoy you slowly and preciously. I can't do that now.

I believe we will have a tomorrow. We have to believe that. We have to be at the Globe but here's a promise. I will be with you in every way, at every level of consciousness, spiritually, sexually – our bodies will continue into immortality. We will walk the earth for millennia and our paths will intertwine always'

These words echoed continuously through Cathy's mind as she climbed the stairway to heaven in astral transport minutes later, she was close to Andromeda's murky swirl, spinning in its maelstrom – her body removed but her mind noting the incredible suction of the gravitational field.

Matt was near, his mind a bead of thought away.

'What does the Black Widow particle look like? Does it have horns, is it a she-devil? Wreaking havoc on unsuspecting humanity or was it the stuff of earth formation?' thought Cathy

Did the Black Widow have the ability to form a super galaxy? A melding of galaxies, of alien beings, rather like the film, Total Recall and Arnold Schwarzenegger's Mars, different bodies and faces, noses and ears skewiff but all committed to their common song – that of thought and reason?'

Cathy Burkert and Matt Mallard were one mentally, as they approached the supermassive black hole, sensing the mouth of the wormhole close now. The other two cosmos-nauts were included only in the audio-loop. The Black Widow particle was blue reports suggested; a blue spirit set aflame, a litmus paper dipped in eternal blue.

'I don't know if I have the strength of mind to take them there,' Matt communicated to Cathy

'I will follow your lead. Let's do it'

The inky-black started to get light, deeper and deeper they swam rather like ancient hieroglyphics depicted on a cave wall, touching the sides now and again starbursts deep within, supernovae their colours frozen in prisms, the blue light of Black Widow not visible as yet.

The laws of physics were no more, they had only blind instinct.

'Cathy, Chandra and Sergei, if we have learnt anything from recent events, we must control it through pure reason – give the darkness a reason for earth to survive.

Think deeply, concentrate and focus on the earth, divorced from human greed, think birds in the air, fish in the waters, the perfect marriage of animals and insect life, the majesty of trees and flowers promising both innocence and sexual fulfilment in the fruit they bear - and us to tend all. Humans must survive to look after all these things.

For all will surely perish in the climate we have set upon the universe.

Thoughts of survival engulfed all 4 minds. Not a glimmer of blue yet.

Voices from CERN were impinging. They had to come down. A calamity had occurred at the facility.

Mallard instructed the others to descend but he stayed for another 5 minutes.

The earthquake measured 7.5 on the Richter scale in canton Valais, Switzerland. The Philistines, people indifferent to artistic achievement, said that the LHC was responsible because it presented the biggest magnetic field on earth and therefore could be linked to large-scale seismic activity. The Philistines were partly right.

The LHC had been running at maximum capacity in the last week as the countdown to the Black Widow began. It could have engendered a shift in the Eurasian tectonic plates, causing the devastation. Half of Switzerland and its neighbouring countries, France, Germany, Italy were experiencing tremors and quakes.

Geneva had suffered little in the aftermath. Personnel at CERN were still going about their daily duties but communications were severed for the next hour. An army of technicians were working to fix the problem.

The countdown to Armageddon, the collision of the galaxies had started.

Without any electronic communication, all were themselves in a black hole, unable to see beyond the space divide.

Matt Mallard realised his cell phone was jammed, probably due to the volume of calls the networks were experiencing. He had to speak to the MI6 man and the Opus Signori but was unable to get through. He had to tell them of the alien life he had the incredibly good fortune to meet.

The last five minutes near Andromeda, he had been alone and pushing deeper, astrally drilling deep, revealing a disk of young blue stars swirling around the black hole in Andromeda, M31 in much the same way that the planets in our solar system revolve around the Sun. Matt was pleasantly surprised to discover the stars, for in such a hostile environment, the black hole's tidal forces should tear matter apart, making it difficult for gas and dust to collapse and form stars.

Matt started to follow the others back when the star outside earth's solar system 51 Pegasi appeared directly through his goggles. A white circular mass, orbiting the star, a distant ball resembling a giant marble was sending out a planetary signal in Matt's thought antennae.

He had christened the planet, 'The Bard's Muse and Shakespeare's Caesar responded:
"I am constant as the northern star,
Of whose true-fix'd and resting quality
There is no fellow in the firmament."
Julius Caesar (III, i, 60 – 62)

A divine pressure- was it God- on his cerebral awareness.

Divinely ordained - extraterrestrial life, through the centuries, from Greek antiquity to Newton had been debated and now Matt felt confused.. the need to believe in this strange new world of burgeoning existence was overwhelming.

Science and fossils stated that man existed 300,000 years ago but the thought communiqué from the Alien life, that he found himself fascinated by, was of life long before that, humans that did not fossilise but continued to evolve as pure spiritual thought, alongside this new life on the Bard's Muse.-

The Alien life, Ebony not of wood but of mental fluidity. Matt Mallard found his mind infused, no just plain dunked like his favourite Earl Grey tea with thoughts of all that had gone before. He was informed of the future and the need to be a prophet, the town-crier for mankind.

Mallard had returned with just that intention. He must tell the Opus Signori. They would know what to do.

Downtown Geneva

The MI6 man, let's call him Jim, threw the mobile on the bed. There was no signal. The room phone was not working as well. Reception suggested that in the light of the earthquake, the networks were being jammed with the volume of calls.

Just before the earthquake struck, he had managed to trace the machine to Al-din. The name was very familiar. Jim had overseen the direct link Al-din provided to Russia. Al-din in effect reported to him. Was that bastard turning rogue and doing the dirty on his puppeteer?

Al-din owed Her Majesty's Government a great deal. Not only did he escape prison in Cyprus for doing Cathy Burkert's head in, but the Turkish Government had overlooked his deeds under pressure from Britain and Cyprus.

Instead he would provide a direct line to the Kremlin. He had played the game so far.

This new intel had to be chased up. Jim drove to The Geneva Centre for the Democratic Control of Armed Forces (DCAF). He knew a man who was in charge of security. The man would put feelers out. It was crucial that Al-din was stopped, forthwith.

Cathy watched the news whilst waiting for the electric grid to be restored. It was a circus. The entire world's media had based themselves in Geneva covering quake stories in France, Germany and Italy. Spinoff stories blaming CERN for their testing had started to be reported within minutes, which brought the reporters swarming around the CERN complex.

They had got hold of the latest news, the five projectionists' photographs, their life histories and the reason for their astral flights. Panic had set in. The entire world's press were camped in every room. Religious leaders all over the world were leading their flocks in hysterical and fervent prayer beseeching God for salvation. Government heads were sending their armies in to patrol the streets in the madness and mayhem that had ensued press revelations.

A tsunami of human emotion swept through every landscape.

The rich man dreamed of expanding his corporate holdings in a new world, he commanded his henchmen to draw up plans for the event of the merger of the constellations; he needed to know climate, geography and natural resources. Perhaps he would be a pioneer, a true colossus in a fitting landscape. Confident and fearless, bolstered from every comfort of background and breeding, he wished to prove himself again, chisel that new empire. A shared podium with the Gods?

The poor man thanked his God for the little he had, resigned himself to death – life had been pretty hard – but; he had a tiny dream, it flickered, was licked out of its resting place and with a pulse for life, faint still but beating stronger now, he wished for a little of what the rich man had. Perhaps they would survive and the new world would give him a chance. He needed just one.

The sick hoped for death with dignity, an end to pain and suffering but in the deep quietness of their pain-ridden world, was there a thought of new cures, magically made immediate, in the new world?

Embossed with the motif of Hope, deeply interknotted in the skeins of the fabric, of the sumptuous tapestry of human life; yearning unravelled and was laid bare, as all gazed to the heavens.

The photographs of the Universe that Cathy and Matt had taken with their minds were on every Television channel. Luckily, the shots of the silhouettes had never been released.

Cathy and the other cosmos-nauts went to ground. All were deeply alarmed. They could not be transported astrally. They found it impossible with the sheer crush of numbers to raise their levels of consciousness. Everyone seemed to be doomed. It was 4 hours to collision.

Chapter 8

JUNE 2012

CERN, Geneva:

Mallard looked across at Cathy as she pushed the long black hair away from her face. They were in the clinical office with the Swedish furniture. There was a guard outside the door protecting them from intruders who wanted a piece of them. The electricity had just been restored.

Hektor Xanthis was introduced to Mallard. Matt recalled he had met the man before. Xanthis was an Opus Signori.

Katherine Jenkins' voice singing 'Ave Maria' in the background, as he and Cathy attempted to relax their minds, provided the paradox to what Mallard was feeling. Heavenly music as opposed to the feelings of rage within Mallard's breast. What was this vermin doing here? He had known there was a man in Cathy's life, someone she was deeply involved with.

That's why he had held off approaching her, revealing all that he felt, all these years. Just recently, he thought he had stood a chance. Now this man was all over her like a rash.

He needed to get out. He went to his hostel room.

Mallard had known Cathy only through their shared telepathic abilities until she had walked into his surgery two years ago. He had taken one look at her, her energy had captivated him. He employed her, training her in all aspects of his latest venture, projection amongst the stars and other psychic phenomena. He began to love her, to want her and need her constantly in his life. They were of one mind, usually, unless he switched her thoughts off on his machine.

Suddenly an idea occurred to him. *Of one mind.* What if he could raise world consciousness through the machine? Shared telepathy from billions on the planet, to aid his and the other's astral flights.

His photographic memory served him in good stead.

When making adjustments to his machine, he did research on new parts available and Wikipedia had an interesting story. The United States Army Research Office budgeted $4 million in 2009 to researchers at the University of California, Irvine to develop EEG processing techniques to identify correlates of imagined speech and intended direction to enable soldiers on the battlefield to communicate via computer-mediated telepathy. Mallard's machine was streets ahead.

Mallard knew that he would have to use all three machines in existence. The MI6 man had denied his machine was still functional but Matt knew otherwise. Matt knew that the machine in the British Government's possession had been used for many a potential terrorist threat – to convert and influence thinking in minds that harboured the intent of chaos. Matt had silently witnessed the read-outs of MI6 operations that his superior machine recorded. Hitherto, he had known if MI6 became aware of his specialised equipment, they would lock him up and throw away the key.

Now there was no way out. He had to confess and explain the need that all machines had to be used to enable global thought transference. It would mean the British Government would know of his super machine but with 4 hours on the clock, there was no choice. It was of the utmost urgency that Al-din's machine was appropriated as well. He tried his mobile phone once more. The signal was faint. He moved to another part of the room. It grew fainter.

Mallard strode outside. He hoped he would be undetected from all the press of people who had invaded CERN. So far, so good. Good signal strength. He was about to make the call when there was a tap on his shoulder. An English voice spoke.

Jim said, 'I need to speak to you, mate. In private. Now.' There was a certain look in the man's eye that brooked no argument. Mallard led him to his hostel room.

Sohrab Reza was outside CERN. The area had been cordoned off. The Swiss military had moved in. Swiss military conscripts were patrolling the streets of Geneva and the other cantons. Sohrab could not get past the roadblocks. His mobile was sizzling with all the calls he was putting through without any success. Access was denied to all outsiders. Sohrab checked into the nearest hotel. He needed to do some work on his laptop. Pop some thoughts in the minds of key CERN personnel.

Hektor Xanthis really listened to what Cathy was saying. Usually his mind was preoccupied, with business affairs, presidential prowess and his country's state of play in the world. This time he was paying attention.

Cathy said, 'Hektor I have to tell you the truth. The reason I have not been in touch all these months is because I believe I am in love with someone else. I'm so sorry. I know you made plans for us and I hate to disappoint you but I must be honest with myself and with you.' Cathy apologised again

Hektor looked shaken and stood staring out of the window for a few minutes. He turned back, took Cathy's hand and kissed it.

'You will always be in my heart', he said. 'Don't give up on us just yet. With life, you never know. I will leave now. If you need me at any time, just call. I will help'.

Chapter 9

JUNE 2012

CERN, Geneva:

3 hours to go. Cathy was having a much-needed sandwich and a coffee at the CERN canteen. Matt had been closeted in his room for an hour and he had just phoned. He needed to talk to her urgently. Make your way over.

Cathy gulped the last of the coffee and hurried across to the CERN hostel with a quick loo stop on the way. Thoughts of their last meeting in the hostel were uppermost in Cathy's mind. They had comes within a heartbeat away from making love. Cathy wondered what it would be like. She could feel her tummy clench with a high wattage incandescence. They shared this incredible electrical energy and surely the experience would be elemental.

She gazed at herself in the mirror. Long night- black hair. Skin, the diffuse liquid richness of sunlight, eyes, aquamarine now like Neptune's cove. Her eyes were her best feature – sometimes they were pure emerald green. Now with excitement shooting tendrils of electric charge deep in her bloodstream, she wanted her eyes to beckon, to burn. Her lips were moist, open as if about to be kissed. Her bottom lip seemed to tremble. The lip-gloss, red, slid over the flesh.

Cathy had decided.

She needed to tell Matt that Hektor was a thing of the past. She really hoped he would welcome the information. Matt was her alter-ego. Hektor had dominated her mind, she had needed him – so much. She had been so vulnerable after her childhood experiences, but now her mind was absolutely clear. She had grown-up.

She knew what she wanted. Hektor brought back memories of being brainwashed in Cyprus. If she stayed with him, would she be open to the same or similar attacks? After all, he would be Cyprus' next president.

Cathy's instincts for survival dominated her thought processes.

With the thought of the world being annihilated within hours, she felt life was knife-edged - a steely precipice where every emotion was exaggerated a hundredfold. Cathy was feeling the pressure.

Matt seemed cool and calm when she greeted him. The machine was issuing the printouts and he seemed to be concentrating on them. He put them to one side and said,

‘Sit down. I need to tell you something’

He related the story that Jim had told him. Al-din’s machine could not be traced. Al-din was clean. He had sold all his businesses off months ago. He was retired, only involved in Turkish politics these days. He, after some choice persuasion, did admit that the blueprint for the machine could have been stored digitally by his staff.

Cathy, Jim is MI6. They traced the company that could have housed the digital signature of the machine. It was traced to an Iranian holding company. Cathy, I’ve got a bad feeling about this. I’ve had it for some time now.’ He explained about Nostradamus’ quatrain that had popped into his mind and the feelings of enmity he’d had towards one person recently. One of the Opus Signori.

‘The only trouble is that the group- the Opus Signori are the only ones who have sworn to protect us. And we will be hounded Cathy, I know it, if we survive today. I wanted to tell you so we could formulate a plan. But, first let me tell you about the machine. I have already told Jim of MI6 and he is bringing his machine over now to add to the energy I am trying to create- a rotational kinetic energy tapping into tidal power. I am hoping this will provide astral lift-off for us within the next half an hour’

At Cathy's incomprehensible look, he waved his hand and changed the subject.

Matt then explained how he had had to confess to Jim that he had built a new machine from 5 years ago and how he had been able to monitor the machine in MI6's possession.

'Jim didn't like it but we have other things to be concerned about. It is really worrying that Al-din's machine was traced to Iranian soil given they are responsible for exploding the missile in outer space and causing the contretemps of Black Widow and Damocles.'

The deadly names reminded Cathy of something very important she had to say to Matt. Her body was tingling, she was so sexually aware of him. She said without preamble, 'Matt, Hektor Xanthis is leaving..'

He interrupted her, 'Sorry Cathy but I'm just picking up on the other machine that had gone AWOL, it's not on Iranian soil, its right here in Geneva. I've made all the calculations. I am absolutely sure. The enemy is here and what's more, he is using the machine right now and I know on whom. Thank God, I am able to monitor the frequency he is using. The printouts are bloody accurate. I have to call Jim and I must tell the other Opus Signori that one of their members is a terrorist.'

Cardinal Jules de Fleury, Mallard's contact at the Opus Signori listened without interrupting whilst Mallard was speaking.

'These are only suspicions. What proof do you have that the man in question is Sohrab Reza, one of us?'

'British Intelligence has traced the corporation that Al-din sold to Reza. It has to be him. Believe me Cardinal; my extra sensory powers are never wrong. This is the man that caused the missile explosion and he is the man who is at present controlling minds through technology that he must have constructed from Al-din's carelessness. The fact that the authorities allowed Al-din to retain such extremely sensitive information which can be of deadly use in the wrong hands is incomprehensible.'

'What is his purpose, if the world is to end in 3 hours. What can he do now?'

'Cardinal, the world can also be merged into a supergalaxy. Now wouldn't you want to be the first with advance knowledge? Why any country could play grabs with any territory they chose in the New World –habitable space where humans can expand their borders. New habitable planets where each country would be granted territory- but, think of the villains who could proclaim themselves as conquerors and squeeze their enemies out of a new homeland. Iranian plans regarding Israel would be served.

I believe he has a good reason to monitor minds. I have spoken to MI6, their man here informs me that the Swiss police are heading to the location we think he's at.'

The Cardinal said, 'I will have to remove him from the loop-feed. I will also have to inform our Israeli Opus Signor, Ben Efraim. You know, we have fifteen of the members on a loop-feed connection. They receive the latest information. We, the other five are here together'

'Don't do anything to arouse his suspicions. Limit the feed to the others for now. Please keep this to yourself.'

The printouts of all the minds of the Opus Signori continued to be logged on the machine in Sohrab Reza's possession. In a minute, he would check the latest information. Their thoughts recorded, every thought.

The hotel corridor was empty as the four Swiss Federal Criminal Police (Einsatzgruppe TIGRIS) dubbed by the Swiss media as Supercops checked The Rovio robot camera controlled by their IPAD as they made their way around the corner. Assuming attack mode, they slid the key in the aperture and burst into the room. It was empty. The guest had left in a hurry.

There was a suitcase full of clothes, and something electrical. They had been warned to be on the look-out for anything like a computer or laptop but there was nothing of the kind, just what looked like an IPOD Recording Docking Station. The officer in charge, a Hans-Pieter Combe, decided to have it investigated. The lab was informed he needed an answer with minutes.

Sohrab Reza pressed the buttons on his IPOD. A vastly modified IPOD. It had the same capability as his very special laptop. It encompassed a remotely activated brain-computer interface – a remote EEG providing a direct communication pathway between the brain and an external device, his IPOD, the wireless handheld monitor that read electrical brain patterns of the two people he most wanted to meet. Cathy Burkert and Matthew Mallard's EEG's, the deviation in their brainwave patterns, identifying emotions which the IPOD transcribed into speech. He was close enough to be able to monitor their minds.

Professor Christoph Benjamin had proved an easy target too.

The Professor was waiting at the gate for him. 'I will take you to the Globe. We have special seating for the dignitaries and more and more want to be added to the list. I quite forgot that you, yourself, had requested a seat two days ago. Ah, I am getting old....

You will be able to view all proceedings from here, Mr. Reza. There are screens in front of each delegate. Once the projectionists view specific stars, the screen will magnify the area to the highest degree. You will see where they are travelling mentally.

Chapter 10

CERN, Geneva

Mallard and Jim, the MI6 man were setting up their machines in the Globe. Mallard had to temporarily switch off his in order to connect the two using a crossover cable. He had disabled the printers so curious eyes would have no idea what the laptops were about. He would have to work in the dark for a short period. He would temporarily lose the live feedback emitting from Al-din's – now Sohrab Reza's machine. Reza was tuned into the minds of the 19 Opus Signori – just one omission, Reza's own.

Mallard decided to reroute that connection. Reza would no longer be able to access the minds of his 19 fellow Opus Signori. Everything else had to stay as it was. The trap was baited to find Reza's whereabouts. He hoped Reza would fall for it.

Jim had received the latest intel from the Swiss TIGRIS. There was a recording in the base of the docking station found in the hotel room. The recording was of Cardinal Jules de Fleury's thoughts on Mallard's revelation of alien life on the planet, 'The Bard's Muse'.

Mallard knew he would be the next target.

Sohrab Reza looked down at Mallard from his vantage point in the ceiling of the Globe. He recognised Mallard from the photos in the press and from the TV news displaying his and Burkert's faces. What was the man thinking now? He checked his IPOD; the screen only recorded thoughts in 20 minute bursts. There was nothing at present. He would have to wait.

Cathy meanwhile was talking to Chandra and Charlie. She was explaining what Matt wanted them to do. Matt had filled her in on his master plan and Cathy thought it sensible to repeat only the bare bones of the planned stratagems.

Heading for the Globe, all three began animated discussions on how to achieve their first goal in the plan - reaching the red stars deep within the double nucleus of Andromeda - a hard task, as the elliptical ring of old red stars were around the supermassive black hole.

Cathy told them of the machines and how they were trying to harness billions of thoughts around the planet to push them through the time barrier of communication- Time, Place, Space, Climate and Noise. They just had to find a way of doing it. Matt was working on it but had not discovered the key component.

'All we know is that we must all together, worldwide, achieve the greatest degree of intimacy – up close and very personal. Matt plans to make a speech, telepathically before he attempts this globalisation of thought. Therefore, everyone will know what we are trying to do. They can concentrate freely then.

The energy of each will form a giant electrical circuit rather like the Giant electrical circuits produced by nature, in the region known as the auroral zone, where strong electrical currents link the solar wind to the ionosphere and charged particles are accelerated and in turn generate the aurora. Thus, the magical open-air light shows of the auroras or polar lights - natural phenomena that form arcs in high-latitude regions like Scandinavia.'

'I was lucky enough to see them,' said Charlie the American projectionist, 'there are breakthroughs every day, thanks to satellites such as Viking and ESA's Cluster, where these incredible displays are visible. They are like plump plumes of turquoise '

'Turquoise means friendship, the stone protects the wearer from negative energy and brings good fortune,' said Chandra.

'Well, let's keep our fingers crossed for positive energy, tons of it' Cathy said firmly. 'Remember Sergei Boystov, our fellow Russian Cosmos-naut who did not have the will to continue. His spirit will guide us through, I'm sure. He has also given me an artefact of great significance, should the end of the day prove life-threatening'

They entered the Globe.

Mallard's machine was set up. So was Jim's, the British Intelligence man. Mallard said, 'Any updates on the machine in Reza's possession. Where is he now, and is he using the machine?'

'Thought you might have that info. We haven't been able to find any trace. Try your machine - it has all the bells and whistles.'

'Can't run them at full capacity with all the onlookers.' He gestured upwards towards the seating gallery.

Mallard added, 'I'm going to go ahead with the team. Make an attempt with the two devices we have. The other cosmos-nauts are in the Energisation chambers. I'm heading there myself.'

Jim patted him on the back, 'Good luck, old chap. Time is running out.'

Sohrab Reza looked around him. A handful of people were seated in the viewing gallery. Only the people of vital importance were there. There was strict security. Twice he had been asked to provide his passport. Twice he had to call the Professor for clearance. The Professor had to be reminded in his mind who Reza was.

Reza's IPOD was working fine. Although there was now a blank from the minds of the Opus Signori.

The astral projectionists were taking their places donning their thermal oversuits, the canopy was being retracted back into the roof, next the four were seen to be entering earth's atmosphere after deep meditation techniques induced by the leader, Matt Mallard.

They were heading straight for the Andromeda co-ordinates. Images were being beamed back to Sohrab's screen. All in the gallery were exclaiming at the speed and energy displayed. Jim, the MI6 man was watching events unfold. The machines were projecting the astral surfers like catapults, shooting them straight to the stars. They were closer than they had ever been before.

They needed to get close to that black hole and the entrance of the wormhole, find Damocles and trace the deadly particle Black Widow-the producer of negative energy density - where particles produce no energy which results in a vacuum. This causes the Universe's expansion to be so great that nothing could exist in it. A scenario before the existence of the Big Bang. Would it recur with Black Widow in the wormhole, hovering on the edge of the Red Giants?

Matt Mallard could feel his breath shortening. Up ahead loomed the double nucleus of the black hole in Andromeda with its red stars hovering. Red giants as they are known as they have exhausted the supply of hydrogen in their cores.

Mallard tried to include the others in the telepathic loop, without success, the machines below them were obviously having some interference. Only Cathy was attuned naturally.

The red stars suddenly appeared to them as Earth's sun, another star that was due to turn red in 7.5 billion years.

A sudden dreamlike state made Cathy and Mallard focus as one. Matt Mallard and Cathy Burkert were creating energy with the aid of the machines that brought an insight into the earth billions of years hence.

A vision emerged. They stood before it hand in hand, like two silhouettes, the sun so very, very close, earth and sky engulfed in the orange glow. A glow that was so intense but it never burned them. The earth was parched, no other beings existed, just the two of them. 'And the quote came from nowhere- a voice whispered. '*And the sun stood still, and the moon stayed, until the people had revenged themselves upon their enemies.....So the sun stood still in the midst of the heaven, and hasted not to go down about the whole day' Joshua, Chapter 10.'*

Sohrab Reza had his 20 minute slot in Mallard's mind. He could read the screen on his IPOD where Mallard's and Burkert's thoughts appeared. They were of one mind. Reza knew God was communicating to him and Iran personally. He was absolutely justified in his actions. Iran would take revenge on its arch-foe, Israel. He willed the two on to find the Black Widow particle, eject it and merge the earth into the Andromeda Galaxy.

Israel would be vanquished. Iraq would be melded into Iran. By the will of Allah, his country would lay first claim to vast new territory.

The black hole of Andromeda seemed to swallow Mallard and Cathy as they hurtled into the gravitational pull.

The screens went blank in the viewing gallery. They could see the 4 bodies of the projectionists below, confirmation was ascertained that they were all alive and breathing but the images of Andromeda had ceased.

‘Probably a glitch in the system, aftershocks of the earthquake’ said the Professor. ‘We will continue to wait. We cannot interrupt now. They cannot be woken up from their surreal state.’

Chandra and Charlie were drifting around the blue stars, in and out of what is known in Latin as the left hip of the Princess Andromeda, also called Mirach a red giant star. The galaxy NGC404 known as Mirach’s Ghost, because it proved slippery to photograph and to be viewed, was visible minutes away. Both Chandra and Charlie could not follow Matt and Cathy.

Mirach is the bright star in the centre and Mirach’s ghost is the glow, up and to the right. Credit & Copyright: Anthony Ayiomamitis

Matt and Cathy had gone too deep. They had always seemed of one mind. Together it was hoped, they would achieve the impossible.

Suddenly, they forgot all about Matt and Cathy as their minds reacted to the vision in front of them- talk about Mirach's ghost! Were they hallucinating? A spirit form had appeared, was it an angel? Pegasus, the constellation was close.

In Greek mythology Pegasus was a white, winged horse, the form in their sights was certainly winged, Chandra's connected it to what he had seen on a visit to Amaravati in Andhra Pradesh, India. Sculputres in the Buddhist Stupa – depicting a bas-relief of the Yaksha Punnaka (Hindu mythological figure) flying through his kingdom on a white, winged steed. Buddha too was said to have left his physical form on a white horse.

Charlie was into the awesome story of Pegasus- the myth embodied the physical and non-physical states of nature. Pegasus was magical, a winged creature, the stuff of enchanted woods and fables. He allowed a hero, Bellerophon of Greek myth to ride him to defeat a monster, the Chimera. His rider however falls off his back trying to reach Mount Olympus.

Both Charlie and Chandra hoped this winged spiritual genie, that was at the forefront of their vision, would let them climb to greater heights, not drop them into oblivion.

They had to help Matt and Cathy.

How could they? Their minds could not advance.

Mentally and subconsciously, they were exhorting themselves to go further.

Pegasus and the winged spirit seemed to provide the answer. Matt and Cathy had to go through to the end. Adam and Eve, reincarnated, forewarned now of the serpent would create that perfect new world.

Charlie and Chandra would support them with all their mental reserves. They focused and a blinding white light flashed for an instant on the screens in the viewing gallery and then all went blank again.

Mallard was in a tunnel and was reaching a near death experience, his body felt close to cardiac arrest – his heart felt it wasn't beating in a regular rhythm. But serenity was absolute.

Cathy was with him, a sudden surge of energy had taken them to the very edge of the red giants. Past them now and delving deep, the black hole loomed closer– thoughts of God and infinity! Mallard, his mind in the rarefied ether, among magnificent spiral galaxies similar in shape to the Milky Way with the red giants peppered across his field of vision, red stars in their declining years. His view through his goggles, fitted with the latest Hubble telescope technology gave him a detailed insight into Hubble's Ultra Deep Field. The glow of distant galaxies away from the glare of the Milky Way, blues and pinks and bright orange glowing in the black velvet of infinity. Mallard, his heart stopping in excitement felt the power of an almighty hand and all creationist beliefs were being explained.

How about 'the survival of the fittest?' was the natural interjection in Mallard's mind.

Darwin intruded. An extract of what he had read when he was researching the interconnection between all things, cosmic and earthly including the stuff Darwin studied on his voyage around the world in 1831 exploring for three years and three months on land: Mammalia, Birds, Fish and Reptiles which had helped him put forward his theories on evolution.

In 1859, Charles Darwin had set out his theory of evolution by natural selection. He defined natural selection as the "principle by which each slight variation, of a trait, if useful, is preserved".

The concept was simple but powerful: individuals best adapted to their environments are more likely to survive and reproduce.

As long as there is some variation between them, individuals with the most advantageous variations survive.

If the variations are inherited, then the disparity in the offspring will lead to a progressive evolution, and populations that evolve to be sufficiently different eventually become different species.

Hang on a minute –Mallard closed his eyes and tried to recall what he had read - wasn't there excitement amongst the biologists recently of the hot topic of 'epigenetics'- whereby rats were injected with nicotine when they were six days pregnant (22 days is their pregnancy term), allowed to give birth and the pups raised to the age of three weeks, before some were examined. The rest were allowed to mature and breed, and their own offspring were similarly examined. There was however, no further administration of nicotine.

The pups of the treated mothers had asthmatic lungs and so did the grand- offspring proving according to the researchers, a case for epigenetic modification; that nicotine is not only affecting lung cells but also affecting sex cells in ways that cause the lungs which ultimately develop from those cells to thus express their genes in the same abnormal ways. Epigenetic switches throughout the generations – the biblical curse of the sins of the fathers (or in this case the mothers), will be visited on the sons, even unto the third and fourth generations.

Darwinism would be disproved somewhat, as it would permit characteristics acquired during an organism's lifetime to be passed on to its offspring, not as Darwin stated, inherited ones.

What if Mallard and the others, their DNA acquiring characteristics of the alien force would as in the prediction of particles in physics break the probability cycle and a new species would emerge? Mallard knew he had not imagined the alien life-force. He felt infused with the God particle. Creation without end.

Now the answers came to him thick and fast.

The blackness gave the male and female who were of one mind, Matt and Cathy, every DNA sequence of every living creature, every thought and trait of every living being was stored in their corpus callosum, the neural fibres that connect the right and left hemispheres of the brain and then transferred below to the ancient pathway beneath- the anterior commisure, the animal brain.

Matt Mallard knew what he had to do. He would have to separate the two hemispheres. He also knew where the Black Widow was. CERN had communicated feedback on the images in the

Hubble's Ultra Deep Field he had viewed minutes ago. Hubble's Telescopic goggles had identified the entrance of the wormhole amongst the red giants.

He signalled Cathy. They were to descend. Mentally he drew on years of training, taking himself and Cathy back to a consciousness of normality. Together their acute intuition had accessed spheres of foreign phenomena but now...Mallard gritted his teeth.

She would have to be a separate entity from now on.

Sohrab Reza recorded every thought on his device. Separation of the female in Islam was according to the prophet Mohammed to do with chasteness and headcoverings over female bosoms...he looked at the women around him, some of them showing their attributes, it was summer and according to the general trend, bareness was a celebration of glorious female form, worshipped throughout the ages.

Sohrab Reza was out of tune with the general populace. He tweaked his machine so it concentrated solely on one male, Matt Mallard.

Descending from the ether, Mallard's mind refocused on terra firma, he had a sudden insight- he knew where the other machine was. It was right there at CERN.

Jim, British Intelligence, looked across at Mallard. They were in Mallard's room. They had two hours. Mallard was confident of success but they needed the third machine.

The Swiss TIGRIS were combing the complex at CERN, everyone was being questioned. Laptops were being examined, computers were investigated. Only a matter of time, they said. Time however, was of the essence.

Mallard said, 'Jim, I have to take care of something very important first. Sorry I'm going to have to ask you to leave for a while. I'm incommunicado for the next hour.' There was a knock on the door. It was Cathy.

Jim left and Cathy walked in. She looked silvery in the tank top and fitted trousers, long black hair and of course those green eyes with the tantalizing promise of eternity.

Mallard, his senses heightened by the machines, knew there was only fulfilment. He had waited too long. He had to ensure she was strong and alone.

Cathy was in his mind. She gravitated to him and as arms embraced, tongues intertwined, clothes were divested and an elemental surge engulfed them. Steely sapphire and sparking electricity surged through their naked bodies. To Cathy, he was

Christmas and birthdays rolled into one. Her pores were assailed by a rarefied atmosphere, crystal clear and pure. They were on the bed, flesh, bone and sinew-slaking their thirst and hunger for each other. Cathy felt her breath stopping as he fitted his body to hers. Cells, tissue and excited nerve-endings were aroused to fever-pitch.

Her body's reactions felt like a valley- ripe, verdant, carved out with a giant ice-cream scoop, where mountains appear in Rushmore groups – a crowd of giants, and rivers topple over edges before plummeting into invisible channels. He was definitely hitting her G-spot. His male scent and skin was so erotic as his chest rested gently on her rounded breasts and then he was arching back as he felt her body attune to his driving rhythm.

They reached their climax as one but it was not enough. They needed fusion once more. Then, words had to be spoken tenderly, of love, of need, of infinity and of separation.

Mallard told her what he had to do.

Jim, MI6, was puzzled. He had switched on the machines at CERN with the printouts turned back on. He had the place to himself while the projectionists were taking a break. The viewing gallery was empty for the mo. The printouts on Mallard's machine were still recording thoughts, the

Opus Signori that Mallard had rerouted, and thoughts of the projectionists zig-zagging through, although Reza's machine had ceased operating. Where the devil was he?

Mallard had said to investigate all personnel at CERN and that's what the Swiss unit TIGRIS had been doing, every laptop had been checked, every computer. All were in the clear. There must be some other device. Jim got hold of the R&D Lab at SIS.

Cathy looked at the man standing in front of her. A striking looking man. Middle Eastern, she thought. He was smiling at her. He asked if he could talk to her. He wanted to know how she projected astrally. He was very interested in the paranormal. He had been one of the fortunate few to witness them take flight.

Cathy knowing how exclusive seating in the viewing gallery was, felt more comfortable. He must be somebody important, in a position of trust. She said, 'I'm heading now for the Globe. I will walk with you there.'

On the way she chatted happily. Cathy was quietly happy. She knew she was loved in every way. She spared a brief thought for Hektor. She knew he would wish her well. He had had her time and her heart for many a year.

Life was good. And if they were to die....Matt had said not to contemplate such a thing. They were about life and living, he had a plan – not a cunning one as in Baldrick's view, thought Cathy full of smiles despite the impending doom- but one of survival for all mankind.

Sohrab Reza escorted Cathy indoors. He said goodbye and wished her well. Out of his breast pocket he withdrew what seemed like an IPOD. Cathy looked at him, slightly curious. She had been doing some research on them recently as she had intended to purchase one.

She must ask him how he liked it. Reza looked at the screen. He was pressing buttons. Cathy felt weird because she quite forgot what she was intending to say. There was a pause, an absence in her mind, she had no idea what had caused it. Cathy's ESP kicked in. Something was wrong. Something that was reminiscent of the machine used on her years ago in Cyprus. She must tell Matt.

Sohrab Reza needed to talk to the Guardian Council. He also needed to touch base with the Opus Signori. They had gone completely off the radar on his machine and he needed to find out why. Were any of them on to him, hence the lack of the loop-feed? Had they deliberately severed all connections to him? He had to know. The IPOD perhaps was not powerful enough. It was a recent acquisition and untried until today. Perhaps he needed to get to his laptop. It was safely tucked away in his car in the car park, hidden from the Swiss TIGRIS hunt for it.

He tapped a question into the Professor's mind. He had ten minutes before the next launch. He would get the laptop.

Matt Mallard heard what Cathy had to say. She described the absence of thought. Mallard took her by the arm urgently and said, 'Where is the man?

Cathy pointed upwards to the viewing gallery. There was no one there. A description of Sohrab Reza was circulated immediately. He was to be apprehended on sight.

They traced the vehicle. The car was abandoned, the doors were wide open and there was no Reza and no machine. TIGRIS, the Swiss supercops searched nearby, powerful GSM signals emanating from their vehicles but Reza had vanished.

They would get him. He couldn't get far on foot.

Mallard had baited the trap for Reza. The Opus Signori's minds had been rerouted. He knew Reza would need to know what was transpiring with the rest of his elite group but Reza had not swallowed the bait. Reza had escaped and his machine could not be used in conjunction with the other two.

Mallard needed to find an alternative source of energy.

He was in the right place. The world's leading physicists were in the vicinity. Seven thousand, nine hundred and thirty one of them.

ISRAEL

Ben Efraim listened to the Cardinal's voice at the other end of the phone. He had had his suspicions about his fellow Opus Signor, Sohrab Reza, even though Reza had been at pains to be charming and friendly, even including him on some choice business deals.

Now his wariness towards Reza was justified.

Reza, according to the healer, Matt Mallard was spearheading a plot to monitor minds. To what end was unknown? Mallard had told the Cardinal about the supergalaxy Earth could be heading for. Mallard's surmise that Reza might want to be at the forefront of a land grab, excluding Israel completely was also of great concern.

Ben Efraim rang his contact in Mossad. There was utter silence for a minute, and then all hell broke loose. The voice at the other end of the phone almost shouted. Efraim must get the latest information. There had been troop movements spotted by OFek 9, their spy satellite, near the Iraqi border. What was Reza's location now, at this moment??

Ben Efraim told him. He was told to keep in direct contact with Mallard. Immediately. Report back, was the terse instruction.

CERN, Geneva

Less than two hours till the end of the world. Cathy watched Matt as he spoke on the phone. She glowed inside. After their unbelievable lovemaking, he had left her sexually complete but still stimulated, wanting yet more. The calamity of this day intruded, they had to be business-like. It was hard to acknowledge death when the world seemed so bright and beautiful. Today was June 20th, the day of the summer solstice. The day was warm and the sun shone.

The physicists had decided to make use of that sun, the longest day when the sun was at its peak, to try and harness its energy so that they could accomplish the task that lay ahead.

Matt had told them of his idea garnered when he was in the depths of Andromeda - of the separation of the two hemispheres of the brain. The learned minds accessed others globally. A plan using genome research - genetic inheritance of human beings recorded in vast databases by governments around the world, and in projects like ENCODE (Encyclopaedia of DNA elements) was decided upon. The rest of the world's scientific institutions were at the ready to share data.

The neuroscientists and the computer geeks suggested a technique called voxelation.

This involves dividing the brain into spatially registered voxels or cubes, replicating the voxels of selected genes in the spatial maps in billions of people on the planet. A deviation in brainwave patterns, from the stored data, signalling neuron firing - electrically excitable cells converting to energy, would then be identified.

Electrical stimulation via the LHC would be applied on the selected genes by the scientists and the CERN technicians, who would compute it all on the special machines of Matt's and British Intelligence. Input would be next.

First they had to, via the remote fMRI in the machines, make the brain blink – a kind of burst suppression; generating alpha waves in the back of the brain, thus cutting off visual information, allowing the bubbling up of the programmed idea. Then the machines would target the right hemisphere of the brain, for a twentieth of a second, just long enough for a burst of neural gamma waves to register that idea: 'Eject Black Widow'

Screens prompts would jog the associated memory of that one focused thought by employing a mathematical trick called the Granger causality test, which makes it possible to determine how one sequence of data points affects another; The neuro-boff's felt that would be sufficient for every individual to project a single thought transference which would enable the black hole in Andromeda to suck up the Black Widow particle and Damocles from the wormhole. Billions of people having just one thought, recurring again and again.

They realised that like the prediction of particles, the thought might be deflected from mind to mind and evolve into world antagonism towards such a process. Therefore, they input a glimmering of the dire consequences if such a path was not undertaken. Focus on getting Black Widow out of the wormhole into Andromeda-hold that one thought! A global 2 minute silence would be imposed to aid concentration.

The scientists thought the energy needed to access billions on the planet might be accomplished with the aid of the LHC and the two machines belonging to Mallard and British Intelligence, plus the satellites harnessing solar power and last but not least, Dynamic tidal power –exploiting the differential between potential and kinetic energy in tidal flows with the aid of the world's tidal power plants.

Mallard, Cathy, Charlie and Chandra were being superenergised before lift-off. They made their way to their beds. Reza tuned in to Mallard's mind carefully. Mallard must not suspect a thing. Reza had his twenty minute slot again. He was hiding in one of the hostel rooms. He had broken in when the entire CERN personnel were gathered in front of the GLOBE. Thousands waited for word of what was happening inside. A relay of information was being conducted on a need to know basis.

Reza had his laptop and his IPOD. He connected both. Together the machines would pick up on the activity of the 2 main projectionists continuously.

Mallard settled into his elevated consciousness whilst the Globe was humming with activity from hundreds of extra computers hastily set up, manned by a hive of choice personnel. Mallard's and Jim's machines were ready to start feeding the one thought to the billions: 'Eject Black Widow from the wormhole into Andromeda'.

The UNEP power grid in Geneva, in conjunction with the physicists at CERN had quickly formulated the means to harness solar and tidal power. Everything was good to go.

Mallard was getting good at raising his consciousness within minutes. The others too. The music in the audio-feed was of spiritual healing and shut out the background noise. The technicians were excluded from the audio-feed in their headphones.

For a moment the memory of the alien life he had sensed in Andromeda, teased at his recall. He knew the creatures, ebony and fluid could not be seen apart from in the mind. They had no form. When the thought of their shape had formed in Mallard's mind, the alien life-force had projected an image that the human brain would feel comfortable with. A fluid human shape – the outlines of a head, a body rather like a carved statue - a Hollywood Oscar statuette, without distinguishing features. They did not wear clothes but nevertheless were sheathed in an ebony lacquer.

That was how he had described the forms to the Opus Signori.

Ben Efraim, the Israeli Opus Signor, had called him regarding the latest intel on Sohrab Reza explaining his country's concerns regarding that individual. Mallard felt no need to withhold any information.

Suddenly Mallard jerked. He tore off his headphone and said to Cathy in her mind 'Quickly now. Come with me'

Chapter 11

CERN, Geneva:

Cathy quickly followed him as he had a quiet word with Jim. Mallard headed for his special machine. Jim followed closely.

‘The bastard is in my head. I know it. He knows everything. Switch off all the machines, all the equipment everybody. We cannot continue. We have to find Reza. If not, he will have the means to convert the thinking of billions of people. We will have given him access through the messaging being set up in billions of minds’

Jim said, ‘I have an idea, we might succeed in drawing him out. Contact the Opus Signori for all information on Reza’

England

Cardinal Jules de Fleury pressed the send command on the email: The file contained all the information on Reza. As soon as Mallard had informed him, hours ago, of Reza’s calumny, he had scoured the network of informants that the Opus Signori had at their disposal and a composite file resulted both in Iran and in Canada. It was difficult to get information in Iran and available intel was only accessible via the local Chaldean Catholic Church.

The reason the Cardinal had met and included Sohrab Reza in the Opus Signori.

It had been Friday June 10th 2011, and Pope Benedict XVI was erecting an eparchy (a Diocese) of the Chaldean Catholic Church in Toronto, Canada. Archbishop Zora was present and it was the Archbishop who had introduced an illustrious and noteworthy individual, a recent Catholic convert from the province of Anwaz, Iran, the archbishop's old stomping ground - Sohrab Reza.

Reza was a prominent citizen of Anwaz, visiting Canada as he was wont to do, on business interests. He was honorary chairman of the steel facility in Anwaz, a great philanthropist and well-known by the local Church for his good deeds. It was considered a great feather in the Church's cap when he converted.

Just today acting on Cardinal de Fleury's orders did they probe further. A Catholic assistant of Reza's, did some digging within the military archives. Reza was still very active within the Iranian Guardian Council. In fact, he was greatly valued by the Ayatollah Ali Khomeini.

Rumour had it he was the architect of the policy that encouraged martyrdom in the Iran-Iraq War of 1980-1988. His plan had been put into action of launching 'human wave' attacks on Iraqi positions.

The Iranian soldiers, raw recruits really, with only a week's basic military training were given 'passports to Paradise' and sent to the front. They all died of course.

Reza had reason to hate Iraq. During the same conflict of 1980-1988, Iraq had tried to annex his hometown of Anwaz. Anwaz was close to the frontlines and Reza had lost his entire family, as the war encroached heavily on the city.

Cardinal Jules de Fleury believed they had uncovered the reason for Reza's perfidy. He looked around at the roomful of people. All the Opus Signori had been summoned ten hours ago as soon as Mallard had started reporting. Each had flown in on his private jet. One member flew in on his country's latest acquisition – The Hypermach Sonicstar, flying at twice the speed of Concorde.

Five members had been present all along. Here at Chartwell, Churchill's former home. The Cardinal turned to one of the five. A Mr. Robert Anderson. They had known each other at school. Gordonstoun. They had both aspired to be 'Guardians' – Headboys - but Anderson had won. A man still on the winning side, heading the security of a nation. Great Britain.

The Cardinal took him to one side. He said, 'How's your boy getting on in Geneva?'

‘Bad business, those mind machines. Reza is out there and knows all of it. That knowledge is lethal and it is in the wrong hands. With access to practically every mind on the planet, he could rule the world.

Can’t find any trace of him. They have started a room to room search but that will take time. Did you manage to get anything on him in Canada?’

‘Nothing much. Just above board business dealings. I plan to speak to all present in five minutes. Let us go in to the dining room. We will have to squeeze everyone in there.’

Ben Efraim knew he sounded loud but the pressure was reaching scorching point. ‘We are the men in charge of the world and we cannot find this cockroach. We have repeatedly in the past and are able to currently use all manner of persuasion, including termination to further our causes. We have armies, in some cases at our disposal and we are helpless. We have to rely on astral projection for our survival of the Merger between the constellations. I have never heard of such ‘dreck’ (crap). Why don’t we send a missile up and blow up the fucking wormhole?’

‘You know it can’t be done. The sub-dwarf star will be even nearer to earth as a result. Let’s all remain calm.' The room quietened down only to erupt into an uproar at the Cardinal's next words.

'Gentlemen, I have to tell you a matter of great magnitude. Until 2 hours ago, our erstwhile member, Sohrab Reza and to some of you, he was considered a friend -has been monitoring our minds. With a mind-control device.'

I must urge you all to be calm. Please!'

Robert Anderson stood up, 'I knew about the existence of such a machine but I had no clue that Reza had got hold of such technology. I genuinely believed there was only one of its kind and that one was with Her Majesty's government'

'You were obliged to tell us. You know there are no secrets amongst the Opus Signori. Our motto is: Transcend self, transcend nations. In order to control the world's destiny, we have had to be above and beyond the call of petty politics, of greed, of corruption. Every thought has to be a noble one. Reza could not have found lesser thoughts in our minds'

'That's exactly what Reza is thinking. He believes his country's cause is noble. Iran has been vilified by sanctions and limitations for a decade or so. Their oil is being produced and stored – tons of barrels and the world has refused to buy any. They are ostracised and live in a state of near poverty. Reza and his country believe Israel is responsible. Iran bitterly resents support for Israel from most of the globe. Another major factor is Iran having the nuclear option- such a threat has convoluted global thinking' said Hektor Xanthis.

'Why can't the tables be turned? Convolute Reza's thinking.' said Ben Efraim

'We can't access him. He has taken great care to be completely off the radar. No trace of any recorded brain activity for us to target him'

Ben Efraim and Robert Anderson said in unison, 'His homes, his phones, his email – have they been bugged? We must get to him somehow'

'Yes, two hours ago. We can't get into his home in Iran although the Catholic Church is trying but his mobile phone that he usually calls me on is subject to investigation as we speak,

'Who is handling that?'

'Cyprus is on top of it. We have a crack team. They are working with Robert and MI5'

'How much time do we have left before the collision of Andromeda and the Milky Way?'

‘CERN has issued a revised estimate – about two hours from now. I should have more information within the next few minutes’

Karoo Region South Africa

Hal Heinberg scratched his head. He had done what Reza had asked him to do. He had fired the missile from Teheran. It wasn’t his goddamn fault that the missile had gone astray causing radiation of such megamass that the dwarf star, Damocles created the Black Widow particle. Mankind was doomed and Hal Heinberg was to blame.

He had to redeem himself. Reza had told Hal of the incredible discovery of Alien life. Knowledge garnered from sources within CERN. Hal needed to target those sources.

Mallard and Burkert - they were of one mind.

Reza had said that Mallard was on to him. Mallard’s machine at CERN had been switched off. Reza realised that his machine and his IPOD could not function on their own. There was no way that Reza could get through. Mallard’s machine acted as a superconductor and Reza started to panic.

Reza needed Mallard’s machine to be turned back on. It was vital that he had to be tuned in when the merger took place between the two constellations. Iran *must* be unparalleled in their power.

If the alien race Mallard had sensed was pure thought without form, Reza's machine could take undue advantage of the situation. With his own and the other machines at CERN, Reza could influence that pure thinking – the thought processes of the alien beings.

There would be a race globally to be the first to encounter such life, and Reza and Iran would be the first to cross the finish line.

Hal Heinberg needed to turn the tide in Reza's favour.

Reza's instructions were explicit. Attack Mallard and Burkert. Use the IRI- Ionospheric Research Institute -their high power, high frequency array radio transmitter would tap into the pair's minds.

Target their emotions.

Hal was ready to comply. He had done his homework on mind control and the IRI. He knew the basics: the radio transmitter electromagnetically induced a shield in the ionosphere which emitted ELF waves (extremely low frequencies), the same as the human brain.

If an external signal, like the one Hal was due to input- electromagnetism- interfered with the ELF in the human mind, emotions could be controlled. These could be synthesized and stored on a computer. Hal had done the spadework. Mallard and Burkert were of one mind and were sitting ducks.

CERN, Geneva:

Reza could not use his phone. The last communication from Mallard's mind was that Reza's fellow Opus Signor knew of his deeds. They would be monitoring his phone. He needed to speak urgently to his compatriots in the Guardian Council and to Hal Heinberg. He must break cover and find a telephone.

Israel: Mossad Headquarters

Colonel Daniel Barak picked up the phone and barked into it. He was livid. All networks were busy. He was currently using his country's hot line. He couldn't speak for long.

The world was in terror. Panic had set in. The armies of every country were keeping law and order so far. Communication networks were overloaded as televisions with news updates were devoured by the waiting billions. Texts and emails were being exchanged frantically as people tried to reconcile themselves to death. Churches, mosques, temples from the hills to the plains, from valleys to mountain tops were groaning with the multitudes, praying and chanting for survival. Most were prostrate with fear.

Daniel Barak knew he had seconds and then Ofek9 would be out of range. The images were being sent to the bank of screens in his office.

He roared at his assistant. The young Major adjusted the screen and spoke with deference.

‘Sir, the thermal imaging camera is on. All bodies at CERN are reported to be outside the GLOBE. The army is positioned at the entrance and patrolling the complex. There are no bodies in the buildings. All mobile phones are being confiscated as we speak. We have just one heat source at CERN Hostel reception. The outline is male. I suggest we get someone to check him out.’

Hans-Pieter Combe looked at the man closely. The man was dressed in the overalls of one of the technicians at CERN. He had just put the phone down at the reception. He answered Hans-Pieter in perfect French. ‘Yes his mobile phone was not working. That’s why he had to call his elderly mother from the reception phone. She was on her own and was very distressed’

‘I need your mobile phone.’

‘It’s in my room. Officer, I have to hurry. I really am needed at the Globe. I have to help with the computers’

The man described exactly what the next attempt was going to be. Even Hans-Pieter hadn't known about the brain messaging.

'Off you go. Hurry. I will get your mobile. What is your room number?'

For a split second, the man hesitated, then gave the number and walked away.

Hans-Pieter took the stairs two at a time. He reached the room. Something was nagging at him. Something about the conversation. Why had the guy hesitated?

The room was empty. No mobile. Hans-Pieter talked urgently into his walkie-talkie. Within minutes every room in the hostel was being searched. They recovered a laptop which was taken apart. It was the machine. Reza's machine. But no IPOD. It must be on Reza's person.

Hans-Pieter raced to the Globe.

Chapter12

Matt Mallard and Cathy Burkert snatched a few private moments. They were in the clinical office, waiting for word that Reza and his machines were apprehended. The phone rang.

Mallard put the phone down and held Cathy close, his mouth in her hair. She smelled so good. He talked to her about the separation they mentally had to undergo.

'Cathy, my darling, as I explained earlier, in order to protect you, we have to be different entities. We cannot project in one mind. I have already reconfigured the machine. Reza is currently able to access our brainwaves. He still has his IPOD which will register our thoughts at intervals. We cannot wait for the police to get him. We have no time.

We have to try the brain messaging on the masses.

I believe I can withstand the pressure from the IPOD- its range is not as effective as the laptop but I'm concerned that you couldn't - not after what happened to you in Cyprus. I wouldn't put you through that again but the urgency has overtaken 'immediate.' We must proceed. Do you understand?'

Cathy kissed him passionately. She said, 'I love you. I believe we will walk the earth for millennia. I am not worried'

'We have to go.' They walked to the Globe surrounded by an escort of armed Supercops.

England

Cardinal de Fleury looked at the men around the table. His fellow Opus Signor.

He said, 'I have nothing much to report. Just that the laptop was recovered and there were detailed records of all of us. Our minds, our business dealings, our IMF and World Bank transactions, our wives or partners, all of it on Reza's laptop. The files on Iran were deleted; they are trying to recover them from the hard drive. There is, however a connection mentioned and I need to speak to you about this..'

He turned to Joseph Tinibu, the South African Opus Signor- 'I believe you might be able to explain the link. It's extremely tenuous but the Swiss believe it might have some bearing on Reza's activities. Have you heard of the IRI facility in your country?'

CERN, Geneva:

Reza had stripped off the technician overalls. He melted into the crowd waiting outside the Globe. He still had his mobile with him but it hadn't been switched on. That way he couldn't be traced.

Earlier, he had spoken to the Iranian Guardian Council. Praise was being heaped upon him from the hierarchy. Do whatever it takes was the instruction.

Hal Heinberg had proved elusive. He didn't know whether Heinberg had managed to get into the IRI facility and had succeeded in programming the computer targeting Mallard and Burkert. He must speak to him. He would find a phone again.

He was waiting for the next astral flight. They had just been informed that it was due to take place at any minute. That meant Mallard's machine was likely to be switched on to attempt the global brain-messaging. Reza would wait to make his move in the thick of the crowd's intense participation in the activity whilst they were given detailed reports on progress within the Globe. Select Television crews were camped outside and were capturing the images of the hushed waiting. Occasional gasps and wailing sounded from the fearful throng.

Reza knew that if he used his IPOD on Mallard now, Mallard would recognise the interference. He was waiting for Mallard to go into an altered state of consciousness prior to the next astral flight before he touched Mallard's mind. Now he would tune into Burkert's mind instead.

Reza could barely contain his excitement. He would be plugged into literally billions of minds at the touch of the little button on his specially configured IPOD.

Cathy stared through her goggles at the canopy above her. She was alone in her mind. It felt strange without Matt's constant presence. She could hear him, Chandra and Charlie through the audio feed. Chandra and Charlie sounded nervous. They talked softly exchanging quiet memories.

Matt was communicating with Jim, the MI6 man and Professor Christoph Benjamin who was the spokesman for the physicists and technicians gathered in front of their computer screens.

Five minutes and they would be at the crossroads of complex interrelations between solar power from the satellites and tidal power from the world's tidal power plants. The LHC and Matt's and British Intelligence machines were up and running. They had tuned in the newly-acquired laptop found in the CERN hostel. The one that Reza had abandoned.

The countdown had started. The Global mind-messaging was due to begin. Matt had provided a spark –a slight touch in every mind, an allusion of the importance of the recurring thought. 'Eject Black Widow into Andromeda'

Cathy settled into her trance-like stasis. The audio-feed was now sheer, heavenly music. Different strains for each of the four, each a personal favourite.

Cathy could see a familiar white light as she left her physical body. She could see herself looking down at her form. She was close to Andromeda. She felt adrift without Matt in her mind.

She was approaching Alpheratz, the brightest star in the constellation of Andromeda. Coming up close, Cathy could see it was actually a binary star, composed of 2 stars in close orbit. The Alpheratz atmosphere was known to consist of high levels of the chemicals Mercury and manganese.

Close by was The Bard's Muse formed in the asterism known as the square of Pegasus. Matt had christened it. Life emanated from it. A quicksilver form, liquid mercury in an alien form – she could see what Matt had described to her, not just the male ebony, but the silvery fluid female version. Alien life around her, projecting an image of themselves, one that Cathy's mind could relate to.

Cathy was overwhelmed with joy. Her thoughts melded with theirs. An exchange of joyous knowledge. They touched her mind and knew her. Mentally every facet of her being was known to them. She listened rapt, remembered James Hopwood Jeans, the English physicist and astronomer's poetic insight, '*the concepts which now prove to be fundamental to our understanding of nature....seem to my mind to be structures of pure thought...the universe begins to look more like a great thought than a great machine.*'

Suffused hitherto by seemingly impenetrable veils, Cathy now felt the incredible contrast as her mind burst through constraints and the veils became diaphanous now – so sheer, as the liquid mercury life-force transferred data – knowledge, as Chandra had said earlier, exceeding every expectation.

Cathy, her brain bubbling with information and exhilaration suddenly shuddered to a halt. Hang on, what was that guttural accent interjecting rudely? It was definitely not through the audio-feed. A foreign voice she'd heard recently.

Sohrab Reza.

His thoughts overlaid hers. She was helpless. The Alien life was answering the questions that were being asked, that of pure thought, of climate, of habitable areas rich in minerals and natural resources. Cathy was mentally trying to instil her own thoughts, to tell them to stop revealing the inner workings of their consciousness. Please, please stop, she said over and over again. They could not hear her. Reza was controlling her mind. He was talking directly to the Alien life-force. His next step would be to convert the thinking of billions- would his little IPOD have the range? Cathy felt distraught with helplessness. She began crying softly, 'Where was Matt?'

Mallard had tuned in to the audio-feed from CERN. Professor Christoph Benjamin confirmed the first round of mind-messaging was in the framework. The results were successful.

The crowds gathered outside the Globe confirmed the common thought of Black Widow ejection. The memory recurring was the second stage. All over the planet, televisions screens were jogging the memory. 'Eject Black Widow into the black hole of Andromeda'

Matt needed to get the others and approach the red giants near Andromeda, the giants at the outermost fringe of the supermassive black hole. There lay the entrance to the wormhole. He spoke to Jim on the ground. Jim started to tune in the others through the audio-feed only. Nothing in their minds.

Each had to concentrate solely on the one thought to eject the particle, the Black Widow.

Reza's IPOD was humming nicely. All the information from Cathy's mind was being downloaded. He couldn't get a fix on Mallard's. He had tried to tune in the billions but he needed Mallard's composite data. He would wait for the next 20 minute slot.

Israel: Mossad Headquarters

Colonel Daniel Barak looked at the young Major. He said, 'Try the GSM on Ofek9 to see if he's using his mobile or the other device – the IPOD.

We have managed to trace a record of an IPOD being sold to a Hal Heinberg purchased in Teheran. Heinberg registered it with Apple a few months ago. Unusual name for a purchase in Teheran. We are checking him out'

The young Major said, 'About 500 IPOD's are being used at the moment in the crowd at CERN. We cannot confiscate IPOD's. We have to trace Hal Heinberg. Unfortunately, we have very few agents in Teheran. I will try and expedite it through our Russian sources. These days Russia is more closely aligned with Iran than ever.'

‘Not after Iran blasted the missile in outer space and caused the current contretemps. The entire world turned against them.’ said Barak

‘Colonel, Sir, I have the Russian contact on line. He is tracing the purchase to an address in Anwaz, Iran. Do we aim Ofek9 at this address? O.K. go ahead with the coordinates’

The Colonel said, ‘Get your contact at the Russian Embassy to initiate a search at the address. Now. They know what I need. All data to be transmitted on the secure network. I do not wish to be disturbed for the next ten minutes’

Colonel Daniel Barak walked into the small cell. Completely soundproofed the room housed the scrambler phone. He dialled a number and spoke in fluent Farsi, ‘Are you in the facility now?’

CERN, Geneva:

Cathy writhed mentally with Reza’s voice in her mind. She turned away in desperation from Alpheratz and headed for the blue stars around Andromeda, thinking by putting distance between her and that star she could escape the voice.

Something drew her to the constellation of Cassiopeia just north of Andromeda. If one were able to observe Earth's Sun from Alpha Centauri, the closest star to our solar system, it would appear closest to Cassiopeia.

Cathy tried desperately to override Reza and think of random stuff – she knew that Cassiopeia had featured endlessly in songs and cinema and normally she would be fascinated by Cassiopeia's binary star but the noise in her mind and the sun's proximity were confusing her. She stared fiercely upward at the sun and made herself imagine the nuclear decay that beamed neutrinos to the earth's surface. The same principle was applied when the world thought the speed of light had been broken in November last year.

Neutrinos, similar to electrons but without electrical charge, unaffected when passing through great distances, were sent from CERN to the Gran Sasso laboratory in Italy, and had purportedly arrived faster than the speed of light.

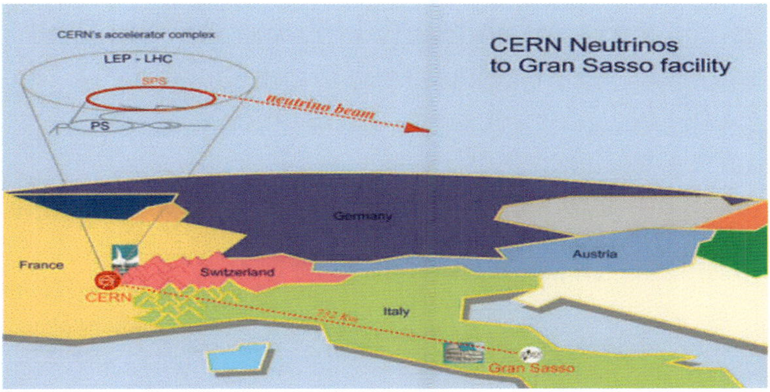

Image: CERN Press Office

Consternation among the scientific community that Einstein's theory was disproved was subsequently allayed when it was discovered one of the scientists, the head of the experiment had failed to plug in a cable correctly, and therefore the findings were incorrect.

But with the appearance of the wormhole time travel took on a whole new dimension. Cathy her mind possessed by Reza in his attempt to connect with the alien-force, tried to recall a paper by Lawrence H. Ford and Thomas A. Roman published in Scientific American, to better understand wormholes when she had first heard of their existence. The reason for her presence at CERN.

Desperately, willing herself into a state of calm, she remembered bits of the paper now: that a space-time bubble, like the wormhole, is the closest that modern physics comes to the 'warp drive' of science fiction. 'Warp drive' indicated faster than light travel. It can convey a starship at arbitrarily high speeds. Similar to wormholes where Space-time contracts at the front of the bubble reducing the distance to the destination, and expands at its rear, increasing the distance from the origin. The ship itself stands still relative to the space immediately around it.

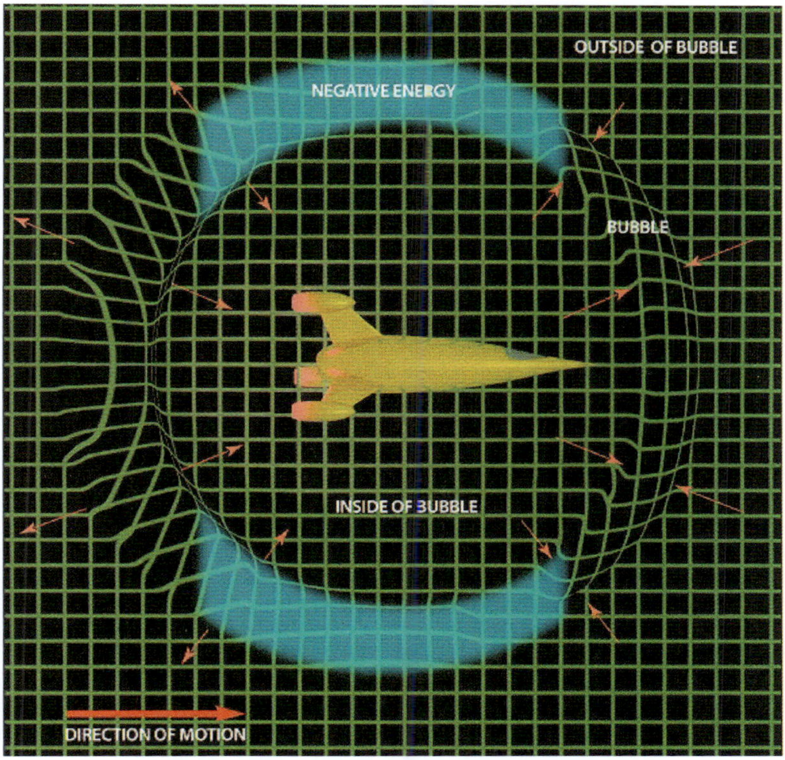

The paper mentioned the physicist, Sergei V. Krasnikov, of the Central Astronomical Observatory near St. Petersburg, who had proposed creating a 'superluminal subway', a faster than light channel, a tube of modified space-time (similar to a wormhole) connecting earth and a distant star. Within the tube, superluminal travel in one direction is possible. During the outbound journey at sublight speed, a spaceship crew would create such a tube. On the return journey, they could travel through it at 'warp speed'. Time travel would be a reality.

Cathy was close to the wormhole now. She would attempt a mental 'superluminal subway' to send information forward in time. She must override Reza's voice. She wondered desperately, if telepathy worked on the same principle. A consciousness where thoughts could travel forward in time arriving in another mind before vocal chords could utter the reality.

The next instant her mind knew pure clarity and the premonition of danger. Just in case, she didn't survive, she hoped Matt would investigate every possibility.

Chapter 13

England

Joseph Tinibu was on the video link and was questioning the man seated opposite him closely. His right-hand man. The man was small and looked reedy as opposed to the big imposing figure of Tinibu but his voice was powerful and sure.

‘I checked it myself, Sir, there is nothing untoward at the IRI. No reports of any unusual activity’

‘Sohrab Reza has never been in South Africa – but there is a connection. I feel it in my bones. Mossad has a hold of his computer files picked up from his residence in Teheran by the Russians. Files are being decrypted as we speak’

Joseph Tinibu steepled his fingers and said, ‘I never agreed with the Cabinet members to have this facility based on our land. HAARP in Alaska have had very negative reports about climate change being caused by the Ionosphere analysis...’ He was interrupted by the telephone ringing. The small man watched as Tinibu picked up the phone.

A moment later Tinibu smiled and hung up, ‘They have a name. A German national living in South Africa – a Hal Heinberg, our IPOD registered man in Teheran. Check if he was or is at the Research Institute.’

'Straight away, Sir.' The small man left the room, hurriedly.

CERN, Geneva:

Matt Mallard tried to raise Cathy on the audio-feed. She wasn't responding. His every instinct felt as though she was trying to get in touch. Charlie and Chandra moved with him towards the red giants and the entrance of the wormhole. They told him they were going to attempt the wormhole with him.

Where the devil was Cathy? He was receiving a message of import from her. It was odd, strange, a thought without a presence. A disembodied Cathy.

He hoped she was alright. He couldn't wait. He was going to have to go in to the wormhole without her.

Suddenly, an emotion took hold of him, sheer hatred. His mind couldn't make sense of it but nevertheless, the feelings tore through him. He hated the alien beings. He needed to exterminate them.

Matt Mallard trusted his instincts. If he was feeling this antipathy, it was for a reason. He must try and find a way of killing this species. He felt sure they were going to harm mankind. He couldn't trust anybody else. He must do this alone. Deeper and deeper he went into the wormhole. All was impenetrable blackness.

The blackness calmed him. The rage still swirled but reason was trying to override. He prayed like he never had before. He prayed to expunge the hatred. He prayed for sense.

And the blackness of fluid ebony, intelligence without form gave him an answer.

'Be amongst us. Spend time with us. Learn our ways'

Mallard, his prejudice still riding high, his hatred without reason - Suddenly and with utter conviction he knew this was just the beginning.

He knew that there would be a merger of constellations. Andromeda and the Milky Way would be one. Earth would be absorbed in the merger. His feelings of rage and antipathy were a foretaste of how the entire human race would react to the aliens. They would try and dominate the pure thought of the alien race. They would convert it and twist it into snake's coils to suit their own advancement. What's more, they would use the technology he had pioneered. His machines would have to be destroyed forever.

First, the Black Widow. The rage was still with him. It came in bursts. Use the rage to find the Black Widow.

The Black Widow was suddenly blinking a tiny blue glow. Similar blue flashes now became visible. All Black Widow particles? There appeared to be more than one. The energy from the billions on earth was working. They were helping Matt and the others to create enormous electromagnetic fields. The electrons present in the atoms needed just one gargantuan kick. The Black Widow could be ejected. First, Matt had to trap just one for analysis at CERN. Remotely, his mind controlled the joystick image in his visor with adroit manoeuvres, trapped one for observation, stored it as data, and then CERN took over with composition and analysis.

Mallard with a hate so strong he could taste it, was aware the Aliens jiggled in the atoms of the wormhole with their own life force. Would they help to create that extra surge to move the Black Widow out of the wormhole into the conduction band and catapult it into the black hole of Andromeda? Was his emotion a barrier to all working as one?

A thought kept recurring in Mallard's mind. Use the hatred. Think Antimatter. Think hatred as antimatter. In normal matter, a hydrogen atom comprises an electron bound to a proton. In the anti-form, the mirror of an electron - a positron - is bound to an antiproton. Together, these two particles make a neutral anti-atom.

Mallard's discussions with the physicists at CERN were paying off. CERN can make antimatter particles routinely but until now they have had great difficulty in retaining this material because it will instantly annihilate when in contact with containers of normal matter.

The burst of hate and rage filled Mallard, his anti-atom. He projected it with intense purpose towards the distance. His understanding was that the universe consisted of normal matter too. The anti-atom and the normal would combust and the antimatter would be reduced to dust. Again and again he projected the hate and then he was spent. It was gone.

That was the moment Hal Heinberg was apprehended at the IRI facility in South Africa. Tinibu's man had moved with lightning speed.

Hal Heinberg did not put up a fight. He was happy with what he had accomplished today. He had controlled Matt's emotions, inducing the hate. Heinberg had paid his dues to Reza.

Just one omission. Cathy Burkert was insensate; she was out of the loop.

Hal Heinberg looked at the policemen who were handcuffing him. He decided to cut his losses. He did not owe Reza any loyalty any more. He would sing like the proverbial canary.

Chapter 14

Hans-Pieter Combe heard the staccato voice at the end of his mobile phone. It was Colonel Daniel Barak of Mossad.

Hans-Pieter answered softly, 'I see him. We are approaching him. Thank you for identifying the IPOD. I believe the information came from South Africa. The GSM signals picked up by your OFEK9 were accurate. My men have him. He was on his way to the hostel reception. I believe he intended to make another call. I will fill you in, after he has been questioned. As you may imagine, we are all very anxious here at CERN. We hold ourselves responsible for the end of this hour'

'What is the latest on the Astral projectionists? We have had no updates in the last 45 minutes. Even the televisions are going blank. I think people are losing hope'

Hans-Pieter Combe said, 'I have no more information at this point. I will call you when I know more'

Reza emptied his pockets on the desk. Hans-Pieter Combe counted amongst the loose change and car keys, the IPOD and the mobile phone.

He said to his subordinate officer. 'Rush this through', handing him the IPOD and the mobile.

Reza said, 'It's too late. I have already programmed the alien mind. Cathy Burkert was most helpful.'

Combe slammed him against the wall, 'What did you do to the Alien race? I will find out everything. It's just a matter of time before you give us the information.'

Reza laughed loudly, 'Time is something you don't have. Teheran informs me that we have marched into Iraq as of one hour ago. Thanks to that little piece of technology you have confiscated, the Aliens will secede vast territory to us in the New World. And', he snorted with self-congratulation 'Israel has officially ceased to exist'.

Hans-Pieter felled him with a blow. Reza slumped down unconscious.

Hans-Pieter entered the Globe and spoke urgently to Jim, the MI6 man. Jim listened intently and said, 'We cannot do anything about Iraq. Mallard is in communication with the Alien race. I don't know what's happening. I can't get through to him.

He's tuned me out of the audio-feed. Yes all the machines are at full thrust including Reza's laptop. The power here is keeping the projectionists going. Listen mate, can you check Burkert –the assistants are around her but I need confirmation, don't wake her out of her trance but just check her breathing.

Mallard said he'd lost her in the audio. He's very concerned. I can't have him worried. He needs all his concentration.'

Cathy looked like Sleeping Beauty, thought Combe suddenly smitten. Long black hair, olive translucent skin, perfect features. Her eyes were closed but her breathing appeared normal. The doctor hovering by the bed confirmed she was in a coma. Hans-Pieter vowed to introduce himself when she woke.

Mallard needed the help of the alien fluid ebony, transmitters of pure thought. He needed their minds with their stream of unadulterated energy to be directed at all the Black Widows in the wormhole.

He spoke to them, his brain with its delta of neurons performing with all the grace of an aerial ballet and he hoped he was clear and precise.

They answered with hesitation. Another had come before him, they said. The other had told them of the need for vast territories because all were of one religion and God-fearing. The Alien race liked the concept of God. They believed too.

They would like to help Matt but first they needed assurances on behalf of this other man. They needed an agreement on territory.

Matt recoiled. He tried to explain that Reza was evil but Reza had somehow got to them. They did not believe Matt. They did not understand the concept of evil. What was he to do?

He said he needed to consult with his fellowmen before he could give them an answer. Instructing Charlie and Chandra to maintain their positions he once again checked Cathy in the audio-feed. Nothing.

He needed her in his mind once more. He couldn't do this without her. He would have to go back to a normal plane to reroute his machine to include her. He told the others they were now at the re-entry stage. All would make a fast snap-back to terra firma.

Forty-five minutes before the collision.

Hans-Pieter Combe looked at the 6 technicians that were taking Reza's IPOD and mobile phone apart. Computers were running decryption codes. There was a feeling of desperate urgency in the air.

He said, 'Anything?'

'Nothing yet, Sir'

His phone went. It was Mallard. Combe headed once more to the Globe.

He said to Mallard, 'All is quiet. No reports of movement from the Iranian border. I guess they are waiting like everyone else. There is no sound outside anywhere on the earth as people prepare for the collision. Reports are coming in from all over the world. Everyone is indoors. We have run out of every hope, even prayer.'

Mallard said without preamble, 'Cathy is in some kind of coma. She is not responding to light or sound. I've tried to stimulate her mind via the machine but there is nothing. With all hell set to break loose in the next 45 minutes – the heat and dust alone will be tremendous - I can't move her now to a hospital. The doctors present here at CERN say she appears to be in a deep sleep. I have to speak to Reza'

'You will have no joy there. The man is adamant that he has done the right thing by his people. He has no compunction in contaminating the alien's thinking.'

'Then I must have his IPOD. I know what to look for'

'My technicians have taken it to pieces. There is nothing. We don't know what happened out there before we apprehended him'

'Cathy is involved in some way. I know it. For Christ's sake, Let me have the IPOD, Combe, don't waste any more time.'

Mallard checked and double-checked the IPOD. He ran the files through his machine. No thoughts recorded. None. It seemed to be a normal one. What was missing? He asked Combe, 'What else did he have on him?'

'Just his mobile phone, car keys and some loose change. Nothing concealed on the phone'

'Search him again. Give him a body search. Every orifice. Something is being missed here'

With Cathy comatose, Mallard was in despair. He knew he had to focus. The world was relying on him. He thought the Opus Signori might be able to assist. He made the call.

Cardinal de Fleury was alone. He was deep in prayer. His phone just rang and rang. He did not want to answer it. He needed to talk to God. The phone kept on ringing.

Switching it on, he said with great reluctance, 'Pronto'

Mallard was quick. Did he know of the annexation of Iraq? Yes he did. What was being done about it?

No, Cardinal, Mallard knew the world was *not* going to end. They were going to be one supergalaxy. The Alien life would exist alongside them.

The Cardinal must do something about Iraq. The world must be informed what they were heading into. Iranian world domination! Mallard was trying to stop it. The Cardinal must do his bit.'

The Cardinal felt the lifeblood flowing again. He believed Mallard. Earth would survive. He went to the Dining room where the others were seated and broke the news. Voices sounded, thoughts were aired, plans were made.

Chapter 15

Reza squealed in pain as the gloved hand probed roughly. A scan of his stomach had revealed nothing but now from his backside, a slender little item was withdrawn. A memory stick.

Reza was struck and struck again. Bleeding he fell to the floor.

Hans-Pieter Combe rushed the disinfected stick to Mallard.

Forty minutes until collision.

Good God, Mallard said aloud, Cathy's last thoughts before she went under. Reza was in her head!!!! He had switched off her mind, literally switched it off – he had put her in a persistent vegetative state.

Mallard went to the bed where Cathy was laying, took her tenderly in his arms and held her for an instant. He would use all the machines, all the power to awaken her. He prayed that would work.

It did not.

Mallard went through Cathy's last words again and again. She had tried to tell him something when he was at the Red Giants in Andromeda? He knew he had received a message, a disembodied one, before she had formulated it in her mind. What was the message? Psychic phenomena explained through time travel.

Messages arriving before they were sent. A simple explanation and surely somewhere in that logic must be a clue as to her survival. He just had to find it.

The machine would have picked it up. Cathy had been switched to audio-feed but her thoughts had been recorded on his machine. He needed to go back to the printouts. Mallard expertly skimmed through the ream of paper. A sudden memory of the printers being switched off temporarily earlier explained the absence of Cathy's recorded brain activity. There was no message that he understood. He checked the data from Reza's IPOD again. Just an impression of the sun and Cassiopeia.

What if Cathy knew what Reza was doing. Putting her into a vegetative state. Cathy knew that patients with such a disorder take years to recover. She had become aware of many physical ailments through Mallard's healing surgery. Mallard felt the tension like bunched fists in his belly.

What did the Sun have to do with it? An impression of Cassiopeia – what was Cassiopeia famous for scientifically? Just Alpha Centauri and Cassiopeia being the closest to the Sun. Think, damnit think! Science and the Sun. He would have to ask the Professor.

Within seconds Mallard had an answer.

Something to do with CERN and neutrinos. Time Travel. Cathy knew the antidote to her vegetative state was for Matt to travel back in time to get her to consciousness. That was the message. Use time travel to rescue me.

Mallard rushed to consult with the experts.

CERN and the experiment with the neutrinos. CERN would help to bring Cathy back from her vegetative state. The physicists had ten minutes to decipher time travel. They talked, many languages sounding, of matter, of neutrinos, of the analogy of sending messages to a mirror and the message is reflected back but so quickly that 'past you' receives it.

They had an answer. They would use the black hole in Andromeda. The black hole had a sphere of darkness around it, 30 million miles in diameter. They explained to Matt that mass slows down time, and the black hole in Andromeda had the mass of several suns within it. He would have to circle the black hole. A full orbit, by their calculations would take half the time on earth. Time would be slowed down and he should be where Cathy was an hour ago within minutes. A word of warning- it was extremely dangerous as he could be sucked in, just like Sergei Boystov.

‘We have devised a way to undertake the perfect ellipse. We will aim you to the side of the black hole, to begin your circuit there. We will try and give you maximum speed to prevent you falling in.’

The physicists knew it had never been done before with a human. OPERA (Oscillation Project with Emulsion-tRacking Apparatus) had shot the neutrinos back to the Gran Sasso lab in Italy in November 2011, trying to prove they had arrived faster than the speed of light.

OPERA was going to do the same for him. They were going to get him the speed he needed just like those goddamn neutrinos. First, OPERA was going to provide the surge to raise his consciousness through the machines, enabling the circuit around the black hole of Andromeda. Neurosynaptic computing chips emulating Mallard’s brain cognition were going to create an artificial consciousness on the machines. Mallard personally would experience an absence seizure, a form of epilepsy- a petit-mal, an absence of consciousness. The price he had to pay for going back in time.

The machine would take over. The artificial consciousness would be programmed to undertake the orbit and to reverse all events at a precise moment - backwards in time. Every thought and subsequent action recorded on the machines at CERN would be reversed.

Back to where Cathy was an hour earlier which would put Mallard in exactly the same place, having done the circuit of the black hole, at the red giants in Andromeda. Beam me up Scotty, thought Matt. Levity, however, seemed inappropriate at this dire hour. Inside, he felt like blubbering.

Cathy reconnected to Mallard's consciousness would be swept back too. Back to where he'd received the original message. Back to the past. It made sense. It was the only way he could rescue Cathy and shut out Reza before Reza interfered with pure thought.

Charlie and Chandra would be re-connected at the final stage of the particle ejection.

Mallard told Jim to ring the Cardinal about Iraq – if the message gets lost in time, repeat it again and again. Tell him we will survive.

England

Minutes later, Ben Efraim, Robert Alexander and Hektor Xanthis checked the map on the screen.

Hektor Xanthis said, 'The Shatt al Arab waterway was opened in February 2012 for commercial traffic, and some of its 120 miles share the Iranian border. My Intelligence indicates that Iran is using it now to gain access to Iraq.'

The waterway is providing a maritime passage to transport troops and heavy equipment to invade the harbours of Iraq. The other borders are too heavily patrolled with Iraqi personnel. For the first time in 31 years, the waterway is in use and there you have it, Iran found its entry-point into Iraq.'

'We have the British bases in Cyprus and in Bahrain to fend off the invasion,' said Robert Alexander. 'My sources tell me that Bahrain is home to the UK Maritime Component Command, which supports Royal Navy warships (there are 12 warships in the Gulf, aircraft, and out-stations in the region. There are also Royal Navy personnel within the Bahrain-based Combined Maritime Forces. They have been given the green light. The US Naval Base too is bringing all their forces in the region to bear.'

'Israel of course will provide air and ground support.' said Ben Efraim

'Cyprus will join in with the RAF providing air attack' said Robert Alexander. Hektor Xanthis nodded in agreement.

'Good. Instruct all that we are now at war with Iran'

Robert Alexander had a call to make. His wife, twenty years his junior and very active on Twitter and Facebook, was told she could not, under no circumstances reveal what he was about to tell her of earth's survival.

All the world believed they were close to annihilation. Today.

But Sally Alexander tweeted she would see her friends tomorrow. She knew for certain.

The ruggedly handsome man with the Semtex-explosive friends was just such a friend. He must pay Sally Alexander a visit.

CERN, Geneva:

Cathy stared at the sun. Was this lucid dreaming? Concentric circles of angels, their wings great and white, a barely restrained force and at the epicentre this golden luminosity, almost unbearable in its power.

She was about to go under. Just like in Cyprus years ago when the machine had subjugated her mind. She knew it was Sohrab Reza who manipulated the electronics that made this mind control possible. She must try and defeat it. She must stay awake.

Look to the sun. In the Inca tradition, Inti, the sun-god was the giver of life. Please somebody save me from this machine. Resurrect me! The greyness started to choke all imagination and a voice was in her head. Not Reza's anymore.

Was it an angel- or a whole host of them speaking in one voice, as messengers of God according to the Hebrew and Christian Bibles and the Quran. The angelic voice paraphrased the words from The Phillipians: '*Reflect on good and just and honest things. Hold pure thought.*' Mentally she willed herself to be ready. She could not drift into a vegetative state. She must go to Matt. She tuned into her headphones.

Mallard found himself at the Red Giants of Andromeda. He had left instructions to prompt his memory after his absence of consciousness. Jim in his audio-feed said the time travel had worked; Cathy was on her way to meet him.

They were now back to 45 minutes ahead of the collision and Reza was beginning his attempt to influence the alien life. Jim and the team back at base were checking on the connection of Cathy's mind to Mallard's on the machine. Reza could not get through to both minds simultaneously. Not on the IPOD, it's capacity was limited and needed recharging, and Reza's laptop was firmly in Jim's possession.

Mallard spoke to Cathy softly, words of love and care directing her to him. Then they were together and the alien life, the male-fluid ebony and the female, the quicksilver of mercury were around them and the power surged through them and around them. Jim's voice saying, 'Steady on mate. We are reconnecting Charlie and Chandra and the billions of minds to your charge. Get those fuckers into the black hole in Andromeda.'

The coronal mass ejection out of Andromeda with the Black Widow particles was accompanied by bursts of massive solar winds causing a geomagnetic storm. Back in Geneva, for the second time that day, radio transmissions, satellites and electrical transmission line facilities were disrupted. The technicians scurrying around said it could last for hours. Then there would be worse to come.

The good news was that the Large Hadron Collider that had detected the Black Widow couldn't find any trace of the deadly particle. The Universe had swallowed it up. The wormhole had vanished with it and Damocles, the sub-dwarf star was one of hundreds of billions in the Milky Way galaxy.

However, the merger of the galaxies was right on schedule.

4 p.m. The witching hour had arrived. Andromeda and the Milky Way were one.

For hours the world lay inert as the gas and dust swirled hugely around its atmosphere. There was no electricity. There was no power. The earth's atmosphere consisting of three layers – the mesosphere, the stratosphere and the troposphere- they went slightly awry.

The stratosphere where the ozone layer is located merged at certain points into the troposphere, the area closest to the earth where the ozone layer is bad for you, where human activity has created smog and greenhouse gases. Oxygen would be in short supply as the ozone layer here can also act as a chemical oxidant ripping off oxygen atoms from other compounds, including humans.

The mesosphere was the strata of atmosphere 75kms above the earth. It now descended slightly. Water vapour caused by the dust enabled noctilucent clouds in the mesosphere, made up of crystals of water ice, heralding radical climate change. The UV filter of the ozone layer did not work so well here. The temperature was hot as the sun loomed closer. Solar radiation was intense. A scalding-hot summer's day, thought Cathy, wiping away the sweat on her forehead.

Matt and Cathy did not go outdoors. All personnel huddled within the buildings at CERN. Makeshift beds had been set up in advance. The Physicists had made their calculations hours ago, but with eventualities completely unknown, they were unsure if the atmospheres had indeed merged. Further reckonings and precise empirical data, based on observation and experiment rather than theory had to be assessed.

Their worst calculation had been, if in the collision, the other planets went into free fall. Matt and Cathy had watched and absorbed as the physicists worked their formulae. Earth in the Milky Way, Sun at the centre, earth two thirds of the way out. The solar system works in a spiral and earth is on the Orion-Cygnus Arm of the spiral. Besides earth, there are seven planets in the Solar system.

They would be puzzling at gravity if the planets had become unaligned, where gravity was calculated on gravity of the object alone without taking into account other factors; of intercepts like time or velocity, of solar winds and of kinetic energy which could affect the earth's magnetic field or magnetosphere.

The physicists were terribly afraid.

Mallard's mind went back to when he was near Orion at the stars of Gemini and the words that had come to him- of God and the portent of imminent danger. He spoke quietly to Cathy. For the moment, do not tell the others.

She brought the precious Russian painted lacquer box to him. In the box were the ancient sheaves of parchment, each with a fat red seal, and a document in Russian. Cathy put the document aside for later and ran her hand over the papyri. The last resort that Sergei Boystov, the Russian astral cosmos-naut had entrusted to her. A Bible was brought to them.

They were breaking the seven seals.

The papyri were old and Cathy read six of the seals through with difficulty. She was rusty at translating Ancient Greek. She laid the seventh aside for later.

She said, 'I think I have it but I need to get a book on Astrology and one on measures, since without electricity, we can't Google anything.'

'Tell me what you need. I'll do it' said Matt. Within minutes someone hurried over to them with a heap of books.

Cathy was shivery and cold, despite the temperature of the day. She could feel the weight of history. She needed to arrive at the truth, her idea of truth and it was imperative she communicated the contents of each seal with the insight she had been blessed with. Somewhere in the language was the solution to earth's predicament.

Matt took her hand and said 'Okay, The Four Horsemen of the Apocalypse are described in the last book of the New Testament of the Bible, called the Book of Revelation of Jesus Christ. Revelations to Saint John the Evangelist when he was exiled on the Greek island of Patmos, at Chapter 6:1-8. The chapter tells of a *"'book'/'scroll' in God's right hand that is sealed with seven seals"*.

The Lamb of God/Lion of Judah (Jesus Christ) opens the first four of the seven seals, and four beings ride out on white, red, black, and pale or green (according to the Greek) horses. The four riders are commonly seen as symbolizing Conquest, War, Famine and Death, respectively. The four horsemen are to set a divine apocalypse, a day of judgement upon the world. Most modern scholars see these riders of the Apocalypse as events that occurred in the first century of Christian history.

Cathy, we must hope the broken seals will not release such calamities today. We are looking for clues to our survival, not our destruction.

Cathy said tremulously, nervous of misinterpreting a message of such import, 'Listen, the first seal of my papyri says*:*

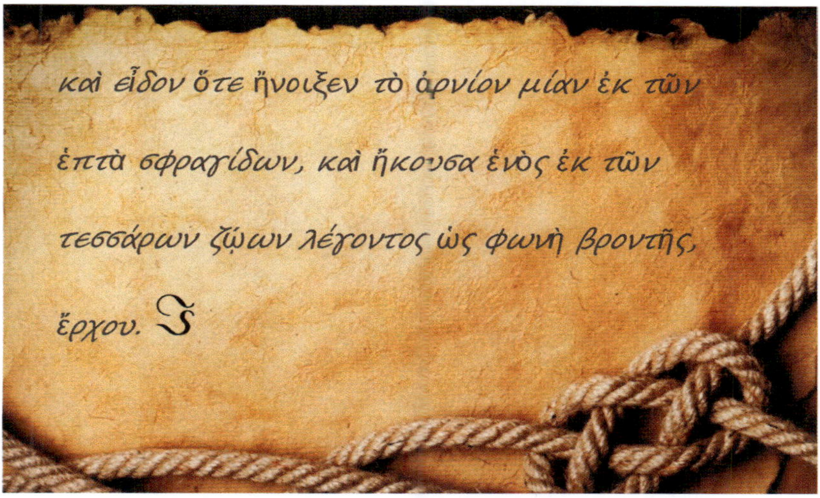
καὶ εἶδον ὅτε ἤνοιξεν τὸ ἀρνίον μίαν ἐκ τῶν
ἑπτὰ σφραγίδων, καὶ ἤκουσα ἑνὸς ἐκ τῶν
τεσσάρων ζῴων λέγοντος ὡς φωνὴ βροντῆς,
ἔρχου.

And I saw, and behold a white horse:

and he that sat on him had a bow; and a crown was given unto him; and he went forth conquering, and to conquer.

Mallard wrote quickly on a pad, ‘We have white, a bow, a crown and a conqueror.’

Cathy said, ‘ Most scholars saw this as Military Conquest but if we see the scroll as ancient eyes looking to the heavens, this seal is the sun, the most visible star in the Milky Way and the corona or crown is seen during a solar eclipse.’

‘I have a picture of a solar eclipse. Look Cathy.’

'That corona certainly looks white,' said both in unison.

'As to conquering: the Roman Emperor Domitian responsible for St. John's banishment to Patmos, (it is the general belief that prophecy was viewed dimly by the Roman authorities) well, the Emperor became very superstitious and minted coins of the god Apollo. He believed only Apollo had the gift of prophecy. Well, the Greek version of Apollo is Helios – the sun-god. St. John, of course is the true prophet and writes of the sun and its corona as a conqueror for future generations, but used the current religious and political allegiances to conceal his true meaning. Domitian would have no reason to suspect his words.'

Matt said, 'You could have hit on something. Religion and astronomy – We have the sun and crown and a conqueror- what of the bow of the first seal?

His fingers rifled through pages, 'Yes, yes - I have it, in astronomy, a planet's elongation is the angle between the Sun and the planet, a bow, as viewed from Earth – another explanation for the bow of the first seal. Cathy I do believe St. John's message to the future was visible in the celestial sphere to the naked eye, he believed Christianity created an underlying message, a portent –it's common knowledge that the sun is due to run out of nuclear fuel in 5 billion years and earth will cease to exist - will Science discover the corona of the sun, and perhaps the bow will reveal seams of gold for man's future and delay the sun's demise?'

'The horses of the seals could be mere methods of transport, in our case, the four astral cosmos-nauts, and the four horsemen could be the Sun and the inner planets – Mars, Venus, Mercury and Earth.' Cathy sounded excited and filled with hope, 'Perhaps this is not our final hour, Matt. Could St. John, who was instructed by Jesus Christ , '*to write of all things that will take place in the future'* have predicted not just events that came to pass in the early years of Christianity but events till the end of time; even our voyage through the heavens and our interpretation of these papyri - Sergei said the old man, his grandfather, who gave the scroll to his Uncle said it would be a force for good not the other way around. Perhaps the message of each seal will change the fate of the earth.'

'Let's do the others in the scroll. The storms outside us are creating havoc with the earth just now. I don't know the extent of the devastation without any electricity- just the diesel generator which will probably run out soon. The lights will go out. We have to be smartish'

'Wait; let me have a look at your Bible. Umm, the words match my papyri but there is a symbol at the end in my parchment, which the Bible doesn't have. I've never seen one like it before.'

'We will have to wait for the power to be turned back on, so I can access it online. I don't have any books on symbols here. Just check if the same symbol occurs at the end of each'

'Ok, the second seal of the papyri:

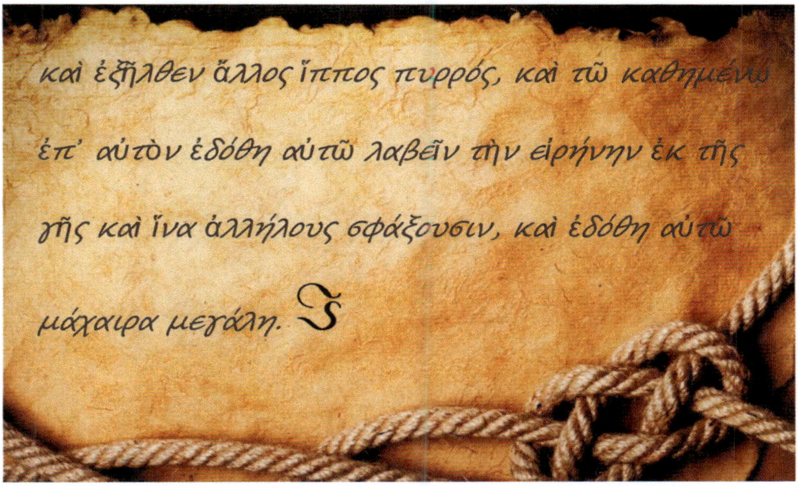
καὶ ἐξῆλθεν ἄλλος ἵππος πυρρός, καὶ τῶ καθημένω
ἐπ' αὐτὸν ἐδόθη αὐτῶ λαβεῖν τὴν εἰρήνην ἐκ τῆς
γῆς καὶ ἵνα ἀλλήλους σφάξουσιν, καὶ ἐδόθη αὐτῶ
μάχαιρα μεγάλη.

And there went out another horse that was red: and power

was given to him that sat thereon to take place from the earth, and that they would kill one another: and there was given to him a great sword

Mars is the fourth planet from the Sun in the Solar System. Named after the Roman god of war, Mars, it is often described as the "Red Planet" as the iron oxide prevalent on its surface gives it a reddish appearance .The Roman God of war, Mars is often depicted with a great spear or sword.

Now for St. John's underlying message – here goes, Mars has two moons, named after characters Phobos (panic/fear) and Deimos (terror/dread) who in Greek mythology accompanied their father Ares into battle.

Ares *was* the Roman god Mars. Today, calculations are that Phobus will be the surface where manned missions to Mars take place – a human exploration first on Phobus, which will act as a catalyst for footfalls on Mars.'

'Matt this is all a bit – well it sounds rather ominous if the seal is read literally – 'power was given to him....to take place from the earth... and killing one another... if you relate it to humans on Mars'.

'I can't transpose the tale to suit mortality. Rest easy.

Photo: Getty

Here's a great shot of Mars with Earth visible to the left'

'We now have the second seal as the first inner planet, Mars and the second horseman of the Apocalypse.

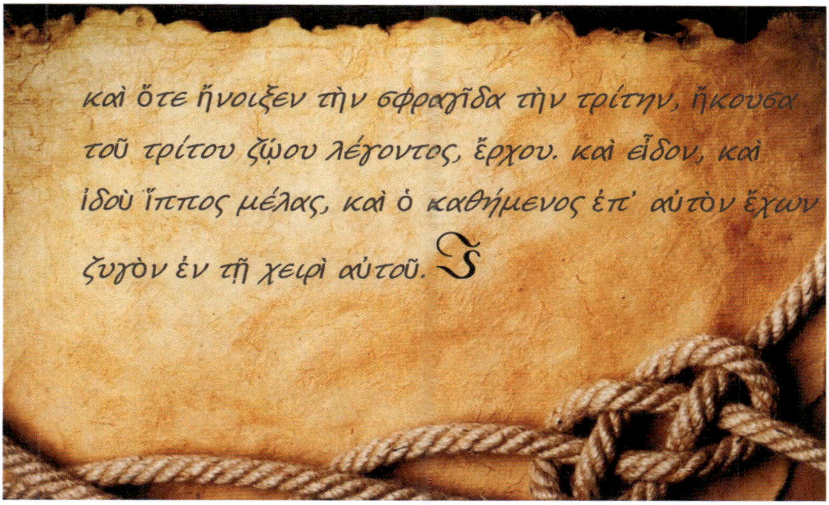
καὶ ὅτε ἤνοιξεν τὴν σφραγῖδα τὴν τρίτην, ἤκουσα
τοῦ τρίτου ζῴου λέγοντος, ἔρχου. καὶ εἶδον, καὶ
ἰδοὺ ἵππος μέλας, καὶ ὁ καθήμενος ἐπ' αὐτὸν ἔχων
ζυγὸν ἐν τῇ χειρὶ αὐτοῦ.

'The third seal is the one with the black horse and the horseman had a pair of balances/ a yoke in his hand. Now 'yoke' was generally understood to symbolise Famine but the word ζυγὸν or yoke can also mean 'balances' in the Greek and the Bible has Jesus saying in Matthew 11:29 '*Take my yoke upon you and learn of me..'* Yoke could therefeore be a bond uniting two or more people.There's that symbol again

Venus and Jupiter in Morning Skies. Credit & Copyright: Babak Tafreshi

Cathy peering over his shoulder said, 'That's a great book you have there. How do you figure Venus as the third seal?

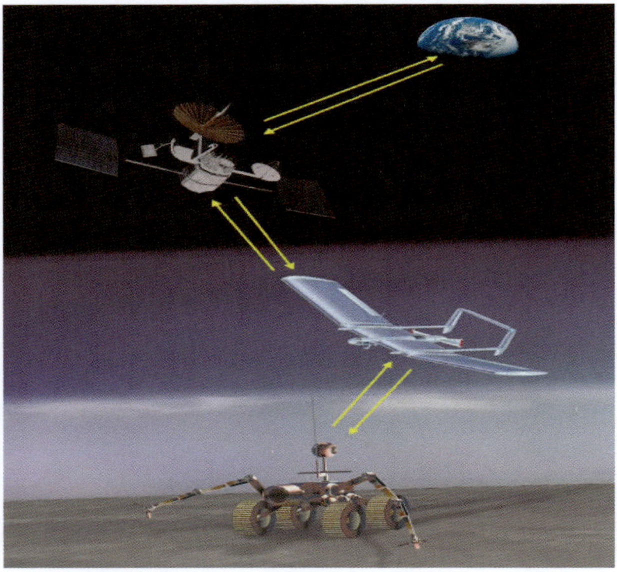

‘Hey, Cathy this is a conceptual proposal that NASA has put together about how we might land a robot on Venus, this planet with incredible pressure and obliterating heat. The article, says: ‘NASA would land a nuclear-powered rover on the surface. Once it started rolling, it would need a way to transmit data through the muck. So, to relay the too-weak signal through the volatile atmosphere up to the orbiting satellite above, it would relay said signal to a solar-powered plane that hovered above the rover at all times, which would then transmit it to the orbiter.

Sorry I digressed.

O.K. Venus is the brightest star in the sky and was named so after the goddess of love and beauty – Venus is so bright, it is said to cast shadows on the earth – those shadows could be the black horse. Also, the reference book I’m looking at seems to indicate the colour black is a polymorph of black quartz, found at meteorite impact sites. Did such meteorites originate from Venus; the science of today deems it unlikely.’

Or did St John mean black sand or shale (there’s a lot of it near Patmos, where he wrote the Book of Revelation) created by an erosion of volcanic rocks and marine organisms – did you know most sand, about 70% is made of quartz, also known as silica, (Fracking- the greatly controversial energy hope of the mo. devours fast quantities of silica) and is sand produced by the grinding and scouring of millions of years of weathering and glaciations. The grains of inevitability!

Hmm, I have a hunch about black sand or shale, I believe St. John in each seal has tried to provide a clue to the future of the planet especially with the merger of Andromeda and Earth, as in Shelley's 'Ozymandias': '*Round the decay of that colossal wreck, boundless and bare, the lone and level sands stretch far away'*.

Is black sand/shale therefore, and I remember Planck, the '*sine qua non'* not of a continuous, infinitely divisible quantity of geological time, but as a discrete quantity composed of an integral number of finite equal parts like an hourglass each measuring a span, a miniature lifetime of each mortal? The whole, including the microscopic life, yet to be de-saturated!

Cathy said, 'For the Emperor Domitian's ears he intimates Roman theology, which he, St. John would be familiar with, and thus hides from dirigisme; perhaps he presents Venus of the balances, as the goddess of love; a yielding, watery female, essential to the generation and balance of life. Her male counterparts in the Roman pantheon, Vulcan and Mars, are active and fiery. Venus absorbs and tempers this alpha male, uniting the opposites of male and female as the goddess of love. A perfect balance!

And the underlying message- the Christ yoke or balances, spelling unity.

I also recall an ode by Horace, the Latin poet in the time of Augustus circa 23BC:

'What now, if Venus returning

Should pair us 'neath his bronze yoke once more' Book III Ode IX.

There - we have our horseman with the balances. She is the second inner planet and our third horseman.'

Matt said wryly, 'I read somewhere that Venus, according to the Mayans, was not the planet of love but of war and bloody sacrifice. Apparently, the Mayans would follow the complex journey of Venus through the sky and time their war rituals and human sacrifices accordingly.'

'I prefer the love angle,' said Cathy. He gave her the reassurance he sensed she needed.

He said, 'Since you and I met, have you felt any pocket of need, any yearning for something, anything unnamed? Cathy,' he kissed her. 'I believe you and I are truly fulfilled. We will have a lifetime, I promise you. Stay focused, don't let the pressure get to you'

Matt winked at her, sensing her anxiety and tension in getting each seal's interpretation right, and added, 'Before you read the fourth seal, there's a bit in the Bible, between the third and fourth seal- which could be a reference to Mercury, the third inner planet - the words in the Bible are: 'And I heard a voice in the midst of the four beasts say *'A measure of wheat for a penny, and three measures of barley for a penny; and see thou hurt not the oil and the wine*'. Let me see if I can find an image of Mercury…'

'Well, according to the book about measures, the ancients could mean Mercury as he is also the Greek God Hermes who was the God of measures among other things. Mercury is also silver, hence the 'penny'.

Well, the very interesting couple of things are measures in ancient times were royal cubits used in Temples and Pyramids – places of worship and the three pyramids of Giza, Egypt are a perfect reproduction of the 3 stars of Orion's belt. Visible to the ancient eye, the 3 stars of Orion, like the pyramids are not perfectly aligned, the smallest of them is slightly offset to the East. The interesting thing is the distance ratios- the measures between the pyramids are similar ratios between the inner planets. Did St. John spend time in Egypt, understand planetary motion and record the measures of Mercury for posterity?

Three stars of Orion: Pink dot below the stars is the Orion nebula
Credit & Copyright: Matthew Spinelli

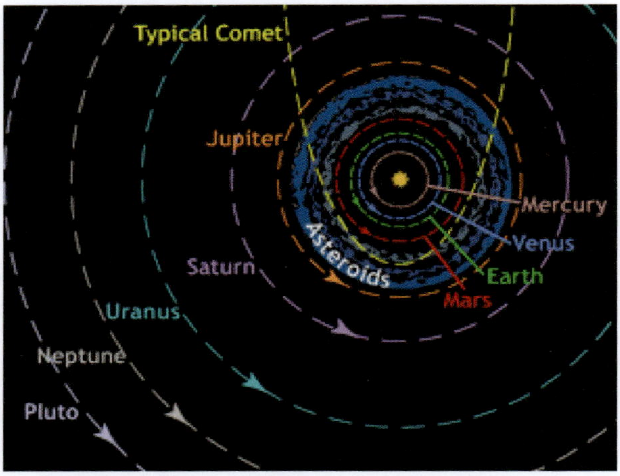

'Here's a picture that shows elliptical orbits and set orbits because of gravity - Cathy, can you see why the scientists are so afraid that gravity is affected? Every basic tenet of science says it cannot be but they have to work with a 'what if' scenario – the heat and dust is tremendous out there'.

'Matt, let's be positive. Let's get back to measures - the later passages in the Book of Revelation are quite definite in their measurements – I'm quoting now – '*and he measured the city with the reed, twelve thousand furlongs...and he measured the wall thereof an hundred and forty four cubits..*' all exact measurements for the Day of Judgement'

NASA/Johns Hopkins University Applied Physics Laboratory/Carnegie Institution of Washington

'This is a NASA shot of Mercury taken by Messenger– it's due to be in the public domain next year, we have a first gander; they used different colours to highlight variations in the rock- normally Mercury is dull silver-grey.

Funnily enough, I did come across something else randomly; I will have to go back to the last seal. Throughout history it has been unclear if St. John in his discourse on measures was connecting the two seals- the third and the fourth – the prophecy affects both, I'm certain.

'I think there is a connection because of the application of *measures* of planetary engineering called geoengineering, a technique aimed at averting the earth warming dangerously which I fear is upon us now. I've just come across the case of the dumping of 100 tonnes of iron sulphate off the Canadian coast that is on schedule for next month in a bid to spawn plankton, which attracts fish stocks and captures carbon, the main ingredient of greenhouse gases. The downside of the experiment is it could at certain depths reduce the oxygen drastically resulting in a stagnant ocean.

What if this deliberate modification of the earth's environment could cause climate changes to the hydrological cycle including drought or floods? What if the repercussions are felt not just on earth but up there in the solar system? Could the planet Mercury with a suffusion of iron sulphate on earth, experience perturbations and react by oscillating and changing shape? That's what happens to the element in electrochemical experiments – a mercury beating heart- as it is known. Could a planetary beating heart worsen solar radiation and cause a runaway greenhouse effect?

Cathy, I believe time will prove us right and St. John in the seals is travelling in time to warn us of tampering with the oceans, not to harm the oil and wine – by controlling emissions of substances like black carbon (relates to the shale of the third seal and shale oil being produced). Believe it or not, '**mercury**' is introduced into surface water and groundwater in the process of shale oil extraction, which could seriously damage the photosynthesis and chlorophyll of plants generally and basic organisms like phytoplankton in the sea.

In other words St John is promoting the balances of the third seal: to protect the coastal fringes of those oceans, where nutrients flow from land to sea, allowing license for plankton and larvae to multiply and fish to assemble in myriad hue and breed thereof. Protect this sunlit layer is the haunting call of the saint from Patmos.

For it is here the temperature fluctuates: and the warm and the cool of seasonal currents bring periods of feast and famine at different times attracting animals, birds and fish to mate, to nurture their young or to feed. Ecological disruption of this system with substances like iron sulphate, shale oil extraction and mercury in our marine world, will be the very mechanisms that would sequester carbon. Rather than a panacea for global warming, I think we would be opening a Pandora's Box.

However, my bet would be on the black stuff – sand/quartz/silica!

Read on, all this will affect the fourth seal.'

'Matt, I'm rather terrified of the next one – this fourth seal. It's us here on planet earth. The colour green would certainly be the green earth. Which part would be the fourth part of the earth?

Let me read it to you-

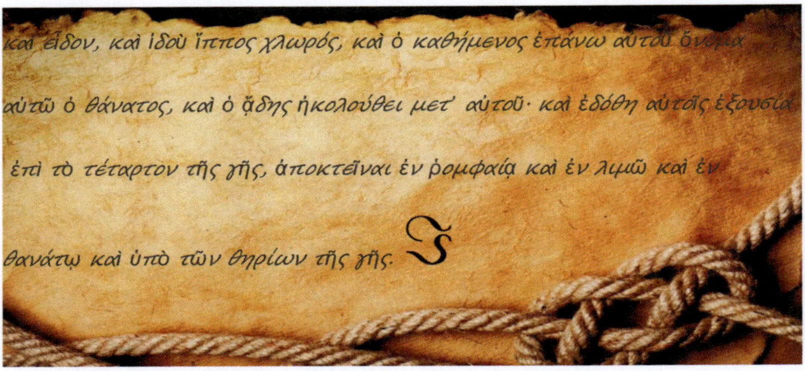
καὶ εἶδον, καὶ ἰδοὺ ἵππος χλωρός, καὶ ὁ καθήμενος ἐπάνω αὐτοῦ ὄνομα
αὐτῷ ὁ θάνατος, καὶ ὁ ᾅδης ἠκολούθει μετ᾽ αὐτοῦ· καὶ ἐδόθη αὐτοῖς ἐξουσία
ἐπὶ τὸ τέταρτον τῆς γῆς, ἀποκτεῖναι ἐν ῥομφαίᾳ καὶ ἐν λιμῷ καὶ ἐν
θανάτῳ καὶ ὑπὸ τῶν θηρίων τῆς γῆς.

'and I looked, and behold a pale or green horse: and his name

that sat upon him was death, and Hell followed with him. And power was given

unto them over the fourth part of the earth, to kill with sword, and with hunger, and with death, and with the beasts of the earth.'

Mallard said, 'I've plucked one theory from this reference book – ancient history had a burning question from the mapmakers and it concerns the theory in existence, of the four elements (earth, water, air, fire).

It was considered then the natural order of the universe, if you think of a set of concentric spheres - with earth at the centre, then water above it, then air, then the fiery heavens, but the facts showed that much of the earth was sticking up above the water.

A standard answer was that God had mercifully made the earthly sphere a bit lighter, so that part of it rose up, like the surface of an apple bobbing in a water-tub: that surface area was the land mass of the three conjoined continents, Europe, Asia and Africa.

This theory made some sense but with the discovery of America, existing as a separate continent, America became the fourth part of the world. I said earlier that St. John connected the third and fourth seal with the planet Mercury and the element too I believe, and measures of geoengineering and here is his message: America has vast quantities of shale and is going great guns with its extraction– is the passage in-between the seals a prompt for the US to be mindful of maintaining the environmental balance?

And Cathy, the fourth seal is relevant to the US, as the fourth part of the earth. Power *is* in the hands of America and let's face it, America has been in the thick of many a battle – and hunger, death and destruction are part of any war. Is this seal a harbinger of many more bloody confrontations? The merger of Andromeda and the Milky Way is going to have every country searching for new habitable space. Will America lead the way; after all it is the most advanced country in space exploration.

‘Cathy, we have to pause and take stock- what if all of this is for us to reveal a new apocalypse- we thought we were saved by the ejection of the Black Widow particles but mankind are bouldering (pun intended) their way through the earth, without checking under the bonnet and kicking the tyres of our planet thoroughly and now earth’s atmosphere seems awry, how do we correct it?..there must be a solution here within this papyri. Here’s an image of the layers of atmosphere’

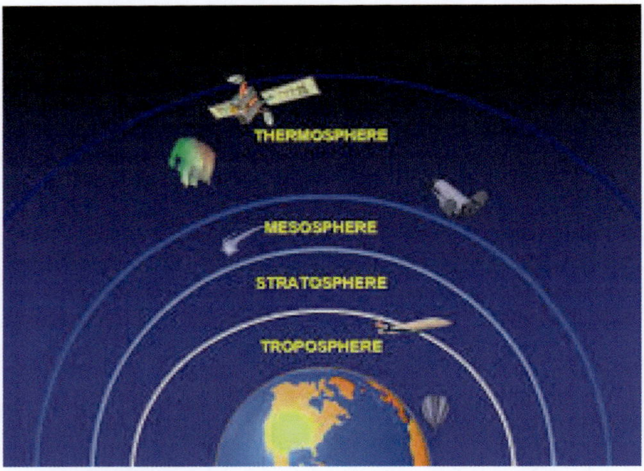

Cathy responded, ‘Look, let’s go on, we have found the sun and the four inner planets, each with a message corresponding to the four horsemen of the Apocalypse and the voice of measures, all visible to eyes from long ago. What of the whole, does it too have a message?’

Mallard uttered an exclamation, 'I've just remembered something, one of the professors was working on a paper earlier, before the galaxies merged and he mentioned a recent discovery, that of almost 30 dwarf galaxies orbiting Andromeda in this regular pattern, rather like those inner planets in the solar system. Orbital patterns in a joyous, sun-dappled affair. Cathy, the solution lies in that discovery.

If galaxies orbit symmetrically, then what of alternate universes - Is this what the papyri are leading us to - supersymmetry of the *galaxies*-parallel or alternative thinking tunnelling through to our dimension, from other universes! Not merely supersymmetry of elementary particles, a theory the professors now say is becoming unfashionable; but a combination of patterns as we discovered– both mind and physics: a twosome we believe, that characterises dark matter in the universe?'

Matt leaned close and whispered theatrically in her ear, 'Shhh now, this is just between you and I - Theoreticists would have my stoopid-woopid head on a chopping block if I suggested such a thing to them!' Cathy giggled as one of the professors approached them

He talked at length to Mallard. Cathy moved away to look closely at the translations of the papyri she had done so far.

The professor gone, Mallard caressed Cathy's arm, he said: 'The physicists here are deliberating, and have established that the pattern of both galaxies, Andromeda and the Milky Way will resume (it seems to be slightly out of sync at the mo) and correct our atmosphere, in time. It could take thousands of years. That obviously won't do- the atmosphere needs a prod straightaway. The boffins have an idea; they are working it all out. Read on but make haste.

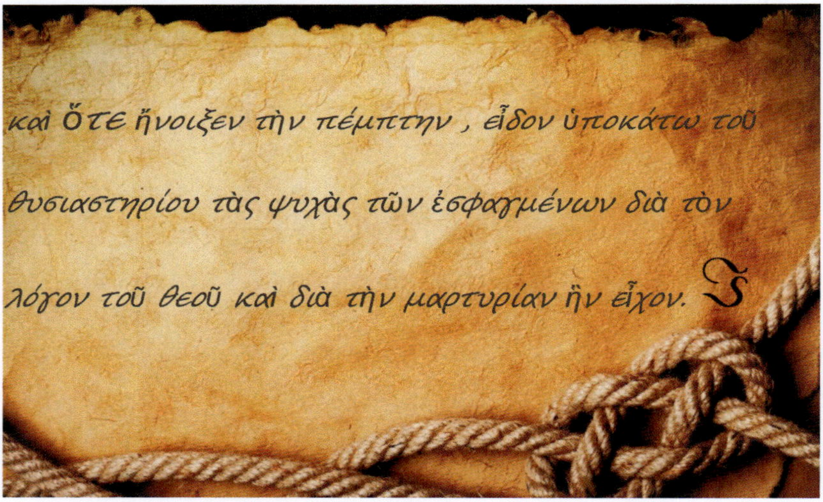
καὶ ὅτε ἤνοιξεν τὴν πέμπτην , εἶδον ὑποκάτω τοῦ
θυσιαστηρίου τὰς ψυχὰς τῶν ἐσφαγμένων διὰ τὸν
λόγον τοῦ θεοῦ καὶ διὰ τὴν μαρτυρίαν ἣν εἶχον.

The fifth seal is to do with Christian dogma but it can apply in the present context, of attacking Christians or any other faith group– there seems to be a general embarrassment in the world today to mention one's belief in God or religion- and the passage says '*And when he had opened the fifth seal. I saw under the altar the souls of them that were*

slain for the word of God and for the testimony which they held:'

As Cathy broke open the sixth seal, the generator started to fail. Light was flickering with candles hastily lit.

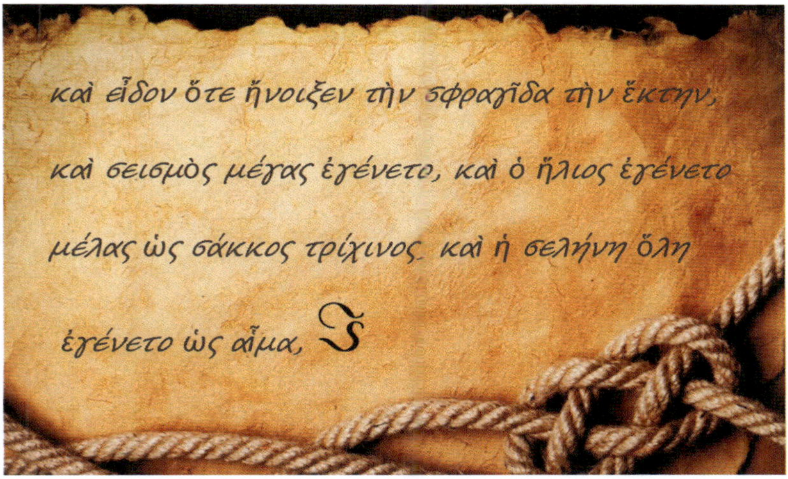
καὶ εἶδον ὅτε ἤνοιξεν τὴν σφραγῖδα τὴν ἕκτην,
καὶ σεισμὸς μέγας ἐγένετο, καὶ ὁ ἥλιος ἐγένετο
μέλας ὡς σάκκος τρίχινος, καὶ ἡ σελήνη ὅλη
ἐγένετο ὡς αἷμα,

She peered at the words and grabbed Matt's hand, 'I think we have to get under the table, now. Spread the word to everyone. HIDE. I will explain.'

Cathy grabbed the candle and ducked under the table. She read aloud, '*and lo there was a great earthquake; and the sun became black as sackcloth of hair; and the moon became as blood.....* Sorry, I can't read anymore. Everything is shaking so much.'

In the darkness of the Globe at CERN, a terrified hush settled for an instant before shouts and screams of prayer filled the room. Some people were panicking but most huddled under tables and in corners, arms around each other. Prayer was all that could be heard as the earth moved around them.

Cathy clutched Matt and they felt the land mass shift and heave as the solar storms affected the magnetosphere- the magnetic field around the planet. Geomagnetically induced currents ran through the earth's surface and through the grid with a shower of positively-charged hydrogen atoms, called protons, causing scientific and communications satellites to short-circuit.

Through a series of chemical reactions in our disturbed atmosphere, the protons drastically diminished the upper-most areas of the ozone layer, a protective blanket mostly in the stratosphere that blocks life-threatening ultraviolet radiation from reaching the Earth. This was the worst outcome that had been calculated by the scientists.

The six seals had been broken open.

All that remained for The Day of Judgement when all manner of hell would be let loose on earth, as foretold centuries ago, was one more seal. The seventh seal.

Cathy, in the upheaval and poor light, laid it aside to open later.

Chapter 16

England

The temperature was soaring. The Cardinal had prepared for this moment for days. NASA had been primed in advance in case of loss of absolute power. NASA's space launch system replacing the space shuttle was a heavy launch vehicle and was being powered up at Kennedy Space Centre's Launch facility running on its 4 engines and fully-fuelled core. It had a complement of trained personnel.

The Opus Signori were chartering the launch vehicle as governments around the world were crippled with inaction. They needed the technicians to get to the International Space Station in the thermosphere of deep space to effect repair to the damage caused to the communication satellites during the merger of the constellations. Earth was in shutdown mode and they needed to power it up again.

The Opus Signori were taking control of the world. Overt control.

Israel

'Land masses have shifted in the last hour. Reports are coming in the old-fashioned way – through messengers on whatever transport is to be had.

Rescue missions are out there but we don't know the number of casualties. People are dying of the heat. The radiation levels are dangerously high. We have the army clad in white protective suits and facemasks dispensing advice to people to stay indoors, the best way to contain the intense radiation'

Voices sounded, the room was buzzing with desperate activity. Men and women sweated profusely in the sweltering heat.

Colonel Daniel Barak listened as the meeting of the War Cabinet took place in the candlelight and heavy-duty lamps.

He snapped to attention when he was addressed by the Chief of the General Staff . The Lieutenant General was dripping with sweat and was curt to the point of rudeness.

Barak said, 'Last intelligence from CERN before Collision was that the Black Widow particle had been ejected. Ofek 9 is unable to function. Before it went cold, we know that the Shatt Al Arab waterway was how the Iranian troops went into Iraq. The only consolation is they will not have gone far. We have no more at present.'

'What was the latest information of the Alien life? Are they around us now? How do we detect them?'

‘I believe they are on a planet called ‘The Bard’s Muse’ part of the Pegasus dwarf galaxy. They are close to Andromeda so they will be closer to us now’

‘So these bupkes (goat droppings) are not here yet!’

‘We are more concerned with the Iranians. We need to know if they succeeded in converting the Alien thinking. It wasn’t possible for Mallard to ascertain this, but our reckoning is the time travel by Mallard erased much of Reza’s influence. All Mallard knew was the Aliens helped to eject the Black Widow particle.’

‘What of Ben Efraim? I believe he is talking to the Knesset on the solar battery operated telephone. Battery banks are running low – corded phones still have some power but to be used only in emergencies. Exactly what the fuck this is...., anyway, I also understand he has plans to restore the electric grid and take charge as the other schmucks are all in hiding.’

Colonel Daniel Barak nodded and said, ‘The hand-delivered messages from my source at the legislative assembly are that he and others in England are coordinating rescue and reorganisation schedules.’

‘Okay, what is the time-scale for the power to be restored?’

‘Two days normally, from launch to docking at the ISS, but we are trying for twenty-four hours’

‘Keep me informed. I’m going to try and take a nap in this godawful heat’

Colonel Barak asked and received permission to use the corded telephone. He had to make a call. There was no answer at the underground nuclear facility at Qom, Iran.

A heavily bearded man dressed in the long traditional Persian trousers called shalvar heard the signal sound from his small cell-like room. He was too busy to take the call. The stockpiles of missiles had come loose and in the darkness, the panic and the shouting of terrified men was predominant. A voice was heard screaming. Be martyrs. Allah promises you a place in Paradise.

‘Fuck that, thought the heavily bearded man, he needed to get to the corded phone, check in and get the fuck out. He had accomplished his mission. In the confusion after the collision, he had set the missiles loose both underground and in the above ground bunkers. In the darkness, it would take days to restore. Buying him valuable time. Next stop Iraq. He had twenty-four hours.

CERN, Geneva:

Cathy looked at the TIGRIS supercop. He was looking back at her with bedroom eyes.

He said, 'You are doing a great job, assisting with the facilities and the food. The darkness outside is not helping, there is barely any light here, and nobody has dared to step outside because of the radiation. As you know, we have had lots of fatalities. Radiation is like a ghost, invisible, intangible but clinging to everything it touches. Luckily the army have been stationed here. They have been burying the dead with their protective suits. We stored enough water but it won't last forever. The news is that they are trying to restore the power. Without it CERN is non-operational.

'What happened to Reza?' said Cathy. She was so hot and desperately needed a shower. She had used a wet wipe just to have some moisture on her face and arms. The water was too precious to waste.

'Reza was shot just before the collision. Don't worry your pretty head about him. I have to go now but I will catch you later' he said with a wink.

Matt was talking to the physicists. He had had several healing sessions with people, speaking calmly and full of hope to those suffering posttraumatic stress. Cathy loved what he did with people.

He walked over to where she was chopping some rather limp lettuce leaves. 'Cathy,' he said and put a hand on her shoulder, 'we need to talk. The top brass here have offered us a couple of protective suits. We can have an hour or so in private. I'll grab a couple of candles. Let's make our way to the hostel.'

They lay in each other's arms, the heat was intense, their bodies were slick with the humidity but their happiness was complete. Two individuals with the gift of prophecy, with their spiritual and physical yearning fulfilled- they had found each other.

Cathy listened as Matt talked softly. He had a task for her to do. They would wait for the power to be restored and then she must go into the energisation chambers and a coolant would be flushed through the system. Cathy would be cooled down and then she had to make one more astral flight. Matt promised it would be the last. They would go back to the Globe now and open the final seal.

Iraq

Shatt al Arab Waterway
Umm Qasr

He was 25 miles from the Iranian border. Just last year the town had been rejuvenated. It was now called Basra Gateway. The U.S. military had occupied it during the Iraqi conflict as a prison camp, Camp Bucca.

The Iranians were nowhere to be seen. The remaining Americans in the camp and the Iraqi's had fought them off. The British and the American naval forces had made their way from Bahrain in the Persian Gulf and had commandeered the Shatt al Arab waterway, wresting it from the Iranians. Latest intel was the Allied forces were heading for Basra

Great fires were burning in the camp. Light was necessary as fortifications were set up in the town. The general public were indoors, keeping out of the radiation waves.

The bearded one had to rendezvous with the Israeli Defence Forces who were heading for Basra. The Israeli forces, suited up, were involved in tactics called LASHAB (a Hebrew acronym for Warfare on Urban terrain) with armoured bulldozers, armoured personnel carriers and radio-controlled drones for intelligence. Small teams of infantry were attacking in close and built-up spaces. They were encountering little resistance from the Iranians who had no battle experience since the 80's, during the Iran-Iraq war.

There was no aerial bombardment as communications were non-existent. The atmosphere did not allow for any aircraft of any kind. All warfare on the ground was as it existed over a century ago.

The bearded one had an urgent communiqué. An order, effective immediately had to be passed on. However, battery operated telephones were a rarity in the field and not obtainable. He hitched a ride on a British military land rover heading for Basra.

An hour later, he had his man, Lieutenant Colonel Cohen spearheading the attack inside Iraq. The message was delivered, a joint communiqué to all allied forces. Iran was for the taking. Just say 'abracadabra' in Syria.

CERN, Geneva:

Dawn was on the horizon and the atmosphere was getting hotter. The storms showed no sign of abating. The wind raged and howled outside. Cathy sitting inside the Globe with a hundred other people went with Matt to one of the theatre boxes for some privacy. She needed to open the seventh seal.

There were 2 sheets of paper wrapped around the papyrus. One was fine with delicate spidery handwriting. The other was a document in Russian with an official seal. The first was in broken English and was from the old man that Sergei Boystov, the Russian Cosmos-naut, had said was the man who had sent the scrolls in the lacquer box. His name was Leonard Sosnovsky and at the time of writing the missive, he was 95 years old.

Cathy read it out loud to Matt, 'I know you are girl I see in my head. I see you for many years. I see you as a child and your picture is sure and clear. I commission portrait of you from picture in my mind and it hangs in my house. My life, it is simple one. I was 6 years old when Nicholas II, Tsar of Russia was killed by Bolsheviks in 1918. My father was General in Preobrazhensky Regiment, the Regiment you know, of Catherine the great. He told me of this scroll which he said Catherine the great handed to him. I have asked my son Dimitri Sosnovsky to keep for you. I have also included in the scroll a document implicating a man in the highest office, President Putinov. It is the proof the world needs that Putinov is the man responsible for Alexander Litvinenko's death in England. It is the report that was put on Putinov's desk of the Litvinenko affair.'

Cathy saw a note in the margin had been added, 'My son, Dimitri was poisoned today...my grandson now will carry this to you'

Cathy read the rest and summarised the broken English aloud: 'One of Putinov's secretaries deliberately made a copy of it and buried it in a mountain of paperwork and kept it in Preobrazhensky barracks. The FSB traced that and other records that the secretary buried. They tortured her, but she did not reveal her secret cache, so they demolished the barracks. Before the demolishment, the secretary managed to retrieve the document. There is a church on the corner of Preobrazhensky square, where the barracks are located, the secretary at great risk, gave it to the rector of the church and believing in my mission, he gave it to me. My son was going to publish it in his newspaper but he was discovered and met his death.

My mission is that the seven seals must be opened, you must do what it takes, you and you alone- the seals and the document will alter disaster. Putinov must be stopped. Putinov is the leader and will lead you to others who want chaos and anarchy. You have the power to stop the world from being destroyed.'

'I think you need to keep this document Matt and deliver it to the Opus Signori.'

Cathy stopped speaking and took Matt by the hand. 'I'm terribly afraid to open the seventh seal. The sixth seal was so accurate. It's absolutely terrifying, the weather we are experiencing!

If I undertake the cooling- what did you call it? – the adiabatic demagnetisation that you spoke of, then that should temper the effects on the ozone layer. It's almost impossible to imagine, this stuff has the likelihood of succeeding.'

'Yes, the scientists are convinced you can do this. It's imperative the atmosphere is given a prod - albeit the capacity of just one body, you my darling, is just such a tiny prod, that it's almost hopeless - whilst the regular pattern of the solar system and Andromeda re-establishes itself. The boff's don't know exactly when this is likely to occur. It could take thousands of years.

Cathy, the scroll with the seals has a purpose. At first, it seems to be exactly as scholars indicated- that the four riders of the apocalypse signify Conquest, War, Famine and Death, all that we are experiencing now - but if we consider instead that the seals are the sun and the inner planets , therein lies the solution for mankind.

The physicists believe the Book of Revelation with the seven seals was intended to reveal to us today, that the pattern of the inner planets orbit in the solar system is unaligned, affecting the atmosphere. A large amount of mass is required –I tell you, Cathy the presence of God in all of this is just incredibly humbling- it just so happens that Damocles our sub-dwarf star, newly resident in the Milky Way could be the key to correct the misalignment of the planets. Damocles is a massive body and its perturbations will impact the planetary orbit. It has to be tweaked sufficiently so that the eccentric pattern of the orbit is redressed.

Trouble is we have to build another wormhole. The first one occurred naturally. This one has to be engineered from the Black Widow particle I retrieved earlier. It could take months or years.

An immediate atmospheric alteration is required.

As you know, normally the solar wind is held off by the magnetosphere, an area that screens out much of the sun's radiation so that there is little direct atmospheric impact. Well, this magnetosphere normally has an 'inflow' of solar energy deposits converted by sufficient energy to an 'outflow' where escaping gravity, it is released downstream in the solar wind in a process called 'ablation' – because solar material, damaging to earth, then has been completely removed from earth and can never return.

Earth has always borrowed order from the wider universe, in order to export disorder – the second law of thermodynamics.

However, the absorption rate since the merger seems to be pretty high, no doubt because of the planets being a bit off-piste-so to speak –there was talk of Damocles' magnetic field colliding with the solar wind and magnifying its effects.

Anyway, ablation in the magnetosphere is not taking place sufficiently, hence the heat. If we introduce you, in a magnetocaloric state, (in short MCE which signifies magnet + calorie or unit of heat) into the magnetic field around the earth – basically you will act as a refrigeration technique.

We will then disorientate you from the magnetic field by the machines we have, using thermal energy, a large proportion of that is our stored psychokinetic energy (my machine holds such in its databanks) which ensures an adiabatic process. The magnetic field will absorb the thermal energy and perform a reorientation. The combination of the two should do the trick. We hope the temperature will drop significantly. The ozone layer around the earth will be preserved.

You will have to mentally circumnavigate the earth confined in a cryogenic chamber, rather like a huge vacuum flask. Your body will be adequately

insulated. It might take awhile. We have done the mental orbit before when we took those photos of the earth with our minds. You will be absolutely fine, Cathy.
Open the seventh seal now. Do it' he said gently.

Cathy opened the seal with trepidation.

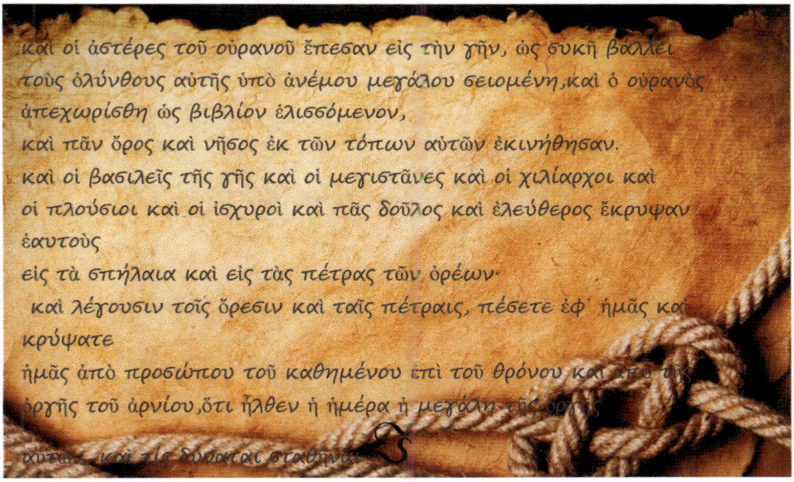
καὶ οἱ ἀστέρες τοῦ οὐρανοῦ ἔπεσαν εἰς τὴν γῆν, ὡς συκῆ βάλλει
τοὺς ὀλύνθους αὐτῆς ὑπὸ ἀνέμου μεγάλου σειομένη,καὶ ὁ οὐρανὸς
ἀπεχωρίσθη ὡς βιβλίον ἑλισσόμενον,
καὶ πᾶν ὄρος καὶ νῆσος ἐκ τῶν τόπων αὐτῶν ἐκινήθησαν.
καὶ οἱ βασιλεῖς τῆς γῆς καὶ οἱ μεγιστᾶνες καὶ οἱ χιλίαρχοι καὶ
οἱ πλούσιοι καὶ οἱ ἰσχυροὶ καὶ πᾶς δοῦλος καὶ ἐλεύθερος ἔκρυψαν
ἑαυτοὺς
εἰς τὰ σπήλαια καὶ εἰς τὰς πέτρας τῶν ὀρέων·
καὶ λέγουσιν τοῖς ὄρεσιν καὶ ταῖς πέτραις, πέσετε ἐφ' ἡμᾶς καὶ
κρύψατε
ἡμᾶς ἀπὸ προσώπου τοῦ καθημένου ἐπὶ τοῦ θρόνου καὶ ἀπὸ τῆς
ὀργῆς τοῦ ἀρνίου,ὅτι ἦλθεν ἡ ἡμέρα ἡ μεγάλη τῆς ὀργῆς
αὐτῶν, καὶ τίς δύναται σταθῆναι

'The Book of Revelation has several catastrophes occurring. I'm going to try and put them together. Help me please.

'Let me read the relevant bits aloud. Basically angels sounded and a mountain burning with fire was cast into the sea, creatures of the sea and ships were destroyed. A great star called Wormwood fell from heaven – I hope it's not Damocles in a manmade wormhole - on the third part of the rivers

– the third part of the sun, and the third part of the moon and the third part of the stars were all smitten.. and a third part of men too were slain. A lot of doom and gloom. And there's that symbol again $\Im$'

'Yes, that symbol is one I've been puzzling over. I believed it to be mathematical, so asked around, '$\Im$' is indeed a mathematical function used, as a basic example, in something called TeX, to find the imaginary part of a complex number or in short: Im.

Oh yes, and to answer the question I know you are going to ask' – he grinned and said with laughing sparks in the grey eyes, 'I'm noted as you know for my psychic powers. To continue: TeX is a computer language designed for use in typesetting. What I could not fathom was this was devised in the 1970's – somewhat later than your papyri, eh? He raised his eyebrows and smiled.

So, dearest it's back to the drawing board. I tried moving the top and bottom strokes around. Still nothing. Why don't you have a go? Perhaps the ancient Greek alphabet will give us a clue. If still flummoxed, I know a chap in London who might 'shed the veils that currently conceal', (the last words he whispered in an exaggerated mysterious tone).

'Matt, be serious. I know you're trying to make me relax, a little less wound up about my forthcoming aerobatics!' Cathy took a deep breath and exhaled softly. 'O.K. Let's get back to this seventh seal. The third part of the world, where the third part of the sun, the third part of the moon and the third part of the rivers are located, is according to the ancient mapmakers parts of Russia, China, India and the Middle East.'

'If a comet or asteroid is due to fall from the heavens- in the Bible's view, a great star called Wormwood (no love, it will not be Damocles, the scientists will be able to control the wormhole with the Black Widow particle now identified and it's volatility experimented on in every which way)– hang on though -Cathy, I'm very afraid to say this but I know this with absolute certainty, I believe there is a prediction of an asteroid called RQ36 hitting earth very soon.

If Wormwood is the asteroid, and in all our present upheaval of the atmosphere and the sun –Jesus, the prediction of the mountain burning in the third part of the world- I'm afraid to say that the asteroid's target would centre around the range of Himalayas. The asteroid would make an enormous impact, like hundreds of the biggest nuclear bombs ever built exploding at once creating a huge crater.

We need to go and talk to Professor Christoph Benjamin. He's well-qualified to shed more light on the consequences of the asteroid hitting the Himalayas.'

An hour later, the Professor adjusted the glasses on his nose and said, 'First I will talk about our situation now. Right now we believe by our calculations, that with the collision, the stratosphere and the troposphere have merged at certain points. We need to get to the cool air in the lower stratosphere and filter it through the tropopause and through to the troposphere. Not have everything all mixed up. We need to alter all the terrible weather.

As to the asteroid, it might have a bearing on our climate for the future. I have consulted with my colleagues and the Himalayas would be the mountain chain that fits the Bible prediction. You see, they are a mountain chain 1,500 miles long and some of the world's major river systems arise in the Himalayas. Their combined drainage basin is home to some 3 billion people. Again as the Book of Revelation predicts, a third of the world's population would be hugely affected.

My colleagues and I think the best possible scenario would be if the asteroid hits the mountain, and it were to form into glaciers, then a massive amount of air, ice and water would begin to move from under the mountain to form the said glaciers.

Of course India and China, in fact, that whole region would be one land mass, all jostling for space. That's the best possible case.

The worst would be if the asteroid which has a breakdown of oxygen and nitrogen in the atmosphere, would result in a chemical reaction forming the molecules NO and NO2 causing acid rain, to such a degree that it would indeed pollute rivers, forests, plants and animals. This is also predicted in the seventh seal. Not to mention the incredible levels of ozone that would be released. Ozone with the sun so close is causing such change to our atmosphere now.

But if, as I said, *if* the Himalayas formed into glaciers, there would be a Sublimation of glaciers where glaciers would be transformed from a solid phase to a gas phase releasing water vapour gases and hence condensation would rise into the troposphere or hydrosphere which could cause clouds with precipitation or rain, much needed with this heat- and could, we hope to God, mitigate warming from the greenhouse gases. A future solution to combat climate change.'

‘But billions of lives would be in jeopardy’ said Matt roughly. Cathy frowned in concern.

The Professor nodded and looked at Cathy. ‘Let’s hope the prediction of the seventh seal is untrue.

Now you, Miss Burkert, if you succeed in the attempt at cooling the magnetosphere, a decrease in the effects on the ozone layer would be almost immediate. You are the lightest in weight to fit into the coolant chamber. We cannot use the others. We hope the adiabatic demagnetisation will be permanent and the atmosphere will correct itself thereafter. I have to say in warning to both of you that only simulated trajectories have been attempted before. Molecular dynamics and adiabatic processes, you know.

At their puzzled looks, he sighed and said, ‘All I will say it has all been only ever done on a computer –we are currently rigging the source codes to the coolant chamber to programme your flight path- So to explain, all these atoms and molecules are numerically determined. They define force fields between particles and potential energy - to affect biomolecules like you and me, living organisms – a lot of physics gobbledygook for you to understand. I see I have lost you.’ He waved them away.

Cathy and Matt thanked the Professor and left to prepare Cathy for the cooling attempt.

Matt said to Cathy, 'I've just had word from Jim. The shuttle is now at the ISS. Power is due to be restored in two hours'

Syria

He was a man high up in government circles. He wielded power behind the scenes. He was also a Christian of the Greek Orthodox faith and he had been summoned to meet the Patriarch Gregorious. Abu Daoud felt the force move within him – was it the Holy Spirit? – as he gazed at the Russian document with the official seal. An old man in St. Petersburg had sent this copy to the Patriarch. The church was the connection, the church on Preobrazhensky Square in St. Petersburg.

The government of Syria has close ties with Russia. Russia was backing President Bashar al-Assad in the civil strife that was beginning to engulf the country. Russia's largest Mediterranean naval base is in Tartus, a major port in Syria and it is also heavily involved in the country's infrastructure.

But Abu Daoud also knew something that was not general knowledge - of Syria's covert plans with Russian expertise, regarding the construction of a nuclear power plant that was already producing 20% enrichment of uranium. Israel had bombed one plant in 2007 but since then four others had been built. Syria had the nuclear capability to build missiles.

Abu Daoud had personally overseen the programme. Now the Patriarch wanted him to scupper the deal and turn Putinov in, thus embarrasing Putinov on the world stage. The world would lose confidence in a nation which condoned the deeds of a head of state. Putinov would be seen as a common criminal.

The document provided the means to do just that. He would obey his religious directive. As soon as the power was back, he would make the call.

The British would be very interested.

Later that day, Abu Daoud rang his contact at MI6, Thames House. The woman called her superior immediately.

A Mr. Robert Anderson who was closeted with his fellow Opus Signor, Cardinal Jules de Fleury.

Chapter 17

CERN, Geneva:

Cathy and Matt breathed sighs of relief. The power had been restored. Engineers had battled the heavy winds and storms, the incredible heat outside to ensure the grid was back on track. For how long no one was willing to guarantee.

The Space Shuttle had docked at the International Space Station and the crew had effected vital links to the satellite systems and communication.

Cathy now had the green light. The physicists had switched on the energisation chamber, redirecting the power from the LHC to just one capsule. The huge output of consolidated energy was directed at the Adiabatic Demagnetisation Refrigerator cycle which was applied to the capsule. Cathy insulated in her thermal oversuit did not feel the chill.

The machines were being activated, Matt's special machine and the others. She was plugged in electronically via the chamber. Computer simulations tried and tested, spurred her to reach Olympian ground. Her mind knew molten gold. The power in her mind was reaching beyond the earth. She was outside her body. Vast expanses of the earth were below her. The colours were of such great beauty that she had to draw breath to go on.

Matt had said to use the analogy of dogs, such as border collies, which are very reliable catchers of Frisbees without being aware of the complex calculations (wind speed, air resistance, etc.) that might be involved. The rule which the dog's brain has subliminally worked out is to run at a speed so that the angle of gaze to the Frisbee remains constant. Cathy had to discount the physics-speak of 'Jeans escape, Polar Wind and Plasmasphere, etc.) and concentrate on the reconnecting the processes that achieved the science of planetary atmosphere. In Matt's words: 'Keep your mind in the magnetic moment'

Cathy was feverish; she was so electrically charged she could have been in an opium smoker's dream. She found herself reaching a consciousness where she was being escorted by smoky silhouettes. They came to her, the quicksilver mercury and the fluid ebony of the alien life and thousands with them, interpenetrating streams of high altitude kinetic processes, achieving uniformity of plasma and energy sources in the ionosphere - the upper layers of the magnetosphere. They seemed to be like angels, of gossamer, thickly feathered and the energy they produced gave her incredible impetus– Two touched her and their minds connected. They had met before. Her skin betrayed her DNA. Sensation after sensation washed over Cathy, unlike any she had experienced before. She felt the very essence of being a woman. Her molecular structure seemed to be triggering a response – the touch of the male fluid ebony seemed to be enveloping her entire body, not just her mind. She felt the beat of another heart, deep within her, in the depths of her womb.

Then, together all three and their companions were absorbed in hemispheric dynamics, decreasing the magnetic field. The magnetopause, the effective limit of the magnetic field, had an inner zone and the thermal energy they produced along with the machines caused the magnetic moments to overcome the field. Stellar ablation was restored. The cooling process had begun.

Cathy did the heavenly circuit, for what seemed like hours. After the injection of coolant at high altitude, it started to move around the globe with the air motions; first in an east-west direction, but also with no time in a north-south direction. Hours later, the adiabatic demagnetisation had spread evenly around the world.

Then the ebony and the mercury said goodbye. The alien life-force were returning to the Bard's Muse. They said they would always be with her, an intrinsic part of her. She was the only human who heard the voice of reason and pure thought. Her and one other.

It would take the rest of mankind another 500 years to reach that plateau. Other humans would search but would never find them again. A human had tried to alter something sacred, an inviolate entity. They would not share their minds again.

England

Fourteen members of the all-powerful Opus Signori were preparing to leave. Five would stay behind. The last 48 hours had been sleepless but a working plan had been put in motion. All governments henceforth would be answerable to one body. Since Reza's duplicity there were nineteen men left. The nineteen men from all corners of the Globe. The Opus Signori. This select group, with each member's life examined minutely to detect their worthiness would always be in the shadows but Heads of governments would know and acknowledge their leadership.

Iran would fall. Armies were mobilising from all over the world. The key to their demise was in the old Aramaic language, buried deep in Aram, an ancient area in central Syria, now in the region of the modern Aleppo, the largest city in Syria.

Aleppo, Syria

The old man wore the amulet. He was a hundred years old and he had travelled far. He was Leonard Sosnovsky and had sent Cathy the papyrus of the seven seals. He had been here in Aleppo for a week. All around him was the unrest of civil war. His body was so tired but he had to be in Syria when Andromeda and the Milky Way collided.

This land was ancient and as his amulet said the word 'abracadabra' in the ancient Aramaic in which *ibra* (אברא) means "I have created" and *k'dibra* (כדברא) which means "through my speech", providing a translation of *abracadabra* as "created as I say' .

And what he was going to say would have far-reaching effects. A conspiracy theory with overwhelming consequences. Putinov would be an international pariah.

On 15 June 2000, *The Times* reported that Spanish police discovered that Putinov had secretly visited a villa in Spain belonging to the oligarch Boris Andronikov, on up to five different occasions in 1999.

Andronikov was the ruggedly handsome man, a friend of Sally Anderson's. Soon after Putinov's election in 2000, Andronikov, then high up in

GAZPROM, to all intents and purposes, fell out with his comrade and claimed political asylum in Britain. That was not the truth.

Putinov and Andronikov set the stage to fool the world. Andronikov was a Russian spy. The richest, most voluble, overtly anti-Putinov, spy. The old man knew this from a connection in the Hermitage museum. The connection, a member of Putinov's innermost sanctum had, under pain of excommunication from Leonard Sosnovsky's beloved Russian church on Preobrazhensky Square, told him the real state of affairs.

The poor bastard Alexander Litvinenko had been a close friend of Andronikov's and formed 'the London circle'. It was he who had discovered the truth about Andronikov and Putinov. Shortly after Litvinenko had been poisoned.

Leonard Sosnovsky knew it had everything to do with Gazprom. Gazprom, the largest oil and gas supplier in Russia. The clues would lead right to Iran's door. Gazprom had ostensibly been ousted in Iran but the latest news was that Gazprom was in talks with Iran about natural gas, despite sanctions by the West. The corporation was trying to win contracts on the Iran-Pakistan gas pipeline, and the Pakistan- Afghanistan-India pipeline as well seeking to influence the whole of Central Asia, by getting into bed with China.

Putinov was the state, so control of that corporation was in his hands.

Re-election as President and Putinov would have then achieved his goal. Complete control of Russia and Gazprom with fingers in every nation south of the Caspian Sea. Andronikov too, would have accomplished his agenda. Britain had included him in the circle of trust along with the Americans. He was in the know, privileged and classified information was mentioned to him without any qualms. The West believed he could exert influence through his former association with Russian oil and gas, to their benefit.

However, Andronikov did Mother Russia's bidding, all the dirty not-so-little jobs in the West. A little matter of cyber spying and loose talk ensured undetected success. He had a beauty of a covert op. prepping at the moment.

To Putinov, Andronikov was worth his weight in gold. Gazprom gold.

Until Leonard Sosnovsky.

The old man, Sosnovsky had a meeting with Abu Daoud. The British had set it up. They had also put him in touch with the bearded one, the covert British operative of Iran and Iraq.

For now, Abu Daoud would know what to do.

Chapter 18

CERN, Geneva:

Cathy and Mallard were preparing to leave. They were heading back. So were Charlie and Chandra. They had already wished them goodbye. Everything was slowly returning to normal. The adiabatic demagnetisation had worked, even though world temperatures were still above average. CERN were no closer to knowing all the answers but attempts to create a wormhole and access Damocles' interactions with the planets were still ongoing. Satellites were restored and flights were resuming.

Cathy in the midst of packing picked up the Bible for one last time. She read again the final passages of the seventh seal where the angel is in possession of a book, and has one foot on the sea and one foot on the land. The seal exhorted the messenger to swallow the words of the book whole and that's what they were going to do.

They would swallow the prediction of disaster that would hit the Asian subcontinent. It would leave a bitter aftertaste, living with such knowledge but Cathy and Matt knew if the asteroid hit the Himalayas devastating the Indo-Australian tectonic plate, the reverberations would move northwest to include the Indian subcontinent mainly India,

Pakistan and Bangladesh. They could not voice their prophecy. Billions of lives were at stake.

The Book of Revelation and the ancient maps of the third world, crumbling each territory in smudged outlines saw waters engulfing the three countries. Science could not sustain the immense populations living within.

Cathy and Matt made a vow to abide by the seventh seal. They would never utter a syllable of their insight. It was for a time many years hence.

Just one thing nagged.

The symbol ℑ. Cathy had an idea and checked it out.

Mallard, on his return, scheduled an appointment in Golders Green with an Aramaic scholar.

England

They were home.

England was at war with Iran. So were Europe, Israel and America.

Russia closely aligned with Iran, Syria and Asia was the unchallenged enemy.

The old, old man Leonard Sosnovsky, tired and worn sat in his hotel at Aleppo and spoke to Abu Daoud. Yes, he confirmed to Abu Daoud that he was the one who had sent him the Russian document implicating Putinov regarding key Russian input into the construction of the nuclear power plants in Syria.

But he had more, much more to tell Abu Daoud.

He spoke with a strong voice, his tones, for his many years, clear and precise as he told of Andronikov and Putinov and the conspiracy theory that Putinov's goal was to ensure Russia had total control of the Middle East and Asia. Even China was in his sights.

The old man knew how the West could bring Putinov to his knees and therefore bring about the downfall of Iran and the entire bloc of countries that aspired to nuclear missile capability.

Proof of aiding and abetting Syria was just one document that would prove to the world that Putinov was to be held accountable. There was another one in the possession of a girl, a Cathy Burkert, a report that proved Putinov had signed the death warrant on Alexander Litvinenko, the Russian who had been poisoned in London. There was a third which the old man had already spoken of – the sleeper spy Andronikov that Putinov had installed in London.

All of this would embarrass Putinov but to bring him down, to completely flatten him was to deliver a *coup de grace* of financial proportions to Putinov's *raison d'être* – GAZPROM.

The old man talked quietly, his voice shaky now. He was relieved when he had finished. He would go back home now, back to Russia, to die.

An hour later, Abu Daoud spoke to Robert Alexander, head of British Intelligence. He filled him in on all that had been said.

Cathy and Matt sat in the plush seats of the very comfortable Daimler as it purred towards their destination deep in the Surrey countryside.

The Opus Signori had been in touch. A meeting was scheduled. Matt Mallard had filed his report and there were questions to be answered.

A quorum of 5 sat around the table. Cardinal Jules de Fleury, Robert Alexander, Ben Efraim, the American Opus Signor John Stanmore and Hektor Xanthis.

The American said, 'In your report, you stated Charlie McCarthy had terminal cancer. We have made sure that the boy is taken care of. He will have the best of care and attention that our resources can provide.'

Mallard said, 'I have agreed to attempt to heal him. No faith required'

The Cardinal said, 'We will pray for him'

It was Robert Alexander, head of British Intelligence's turn to speak, 'I believe Jim, my man on the ground was of great assistance to you in Geneva. Unfortunately, from your report you say he knows I am a member of this group. I would rather he was ignorant but I shall have to make him my personal assistant, part of the Opus Signor Security detail'

Ben Efraim raised his hands in the air, his voice had an icy edge,'You say the machines are destroyed. On whose authority did you destroy them? There were four I believe, yours, MI6's and Reza's and the IPOD – why did you think you could do such a thing?'

'They were my invention. They were never sold or given to anyone. They were misappropriated and as such I had no qualms in erasing their databanks permanently and melting them down for scrap. They will never be used again. No artificial thought transference, not of my creation'

Ben Efraim said, 'There are others like you who will do as you did. Already, there are whispers of a new form of warfare. Computer-enabled telepathic control of armies'

'Shall we move on?' said Hektor. He looked at Cathy. 'All of you present here know I was involved with Miss Burkert. It is no secret that I would still like to be but I think the lady has other plans' He indicated Mallard.

'What do you both intend to do now?

'We will be working in collaboration with CERN and other organisations to correct eternally the atmosphere besides using our powers of foresight to determine new migration destinations for homo sapiens in this merged world of ours.

We cannot do anything about the land mass shifts but we believe it's great news filtering through of Africa fitting into South America like a glove, just like in the Jurassic period a hundred and fifty million years ago - except for the continental shelf - the extended perimeter of each continent and coastal plain.

The preservation of the continental shelf around the Atlantic Ocean and the Mediterranean Sea will give rise to new fortunes. The sea-beds of the bordering lands are set to be the richest of all, a veritable Croesus of oil wealth.

For us, the sands there will reveal eternity- geological time made visible in a process of sand formation: by weathering, then sandstone and exposed liberation- a cyclic process, over and over again. Such quartz sand grains will aid Cathy and I to predict new spaces in our new world of Earth and Andromeda and to paraphrase William Blake's words in 1803 or thereabouts: We would like to see a world in a grain of sand'

'One last item' said Hektor, 'your report mentions the six seals in The Book of Revelation. It does not mention the seventh. What happened to that papyrus?'

Mallard took Cathy's hand and said, 'Do you have your Bible, Cardinal?'

The Cardinal proffered the red clad book.

Cathy took it and found The Book of Revelation: Chapter 10. She showed it to the others. They passed it around, each reading aloud.

The Cardinal said, 'So you are taking a vow of silence'

Mallard said, 'We believe if it is divulged, then cataclysmic events would unfold. The earth would cease to exist as we know it. Whole continents would be erased off the map. We cannot go public with such information.'

'The world is watching your every word and every action as your fame has spread. You two were responsible for saving the earth.'

'We had help- Chandra and Charlie -and Sergei, who died tragically'

'The surviving two will be looked after all the days of their lives. You both will be protected and sheltered, especially from the public eye. Officially you will never be found.' said Hektor.

Cardinal Jules de Fleury made the sign of the cross and said, 'You have my blessing. We will always watch over you. You will never want for anything. Bank accounts have been set up for you both. They will always have funds to support you.'

Hektor left his seat and approached Cathy. 'May I speak to you for a minute?' He took her to the next room. 'Are you alright?'

'Yes, I'm happy'

'Come to Cyprus for a holiday when this is over. As my guest.'

'I will. I will see you again.'

Chapter 19

They talked long into the night like students – young kids fresh out of school. Now as separate entities without the electronic link, they needed to explore each other's minds and put their world to rights. They had succeeded astrally, orbiting their outer- earthly pursuits. Now they needed to affirm their souls, by making sense of what they had experienced.

They talked of Nietzsche and the eternal consciousness they had encountered, when their bodies strayed onto a mental plane, when they drew breath away from the need of each other. A look, fingertips brushing skin, lips sensuously swollen–kissed; the dream of eternity, the desire of form indulged with no restraint.

With their bodies they fine-tuned their sexual responses and their intuitive ability enhanced every movement of their joined flesh. They had found each other, were gifted with spiritual insight and must use it to be of benefit to others. They must help and heal, each in their own way.

They surfaced slowly to become aware of the world beyond themselves.

They talked of a world of science and prophecy, of the Bible and Isaac Newton. Newton, who believed that God was a masterful creator whose divine design of the mutual actions of planets and comets would need a reformation – was this that reformation- the misalignment of planets the solar system was experiencing? God the mastermind adjusting the grandeur of all creation? Newton also believed that prophecy was hidden in the language of the Bible.

'And this is where we came in, deciphering Scripture' said Cathy. 'The Bible is open to so many different interpretations – I read up on Galileo in Wikipedia, the first person to use a telescope. He defended heliocentrism, the theory that the planets move around the sun, and claimed it was not contrary to passages in the Bible that said the earth is stationary. Galileo believed that the writers of Scripture merely wrote from the vantage point that the sun does rise and set and like our ancients of the seven seals, who gazed upwards and saw a limited expanse- just the four inner planets.'

Matt responded, 'Professor Christoph likened the prophecy of the seals – in fact any prophecy to the double-slit experiment in physics where light particles are deployed and directed towards a screen through double slits, producing light and dark bands – an interference pattern on the screen but – here's where the ancients' observation of the planets and the resulting seals comes into the equation.

The light particles respond differently when they are observed, say by a camera - they have no interference pattern. So, researchers tested the theory of observation after the particles were deployed and they surprisingly found the same result- the no interference pattern. It's as if they know they are going to be observed in the future even though it hadn't happened yet.'

'Yet again, Matt, Scripture and prophecy, science and Aliens - and of course our raison d'être, a consciousness that has accessed the dominion of angels'

'Yes, I believe with our striving to attain a higher thinking, we are able to achieve what the Alien life on The Bard's Muse were communicating. Pure thought through the centuries. Perhaps we are proclaiming now what future generations will achieve – our very own quantum mind experiment. Cathy, did you know they touched my mind – the ebony and the mercury -knew my DNA, my genetic map when I was with them at the Red giants of Andromeda. I believe they knew my soul.

They communicated a message of a curious earthly need. I believe they need physical bodies, propagating in the belly of the earth, within the soil, through burial, internment, ashes, rather like every other facet of nature.

All matter, remnants of their world, shaped on earth to mirror that infinite vista.

However, a consciousness of eternal existence, the alien life we met, remaining in the heavens - rather like what Christianity believes – holy spirits, the seven spirits in the New Testament called 'Dunamis' and translated as virtues, they are perceived to be exalted spiritual beings.'

'If this consciousness is far superior to the human mind, can they influence our thinking? Can they determine the path of human life? Do we reproduce at their bidding?' said Cathy.

Matt said wryly, 'I think humans are able to influence their own lives quite successfully. Take the science of human embryos tested for genetic diseases prior to implantation.

Human reproduction without flaws is sought more and more. To me there is room for error in the quest for perfection, after all even a weed bears a flower - but to answer your questions, I do not believe that the alien consciousness can influence human thought apart from communication- but the highest form of eternal consciousness like God can answer human prayer- so yeah, God can influence human life but through requests made by the will of the individual. In other words, we get what we want, but not when and how we want it- that's the almighty's territory!'

Cathy smiled and kissed him, 'I think I'm happy with that'

He bought her wild roses and as they faded, she breathed in the sigh of their perfume. From that lingering sweetness, she knew, henceforth would lie all roses and all summers. Its scent, a heady distillation of gardens and sunshine- intoxication across the centuries would fade. Only her heart would trip, rendered so by the alchemy of these crimson blooms.

Another day, they were together in the shower and mad, passionate fitting of two halves – male and female, perfectly built, each to accommodate the other –hills and valleys, and glorious sex left them replete.

Cathy exhaled softly almost to herself, 'I guess I saw stars just then'

He heard the soft words and the topic of elements of dead stars reaching the earth and Dr. Brian Cox and Stephen Hawking's theories gave rise to a question. Would believers in pure science ever accept the eternal consciousness of the alien life?

‘Yes, if they are also capable of accepting Eternal recurrence in thought alone, not bodily reincarnation but spiritual thought only. We have, I believe, one shot at a body in life and science will advance to such a degree, they will not merely come to peace with such existence but embrace it. Cathy, with all the rewriting of the rules of physics that has been taking place and our survival on earth, we must now talk of death.’

He talked softly, long into the night. A promise was made.

Mallard held her close, ‘We must maintain our belief in Nietzsche’s *amor fati* ‘love of fate’, good or bad, and tell others of it. The Alien life-force would then be protected and not affected by human corruption and greed as Reza tried to do’

‘It’s a fantastic concept and we will always have the Opus Signori to sound out our theories. They are well qualified to draw conclusions and apply them to the world at large. They certainly have the means to do so.’

‘I believe they too have evolved to be a force for good – I believe evil elements have always existed in their ranks like Kennedy thought when he made his speech back in the 60’s –they could have blood on their hands indeed, but I think near extinction of the human race has given them a new mandate.

Having said that, I don't know if I'm entirely comfortable in global power controlled by a tiny minority and not an elected one at that. Still, I hope the evil elements have been expunged. In any event, there is no moral wriggle-room remaining for the nineteen.

Cathy, the Cardinal took me into his confidence. The Opus Signori will never recruit anyone else. They do not trust the base nature of men, after Reza's incredible betrayal. They had surrounded themselves with every safeguard, via men and machines, to no avail. Reza soured everything they stood for. To be above and beyond partisan considerations. The Opus Signori have no one on whom to bestow their legacy. You and I are the only outsiders to know of their existence. That knowledge will die with us'

The five men were heading each to their homes – the Cardinal to Italy, Ben Efraim to Israel, John Stanmore to the States, Hektor Xanthis to Cyprus and Robert Alexander to his young wife, Sally. They would meet again in a month's time.

Sally Alexander had an interesting day.

Her handsome rugged friend, her dear Andronikov, had wined and fed her on the choicest titbits at luncheon. He had been greeted by pop stars and paparazzi, his fame and his wealth were overwhelming. All she found pleasing and flattering. Her friends would be terribly impressed. She giggled at his jokes and revealed too much.

Andronikov made the call. He had Putinov's direct cell number.

A press release was issued the following day. Russia was putting a space mission together for the first time in 60 years. A manned mission to The Bard's Muse. President Putinov's goal had been to send a space mission to the moon by 2018 but recent information had intimated Alien life, so the race to the Bard's Muse was on. Within the year, Russia would revive its space programme. Russian cosmonauts would be space-bound.

The world's press took up the story. The internet sizzled with the information. Alien life was a fact and existed close to the earth – 51 Pegasi was a spacecraft away. Commercial flights on Virgin Galactic were already being mooted. There was a mad rush to pre-book.

The Opus Signori needed to trace the leak. They found it in the person of Sally Anderson. She was remorseful but still tweeted inanely.

The Opus Signori decided to bring forward their meeting. All 19 would meet within 48 hours.

Russia had become an absolute priority. Their support of Iran and the continued loss of life took precedence. The space mission on the hunt for the Alien-life was another. They had to be stopped one way or the other. The Opus Signori knew how, they had the incriminating documents to set things in motion, from the old man of Russia, a Leonard Sosnovsky. Once they had ignited the spark, a conflagration would ensue.

By the end of the week they would be aboard the Space Shuttle. They needed to get to the Bard's Muse before the Russians. They would stop to refuel at the International Space Station, the ISS. The Russians Soyuz capsules currently shuttle supplies to the ISS and would be making a stopover there. The Opus Signori would thwart the Russians at that facility. Intensive dialogue was currently underway with the other nations involved in the ISS – the USA, Canada, Japan and the nations of Europe. Fellow Opus Signori representing these respective countries were now in possession of the relevant details, their task to dissuade the Russians from their quest for the Alien Life.

To the eighteen men of the Work of Lords, they were a dying breed. After Reza Sohrab's calumny, the select group would never admit anyone else to their ranks. With their passing, world matters would be administered by petty politicians.

Just one man, the nineteenth knew differently. Cardinal Jules de Fleury.

Hektor Xanthis contacted Dominic Anderhub, honorary chairman of the Science lab Columbus, docked at the ISS. Anderhub, who in Geneva weeks ago, had informed Xanthis about the photographs taken by Cathy Burkert and Matt Mallard. He would pave the way for them.

Chapter 20

Paris
An apartment on Rue de Montalembert
7th Arrondisement.

Nineteen men, a gilt and rococo ceiling overlooking the magnificent minds below. Lions of their time, protecting the pride of nations, they talked of events that would unfold in the next 24 hours.

The Russian President, Putinov, would take a fall or - he would be malleable. They were going to hit him where it hurt most - the country's income producing behemoth, Gazprom. At the beginning of 2012, Gazprom had placed Convertible Rouble Bonds subscriptions in the market. They were seeking unprecedented investment on the global stage. The book was thrown open and the CB's were available, with the nominal volume of billions, maturing after 10 years with a 3 year call option.

The Opus Signori were exercising control of the World Bank and the International Development agency therein. The American president of the World Bank was known to John Stanmore, the U.S. Opus Signor. He would arrange the transfer of funds for the Convertible Bonds. All would be purchased.

Now within 48 hours the message would be sent. The Convertible Bonds would be exchanged for equity in Gazprom. The Opus Signori would in effect be controlling Gazprom. They would have front men, men who would act on their behalf sitting on the board of directors, to wheel and deal.

The shadows would conceal the 19 men.

If Gazprom tried to buy the CB's they would need billions which they did not have. If they tried to drive the share price in order to protect themselves, insurers would downgrade the debt making it difficult for stock to be purchased.

The downgrading of debt would be in the aftermath of Putinov's exposure to the world press. The root cause of Putinov's downfall and disgrace was Leonard Sosnovsky's documents. They had received two from Abu Daoud in Syria courtesy of the old man. One detailing Putinov's aid to Syria's nuclear capability and the other, Putinov had installed a sleeper-spy Andronikov in London. The last was complicity in the death of Alexander Litvinenko on British soil, handed in by Cathy Burkert. Putinov's credibility would be seriously damaged. Investor confidence in Russia would be at critical point.

The IMF would be unable to bail them out. The Opus Signori controlled that facility. Their reason for denial: the entire bail-out fund had been swallowed up by Greece, Ireland, Italy, Portugal and Spain. The World Bank could then claim sovereign immunity as their charter stated.

Putinov could step down from the Presidential Office Or he could stay. Three reasons would keep him there. Give the order to remove Russian aid and infrastructure to Iran and Syria. Firstly, Iran would collapse without it. The war with Iran would be over. Iran would surrender. Secondly, civil strife in Syria could be resolved without Russian support for the Assad regime.

The final reason was the planned space mission within the year to seek the Alien Life. Cease with immediate effect.

The nineteen men talked and set the world's agenda for many a long hour. Five of them would leave on the Space Shuttle. These five remained behind to discuss their arrangements. They were the handpicked ones from the USA, Canada, Belgium, France and Japan. They were the lucky ones. They were going into Deep Space to seek consensus from their countrymen on non- encroachment of the Ebony and the Mercury thought forms.

The remaining fourteen left the apartment, one by one, heavily protected with their security detail. Cars that resembled panthers almost in a convoy were moving slowly along the river Seine. Barely three blocks away, the semtex hit 4 of the cars. The four Opus Signori in the cars, each with their two armed guards and assistants were declared dead by the doctor attending. The forensic scientist and the police swarmed around them minutes later.

The other Opus Signori in the cars behind saw and heard the explosions. They could *not* be found anywhere near. They had to retain their anonymity. They gave instructions swiftly. They were going into hiding. Somewhere in the organisation there was a leak and they needed to find the culprit. The scouring of ranks began.

Rome
The Vatican

Cardinal Jules de Fleury was morte – the word spread like wildfire through the Vatican. In the 73m tall tower, this is the Tower of the Winds, built by Ottavinao Mascherino between 1578 and 1580, a place where members of the public are never normally admitted; here in the Hall of the Meridian, a room covered in frescoes depicting the four winds, is a tiny hole high up in one of the walls.

At midday, the sun, shining through the hole, falls along a white marble line set into the floor. On either side of this meridian line are various astrological and astronomical symbols, once used to try to calculate the effect of the wind upon the stars. Cardinal Jules de Fleury's inner sanctum.

This Tower of the Winds also houses the secret archives of the Vatican. Hektor Xanthis was taken under armed Swiss Guard to view the Cardinal's private mail deposited here.

He found no reference to the Cardinal's murderer. Just the Cardinal's last Will and Testament to be read amidst great secrecy, by the brethren of the Opus Signori.

Israel

Tel Aviv

Colonel Daniel Barak felt raw today. This morning when shaving, his mobile had rung with the information. He was on his way now to the airport to fly to Paris.

Ben Efraim's body was being detained until his arrival.

Two days later, he had examined every facet of the investigation into the murder of Ben Efraim. There were no clues. He flew home and filed his report.

Suspected Islamic Fundamentalism was the main motive in the killing.

Brazil

Rio de Janeiro

Ernesto Quadros had his spokeswoman in the Brazilian government and the ear of the President Dilma Roussef. The spokeswoman had been vociferous on his behalf in her objections to the Belo Monte Dam. Had his stonewalling the project attracted enemies? Was that the reason for his murder?

The Belo Monte Dam is a proposed hydroelectric dam complex on the Xingu River in the state of Pará, Brazil. The Belo Monte Dam complex consists of three dams, numerous dykes and a series of canals in order to supply two different power stations with water.

The fish fauna of the Xingu River is extremely rich with an estimated 600 fish species, with many species found nowhere else in the world. They would be destroyed by the construction of the dam.

Ernesto Quadros, the Brazilian Opus Signor knew too, that dams in Brazil emit high amounts of methane, due to the lush jungle covered by waters each year as the basin fills. He was the man behind the protests worldwide. Dangers from the carbon trapped by foliage, which then decays anaerobically with help from methanogens, converting the carbon to methane, a more potent greenhouse gas than carbon dioxide.

Ernesto's pushing for litigation and his main objections that the dam will directly displace over 20,000 indigenous people was well-known in certain circles. Whilst in Paris, he was hoping to have a meeting with Chief Raoni of the Kayapo indigenous tribe. He wanted to tell him he would use every effort to further the causes of the Kayapo peoples. It was not to be.

His body was flown home. Motive for murder. Unknown. He left behind a wife and two children.

Greece

Athens

She was blonde and beautiful. She secretly brokered a deal between the dodgy German arms supplier Ferrostaal and the Greek Navy. Bribery to the tune of millions was paid to Greeks in very high places to facilitate the deal. Vasilis Metaxas was rumoured to be getting the public prosecutor's office to look into the affair.

The night before, she was Vasilis Metaxas' companion in Paris. So was her friend, the brunette with the big breasts. Together they had pleasured Metaxas and each other. Tongues dipping and raw sex, his erection made to last for hours with the popping of a Viagra or two. She was insatiable. She left him in the early hours and made her way downtown. Her brunette friend knew a great cafe where they could chill out before her flight home to Athens.

In Athens she heard the news; Vasilis Metaxas had been murdered in Paris. Her contact at the arms supplier Ferrostaal rang to congratulate her on a job well done. She said she didn't know what he meant.

The rest of the Opus Signori were in hiding. Their flight on the Space Shuttle to the ISS was delayed until they could regroup and effect a new plan of action. In the meantime, the word had gone out: Start the offensive against Putinov! They had obtained proof of Russian culpability. The vast resources activated with meticulous ferocity indicated positive cyber trails of Russian digital traffic; the hit on their members had been planned for a long time.

Moreover, the main priority was the continued war with Iran and Allied lives were being lost. There was no time to waste.

Dominic Anderhub called the ISS via the Orbital Communications Adaptor which allowed high speed data transfers and carries voice and video signals. The signal was sent up 90,000 miles by way of a communications satellite.

The astronaut at the Columbus Lab confirmed they knew that OPSEK, the planned Russian habitable artificial satellite, due to be launched within the next six months would consist of modules taken from the Russian Orbital Segment of the ISS before the ISS ceased to exist in orbit, and the missions planned were Mars, the Moon and now The Bard's Muse.

The man behind the mission was none other Vladimir Putinov. He was woken during the night with the news from GAZPROM. He dismissed it and went back to sleep.

That morning, there were many more calls and visits. Putinov and his advisors batted alternatives back and forth. The Convertible Bonds bought by an unknown syndicate who were threatening to dump the stock in GAZPROM came as a bolt out of the blue. Worse still, Putinov had been asked to step down or GAZPROM would go under. Russia's economy and all its oil and gas plans in myriad networks would be null and void.

Compliance was not on the agenda. The master plan was for Russia to take centre-stage in the world. The humiliation for Putinov to step down, and the reasons if made public, would be intolerable. Russia would never recover.

They knew they would have to back out of Iran, but Mother Russia would let their arch-enemies stew for a bit.

One thing was assured.

The Bard's Muse was going to be a project-in-waiting. As soon as the ISS had ceased its operations and OPSEK was the landing pad for manned missions – the Bard's Muse would have Russian visitors.

It was a matter of Russian national pride especially in the light of US withdrawal of its space missions until 2020.

London
Westminster Abbey

Cathy gazed at the nave of this amazing building, it reeked of history, and the only existing depiction of the structure is in the Bayeux Tapestry probably commissioned in the 1070's. The height and simplicity of the gothic architecture of the building she found imposing and yet welcoming.

She felt at home with people she had read about, studied and been of one mind with, through the pages of their books and ideas. Kings, Writers, Poets, Scientists, monks – the list was endless. She felt steeped in the knowledge of their deeds and spiritually she felt a link.

All the greats were buried here. She walked to Isaac Newton's monument, north of the entrance to the choir screen, near his tomb.

The monument features a figure of Newton reclining on top of a sarcophagus, his right elbow resting on several of his great books and his left hand pointing to a scroll with a mathematical design. Above him are a pyramid and a celestial globe showing the signs of the Zodiac and the path of the comet of 1680- Halley's Comet – featured in the Bayeux Tapestry as a fiery star.

Halley's Comet was seen as something of an omen in its appearance throughout the ages but it could also foretell great events as in 12 BC, it had appeared only a few years before the conventionally assigned date of the birth of Jesus Christ. Scholars attributed it as an explanation of the Star of Bethlehem. Science and God yet again.

Cathy had come to the Abbey to hear Choral Evensong. She always felt transported when she heard the beautiful music. She needed her thoughts transported today. She was hoping she would be able to reach through the great vaulting ceiling in the presence of God to the outer reaches of space and to the fluid processes of pure thought. Like

Halley's Comet, she needed to sound the omen as clear as the bells of Westminster Abbey. The Bard's Muse was under threat from human invasion. The Alien life-force should head for Mercury.

Her mind reached for a place that was sacrosanct and Gustave Doree's drawing of Dante's Paradiso came to mind. Cathy's classical background and the words of Dante Aligheri in the Inferno, Canto II resounded: '*Now, I wish to illuminate you, who are stripped in mind, as the surface of the snow is stripped of colour and coldness by the stroke of the sun's warm rays, with light so living it will tremble, as you gaze at it:*

Cathy trembled and the picture in her mind was the physical manifestation of Doree's drawing, she was abjectly humbled at the vision of angels – banks of them, angels with white wings, thickly furred, reaching for the sun, shining and huge in its magnetic field, in the centre of all passion and desire. Sitting in the Quire of Westminster Abbey, listening to the choristers singing paeans of praise to God, amidst the gilt and blue filigree frames, as awe slid into worship, she felt herself reaching out to the great beyond.

Then she fainted.

Chapter 21

Golder's Green, London.

The man was young, his dress of kippah (headcovering) and tallit (shawl), was customary of the synagogue and from where he had just returned. Mallard watched as he peered at the symbol intently. Mallard had mentioned Cathy's belief that the symbol was Aramaic or Hebrew.

The young man smiled, 'Yes', he said, 'it's both' - It's a double Lamed. 
one, inverted over the other. He was drawing

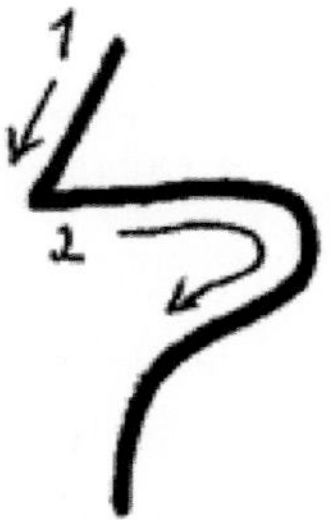

quickly. The Lamed is the 12th letter of the Hebrew Alphabet, with roots in Aramaic. Hebrew letters also serve as numerals so Lamed is the equivalent of the number 30. Do you see how they fit? This is your symbol

and the double Lamed fit perfectly when inverted.

Straight **Inverted**

Umm, you say it was on some old scroll? I have studied many of the old texts, including ancient Aramaic and I have never come across this.'

Mallard then told him of the mathematical symbol in TeX.

'The link between computer symbols and old scrolls,' the young man murmured softly, repeating the words as he took off his shawl and headwear. 'Perhaps, perhaps...there may be something...Do you have time for a cup of tea? I will tell you a story – a very old one, from the Book of Genesis; of the Righteous Ones.

With a mug of his favourite brew on the table in front of him, Matt Mallard listened intently.

‘The Lamed Vav Tzadikim, also known as Lamed Vavniks from the Russian translations – (‘niks’ is a suffix in Russian, like the beat ‘niks’ of the ‘60’s) These Lamed Vavniks are 36 special people in the world – as I mentioned Lamed also is the numeral 30 and Vav is 6 = 36 Righteous Ones.’

The young man steepled his fingers, leaning forward in his chair, ‘This is a concept rooted in mystical Judaism. It is said that at all times in the world there exist 36 special people whose sole purpose is to justify the continued existence of mankind in the eyes of God. Tradition states that all 36 are unknown to each other and if even one of them becomes aware of his true calling, then he dies and his place is taken by another. You see, there has to be thirty-six at all times. Even if one is missing, then the world will come to an end.

Mr Mallard, I see from your expression when I mention this group, you have a strange look; have you heard of them before?’

‘You are mistaken. I have never heard of the Lamed Vavniks. What connection could they be to the symbol of my scroll?’

‘Perhaps the content of your ancient scroll would provide some explanation? If the double Lamed is used, it could signify a cycle of emptying out, getting rid of, terminating.’ The boyish face opposite Mallard suddenly looked mischievous, he said, ‘You are not planning an assault on this group, are you?’

Mallard smiled duly but his expression remained tight. He thanked the young man and made to take his leave. Just as he was about to shut the door behind him, he heard the other say, ‘Oh, by the way, when writing the double Lamed, you would always add a vowel in-between. Perhaps that’s the missing piece in the jigsaw. Goodbye’

Iraq

Lieutenant Colonel Cohen of the Israeli Defence Forces was in the Majlis of the house. The place where men sat and deliberated. The men around him, Bakhtiari's, a nomadic tribe living in Lorestan, in the south-west of Iran, had met him and his company in Baku, Azerbaijan, largest city of the Caspian Sea.
The Lieutenant-Colonel and the corps had made it the long way around through Iraq and Armenia to avoid detection. The flight on the Boeing C17 Globemaster III, a large military transport aircraft, had landed at Yerevan, the capital of Armenia.

There they had been helped by Igor Ahronian, an Armenian who had the misfortune to be related to one Nasr Al-din, Cathy's arch-foe in Turkey five years ago. Igor had braved the concentrated fighting in Iraq, spilling over the Armenian border, and had led them through mountainous terrain.

The Bakhtiari had collected them and arranged safe passage through the north via Tabriz. There, close to the oil refineries, the bearded British one had detached himself from the Israeli elite corps. He was an expert at the US battle plan based on "Shock and Awe", the psychological destruction of the enemy's will to fight rather than the physical destruction of military forces. He was heading for the Azadegan oilfields in the southwest, deep in enemy territory.

The Lieutenant-Colonel and the Corps travelled at night to escape detection. They wore large solid shirts with round collars, typical of the Bakhtiari dress. They blended in with their guides, part of the nomadic tribe, travelling in old beat-up cars.

The Bakhtiari's spoke of freedom and peace. Cohen listened to their ambitions of having a Bakhtiari as President of Iran. They knew of just such a man. He was well-equipped to be the next leader through lineage and endorsement by reformists of the Guardian Council. Cohen respected this purest Persian tribe, noted for the strains of plaintive Luri music playing in the background. They were giving him and his men free passage, in exchange for reform in their country.

Battleweary, the Colonel billeted his men in the quiet town. Communications were set up. One man in the tribe had internet connections. The message was indistinct. President Mahmoud Ahmadi and Supreme Leader Ayatollah Khomeini had announced that the oilfields in Iraq were now under Iranian control. Cohen hoped the British and Americans from bases in Israel and within Iraq would be in a commanding position to wrest control, if the news was accurate and not mere false propaganda.

Air attacks on Iranian targets and the Iraqi positions they held, had started shortly after the adiabatic demagnetisation undertaken by Cathy and the Alien life-force had cooled the atmosphere, and were continuing.

The Colonel told his men there was minimum rest for them that night- they were on the march at dawn. The oilfields in Iran would be the target.

Tit for Tat was the name of the operation.

They would be heading southwest to Khuzestan and the Yadavaran oilfields, swollen with Chinese investment whilst in the south via the Persian Gulf, the British and Americans would be attacking the Zagheh oil fields in Bushehr province.

Teams of Press and Media would be waiting to announce the offensive to the world.

Russia with its billions of investment in the oilfields in Bushehr would need to comply with the Allies demands to cease support of Iran or risk being at war. China would follow suit or risk heavy losses in oil and gas in the region.

Putinov was in a bind, both at home and abroad.

Within 24 hours, Television, newspapers, texts and emails broadcast the news. Putinov had appeared on State Television at a news conference. Russia was joining the Allies in the war against Iran. China issued a similar statement.

An hour later it was all over. Iran had surrendered.

Rumour had it that Putinov was stepping down after his term ended at the end of six years. He would not be 71 years old and still be in office.

Putinov smiled as he entered his innermost sanctum, in the bowels of a nondescript Moscow building. Only one other knew of this room. He would take over after Putinov was gone. The one who signed his name:

It was a joke using the double Lamed. It also acted as an excellent cover if discovered. The words would spell out a word in the text of everyday-folk.

He looked at the machines; technology invented by the Englishman Mallard, arranged neatly around the large circular room, each with their own printouts, fifteen of them. Every thought closely monitored. Nasr Al-din, his Turkish buddy had given him the blueprints many years ago.

He had rid the world of four of them. These fifteen would go the way of their group. Their true calling was now to be revealed to each other and as such, they were destined to die.

They were the Lamed Vavniks and he would hunt down and exterminate all of them, including the remaining twenty-one. So far these had escaped detection.
The 36 Righteous Ones would be replaced with his own men, handpicked and loyal.

He had time. 71 was a few years away.

Andronikov, his comrade, continued to live in London, believing he was trusted to the end of his life. Her Majesty's Government indulged him.

Matt Mallard looked at Cathy lying next to him. She looked so pale, swathed in the white sheets. She was in a deep sleep now. Italian tourists had spotted her this afternoon in a dead faint at Westminster Abbey and had brought it to the attention of the master of the Choristers. Cathy had recovered swiftly but it was thought she would need to be accompanied home. Mallard had hurried to her side.

They had discussed *ad nauseam* their plan to connect with the Alien life-force. Cathy had told

Mallard what had transpired just before she lost consciousness.

She had hoped the angelic vision had accessed the pure thought of the alien life-force on The Bard's Muse. Mallard had held her hand and allowed her her romantic illusions. He was already in touch with CERN. They were formulating plans. Now Mallard knew he had to go back to Geneva and CERN. He would leave Cathy here. He would be back within a month or two, he hoped.

Before he left, he told her of the Lamed Vav Tzadikim or Lamed Vavniks; Opus Signori as they are known to us. His instructions sent a chill down Cathy's spine: Tell the surviving 15 they are being hunted down, one by one.

He held her close and whispered in her ear, 'There are hidden ones, sixteen others, and they would have already had 5 added; after the assassinations and Reza's perfidy, to bring their numbers up to 21.

Always 36 Lamed Vavniks.

They have to be told as well.'

Mallard knew for sure of their existence, after speaking to a young man in Golders' Green; a veil of secrecy had to be cast so deep, like layers of geology, in which crust, mantle and outer core, keep that inner core of giant crystals sacrosanct; so with these righteous beings, constantly at 21 and anonymous.

'Do you remember the symbol from the papyri? Apparently, there has to be a letter in the middle of the double Lamed in Hebrew. I can't work it out. Tried all the vowels and you will have hysterics when I tell you I figured it must relate to the present day use of 'LOL' the acronym for the internet slang 'laugh out loud'.

Well, the internet-speak relates in a way, to the identical mathematical symbol in TeX, developed as a typeset for computer-mediated maths-verbals – hey you, stop laughing, why does it have to be profound - the ancient prophets also had a sense of humour, I'm sure. Perhaps at the end of each seal, they were sending us the other common translation for LOL – Lots of Love – Cathy, stop guffawing - O.K. I give up. It will be found one day but not today and not by me!

I will send it to the Opus Signori and see if they make sense of it.

Mallard hesitated. Perhaps it had better wait till my return.

Cathy had nodded.

Now, Cathy woke to a sense of rightness. Of all being in order for a brief moment in time. For the first time in all of her years, Cathy's intuition played her false.

CERN, Geneva:

Professor Christoph Benjamin and his team sat with Mallard and worked out the experiment. Previously, they had relied solely on Mallard's machine and the MI6 and Sohrab Reza's back-up laptops. Cathy and the Alien life-force had done the rest. The machines were not available now. They had been destroyed. Just the LHC and the other particle detectors remained.

The scientists plotted and planned. They were relying on existing experiments that CERN had conducted.

First they planned the outcome, the goal they sought so that the Alien life would never be disturbed by humans. The Bard's Muse was a Jupiter sized planet, which as a terrestrial mass could drive spiral waves in the surrounding gas or planetesimal disk (solid objects that form planets) causing the planet to migrate. That was the good news.

The bad news was that the planet orbits around a star, Pegasi51, where it has sufficient atmospheric pressure to maintain liquid water on its surface.

Humankind was agog that this was a habitable zone – a planet favourable for life to grow. Probes from earth on flybys over the Bard's Muse proved this to be true.

In fact, they told Mallard, the news recently had been quite depressing. Probes, electronic microscopes in space from space agencies all over the world were hovering around The Bard's Muse, ever since the Russians determination to send a space mission to the newly discovered planet had been announced.

The world was hoping hourly for glimpses of the alien life.

The physicists' planned for The Bard's Muse to lose orbital angular momentum (spin) and migrate beyond the outer edge of the habitable zone.

The planet would then be too cold to sustain liquid water. Humans could not exist in such an environment. Therefore, the Alien life-force would be safe from human invasion and settlement. They were formless, pure thought in motion and as such were safe in the changed environment.

All experiments at CERN were reviewed and the same process whereby Cathy Burkert had been able to introduce coolant to the atmosphere – the adiabatic demagnetisation - was mooted. The physicists patiently explained the process to Mallard. He had to perform and the controls were to be in his hands.

CERN needed to cause a torque, a rotating force from CERN and the alien life would do the rest - provide the interior force, a centrifugal force pushed outwards. That should ensure the planet's migration beyond the habitable zone.

The conclusions of an experiment by Gregory B. Furman, Victor M. Meerovich and Vladimir L. Sokolovsky were adopted. Entanglement procedures in a dipolar-coupled nuclear spin cooled using the adiabatic demagnetisation technique, would do the trick.

The magnetic moment of a magnet is a quantity that determines the force that the magnet can exert on electric currents and the torque that a magnetic field will exert on it. A loop of electric current, a bar magnet, an electron, a molecule, and a planet all have magnetic moments. Did Mallard get it? He did, barely.

Well, they said, a magnetic dipole is the limit of either a closed loop of electric current or a pair of poles as the dimensions of the source are reduced to zero while keeping the magnetic moment constant.

One form of magnetic dipole moment is associated with a fundamental quantum property, the spin of elementary particles. Dipolar moments of these nuclei can be entangled.

A pulsed EPR experiment (electron paramagnetic resonance) which is the interaction of electron spins in a constant magnetic field can also evolve into techniques where the nuclei in the environment can be studied and controlled. You see Matt; we can get to the temperature!

In other words, the physicists stated, temperature according to calculations could therefore be reduced significantly over very long distances

'By the way, EPR, you Matt will be very keen to know, is also an experiment using the same abbreviation people used to describe the Einstein-Podolsky-Rosen experiment (EPR experiment or EPR paradox). Einstein-Podolsky-Rosen designed a thought experiment intended to reveal entanglement phenomena.

He said that if there are two physical elements of reality interacting, each cannot be measured alone, both have to be simultaneously predicted and measured and if this cannot be done, then the description of that physical reality is wrong. Therefore, you and the other cosmos-nauts might just have proved that physics cannot be measured alone, but that physical reality and consciousness go hand in hand.'

We will attempt to do both EPR interactions and thus achieve the temperature control that would ensure The Bard's Muse would be a frozen waste.

Matt Mallard's electrical energy wired into the accelerators at CERN would be the additional boost necessary for the nuclear fission needed for the dipolar- coupled spin .

Thus, they patted him on the back and said, 'We will let you be awesome in the coolant chamber, my friend. We have constructed one your size'

The experiment was scheduled to take place in the next few weeks. Cathy had to do her bit in the meanwhile.

Chapter 22

Cathy was at NASA. Mallard and Cathy had talked through what needed to be accomplished. Their horror at the growing number of space probes demanded prompt action.

Messenger, another space probe was due to be launched again shortly, on a scheduled trip to orbit the planet Mercury.

Part of the mission was the study of microbial ecology which involved collecting DNA micro-organisms or RNA sequences, the encoding of genetic information directly from the environment

That's why Cathy was here. Cathy needed to get to where the space probe was being prepared for launch. The kind professor from John Hopkins University escorted her around. He said they had to be quick.

Cathy smiled and said she just needed a couple of photographs to help with future CERN experiments. She needed to learn the probe's inner workings.

Cathy walked and talked naturally but she was extremely nervous. She neared the probe. It looked huge close up, quite like Star Wars with its solar panels and magnetometer boom. She raised her camera with her left hand. The pin was in her right hand. Surreptitiously, she pricked her finger and quickly touched the boom.

The Professor tutted as did the others working around the probe. Cathy apologised immediately. She smiled in repentance with her big green eyes. They started to look a bit more kindly.

Cathy was embarrassed but did not know any other way to get the message to the Aliens. Now her DNA was on the probe and the spacecraft would be heading for Mercury.

She knew the Aliens would recognise her existence in their environment. With their knowledge of her – a mere touch on her skin with their mental sense had lifted her DNA fingerprints –they could then connect with her mind. She hoped they had heard her trying to send a message from Westminster Abbey - go to Mercury temporarily, human invasion is imminent.

If they tuned in to her consciousness, they would know they must create an interior force, a spin identical to the one the three of them had done to cool the earth's atmosphere.

The space probe, Messenger would be there on Mercury soon with the help of the gravitational slingshot, which changes a spacecraft's velocity relative to the sun, altering the speed and making them go much faster.

Cathy flew back home the following day. Matt was expected back in a month. Cathy looked at her watch. Just about now his experiment at CERN was taking place. It was the first of many. CERN would be repeating the process until, they hoped, data from the Hubble Space telescope would confirm The Bard's Muse had migrated beyond the habitable zone.

The Opus Signori were still in hiding after the assassinations of the four leading members. They were aware of their own mortality. The fifteen men met to read Cardinal Jules de Fleury last will and testament. They came by bus and by coach, no more grand automobiles, no retinue of staff. Dressed simply they sat in a crowded bar under poor lighting. Only their xenon mini-torches, with the gas producing a violet-blue arc of light, betrayed their high-tech accoutrements.

They were then informed of twenty-one more of their rare breed, hidden from all, their identities unknown, even to each other and so it would remain all the days of their lives.

The true purpose of all 36, not to oversee the world as each thought, but merely to prostrate before God on behalf of humankind.

These men swore solemn oaths to use their power and wealth for the sanctity of evolution. They had no-one on whom to bestow their knowledge and wisdom. They would never trust an outsider again. New recruits would be drawn from within their own ranks.

Cathy and Matt were now on the inside, part of their closed world. They had not been in touch but received reports regularly. They knew of Matt and Cathy's attempts to warn the alien life-force.

Cathy knew that Hektor was extremely busy with the presidential elections in Cyprus. She also knew that his life would change. He would no longer be in the shadows.

Huge gas supplies discovered off the southern coast of Cyprus had resulted in his government being inundated with envoys from China and Russia seeking licensing for exploration of the hydrocarbons. Hektor was deeply involved, his ministers were joyful but all had to be tightly controlled with Turkey baring its fangs with threats of warfare and warships. Israel had proved an ally, a protector. They had the clout to act as a sentinel-on sea patrol from Turkish threats. Cyprus' plans for the future were rosy.

Hektor immersed himself in the business of the day. He enjoyed all the minutiae of government but he went home to an empty house. Women abounded and his needs were assuaged intermittently but his thoughts were of Cathy. She was a shining beacon that he had found peace with. He wanted her permanently in his life. He would arrange for her to visit immediately.

Nicosia, Cyprus.

They walked and talked. She was in the corridors of power and she felt dizzy with the underlying energy. Hektor was attentive in the midst of a very busy schedule. She felt flattered with his minders and his ministers paying her assiduous attention. She was cosseted in a world far removed from everyday living. Cathy enjoyed Cyprus, she always did. She cared deeply for Hektor but could not be with him. Matt was her alter-ego. With him she knew fulfilment, in every way.

Besides, her energy levels had reached a zenith exploring outer space. She craved the same drug, not the potential but the kinetic. She was on the move, not poised for movement. She felt like Thursday's child: she had far to go. She must finish what she started. CERN was due to be shut down for repairs lasting two years. Cathy needed a job.

Hektor had offered her a position here in Cyprus. She would be the personalised kinetics in the drilling for that black gold. Cathy was introduced to the experts. They suggested her psychokinetic input, much lauded globally by the success at CERN in saving the planet, would provide a much more detailed understanding of the history of the geologic process and thus have a substantial impact on exploration success and the accuracy of estimating in-place reserves.

Cathy was excited at the prospect but not for the reasons Hektor detailed. This would be the perfect way of analysing the qualities of sand and the effects of drilling in regions proximate to that powdery substance.

Cathy was so tempted to stay on this island of Aphrodite. Matt would be too. He was due home soon. They could work together alongside geologists, on the silica, a substance they firmly believed would dominate the future of the human collective psyche.

Chapter 23

London, England

3 a.m. Cathy woke from a fitful sleep. Again. Night after night, day after day her mind was disturbed. It seemed to be plugged into some kind of electric charger. She seemed to be at another level of consciousness, a state of wakeful dreaming. Scenarios would occur to her, voices sounding in her mind – alien to her thinking. Her mind seemed possessed. Hallucinations where she lay on her bed, unable to move for hours whilst her cast of characters played their parts, tragedy, comedy, thrills and spills. She lay enrapt, eyes dilated, caught up by her mind's machinations.

A great burden seemed upon her with this constant state of mental flux. Her grief seemed to be vast-bloodless and pale, a spaghetti bowl of tortured emotion. She was Heathcliff wraith-driven, haunting the moors, she was Juliet desperately licking the poison on Romeo's lips, she was every war widow suffused with desolation. She keened aloud at times, dreadfully, walking for miles in deserted woods. Black hair wet and tangled, she would return for an hour only to rush out once more, forever seeking surcease from that knotted, visceral pain.

She needed to see the doctor again. She was having another episode. She would start swallowing the pills immediately.

Just as soon as the doctor gave her the thumbs-up.

Cathy waited, gazing blankly into space. Her name was called. Dr. Patricia Murphy looked closely at the young woman. She had been treating her for a few years and she had seen Cathy, mentally beaten after her time in Cyprus, then a period of sedation but happy and fully functional in the last couple of years.

Patricia Murphy realised grief weighed heavily on those shoulders. The girl's mind had not been able to cope. Yet again she had experienced an episode of psychosis- a chemical imbalance. Cathy seemed removed from reality. It was important to bring her back. Her condition demanded her full and focused attention.

'Cathy,' the doctor said gently, 'it's been six weeks – he died, my dear. Can you accept it?'

The stare was blank. There was barely a nod – but it was some kind of assent.

The doctor was encouraged. She continued, 'Your test results were positive. You are pregnant. Your scan is scheduled for tomorrow. Everything looks absolutely fine'

Cathy whispered, 'My mind is slowly coming to terms with Matt's dying.... he was so full of life.... the last experiment at CERN went horribly wrong..... we had so many plans...'

'Cathy, can you tell me about it?'

'The coolant chamber malfunctioned...Matt's energy wasn't enough to override it. He died, Doctor. Oh, the experiment was conducted nevertheless and the planet migrated. So you see they need never have used Matt'.

Cathy tailed off and the doctor heard such a poignant sense of both anger and futility in her voice. She realised the woman's utter incomprehensibility at such a tragic event.

Cathy got hold of a tissue from the box on the doctor's desk and blew her nose, 'I'm really all cried out but I'm beginning to be positive again. Matt and I believed in an after-life, a consciousness that exists beyond the physical body. A promise was made amongst scent-faded roses', said Cathy and the doctor heard almost an angry tenderness in her voice.

‘I know that Matt is always with me. I knew the moment he died; at first there was silence, such a silence that I had never experienced in my whole life. It was as though sound had disappeared from the world.

Then, it was as though his special machine had been switched on and we were sharing each other’s thought processes. My grief overwhelmed me for a time and I could not see beyond it. But now I’m able to recognise our minds seem to be streamlined in the fourth dimension – a sort of hypersphere - it evolves continually. He dwells in my mind and now his baby is due....Doctor, I know I will be alright.’

And so ineffable sorrow is redeemed, thought Dr. Murphy. The mind affording the protective armoury - chemically. She said aloud, ‘Good. What will you do now?’

‘My friend in Cyprus has offered me a home until the baby is born and a job thereafter. Or I could stay in England, my family are here – and I have a group of friends who see the unborn babe as their new life-blood. They want to look after and protect me and help raise the baby’

‘Which would you prefer?’

‘I think I’ll do both. First Cyprus and later I will return. An exciting time for CERN lies ahead after their shut-down period, with the merger of the galaxies. I would like to be part of that. I could bring my knowledge gained in Cyprus to the table.’

Chapter 24

The Opus Signori gazed at the boy seated before them. His mother had brought him to them. She had told the boy all that had gone before. She knew the boy had a destiny and they alone could fulfil it. She would be waiting for their return.

His hair was black and his eyes like his mother, emerald green. They were already obeying his instructions. He was unusual, this boy. At age ten, he had the Wisdom of Solomon and the genius of intellect never seen before by any member present. He was a scholar of many subjects- of the sciences and of literature; each and every discipline was mastered. Music, art and dance were keenly observed and enjoyed. He talked and conversed in many languages-he spoke each and every Opus Signori's native tongues fluently and above all he loved!

Loved the world, every living creature and people most of all. It was uncanny how he knew what made people tick. He talked to all with kindness and consideration. He seemed to know their very thoughts. Like his father, he had the gift of healing. He healed with words and the touch of his hands. They scratched their heads and talked quietly that he knew so much of human DNA. He touched and he knew. So far the Opus Signori had prevented the outside world knowing of him. They knew he would be besieged by needy people the world over.

They crowded around him. They touched his hands and patted his head. The green eyes beamed back, an almost spiritual light, it seemed. He asked a question.

Yes, they answered, all preparations were in place. The Spacecraft was due to launch in the next few hours. The heavy launch vehicle would take them beyond earth's orbit. They would be at Mercury in no time at all. From there, they would attempt to find the Bard's Muse. For ten long years despite several space missions, the planet had proved elusive. Now the Opus Signori would accompany the boy at his request but they were afraid.

The boy smiled. He could read their minds. He knew they wanted to make the return journey but that would not be possible. Not for the next decade, if ever. Their places on earth had already been filled. First the fifteen men had to be educated in the ways of his people as he himself had to absorb all knowledge from the eternal consciousness.

He touched the arm of the man who stayed closest by his side. The one who signed with the double Lamed. : LOL

A man who would know true enlightenment.

A good reason, he thought, to ‘laugh out loud’ indeed.

He would need the other Opus Signori, the twenty-one hidden Lamed Vavniks, when he was ready to return to earth. They would help to make his rule absolute. The world would begin a new age, the age of Supreme Consciousness.

Beautiful Physics and the Absolute Mind.

Now he was going home. His mother had made the promise to the Ebony a long time ago when he had been conceived on a star-studded flight in the magnetosphere.

In return his mother and his earthly father who had died before he was born would be the only two who would ever walk the millennia continuously in physical form. Their DNA profiles would be feather-touched into the same human existence in every generation.

Epilogue

They stood at the edge of the new world. They had walked through millennia, steps without trace. The earth now was parched, not a single blade of grass, not a tree standing. Orange and sandstone in colour, it stretched endlessly.

The sun was hot in this new world and they lived with it.

Knowledge in every pore, skin finding a sequence in the DNA of long tresses, bone and sinew, the earth had absorbed their bodies over centuries and they were made anew each time. They possessed the genome of every plant and tree, of every animal, every living creature.

They chose again lands where certain peoples and plants could survive. They chose the skins of climates and geography. They chose the animals, birds and insects to live in the wild and the tame. For they remembered when the world was populated, long, long ago. Their minds imbued with knowledge of all time knew a mind before war, hate and destruction. They would build that world again. They would ensure the child growing within her womb would inherit the peace of all peoples.

They would no longer be alone.

The End

Bibliography & Acknowledgements:

King James Bible

Judith Butler: *Giving an Account of Oneself* (2005)

Stephen D Snobelen: *Newton's science and Religion* (Ashgate 2004)

*Brenda Dunne and Robert Jahn: *Quirks of the Quantum Mind*

**A special acknowledgement to Brenda Dunne for encouragement and inspiration.*

*Jack Benton CERN, MPhys

**A special acknowledgement to Jack Benton for answering many a question with patience and generosity.*

*Matthew Coombes CERN, MPhys

* *Full Page 3 acknowledgement to Matt Coombes.*

Rev. Dr. Richard Buxton:

**A special acknowledgement to Richard Buxton for advice and a sounding board.*

Dr. Marek Kukula. Public Astronomer, Royal Observatory, Greenwich: *for inspiration and encouragement.*

*Gregory B. Furman, Victor M. Meerovich and Vladimir L. Sokolovsky: *Entanglement in dipolar coupling spin* (2011)

**A special acknowledgement to Gregory Furman for answering questions with patience and generosity.*

*Lawrence H. Ford and Thomas A.Roman: *Negative energy – Wormholes and Warp Drive* (Scientific American – January 2000)

**A special acknowledgement to Larry Ford who answered many a question with considerable patience and generosity.*

Thomas Caddick, Banker

William Shakespeare Complete Works: Bate and Rasmussen

Wikipedia

NASA Images

CERN Images

Printed in Great Britain
by Amazon

30322294R00197